Praise for *Mundaca*

'Mundaca *is a wonderfully compelling tale, a mixture of romance and intrigue woven into the fabric of Basque history, local characters and personal tragedy. This adventure is told against the extraordinary natural beauty of the town's location, including one of the most unique waves found anywhere in the world. It's extremely rare these days to read something that gives genuine insight into what those early years of travel and cultural upheaval were like. Owen Hargreaves has eloquently captured something of those times, and done so from a deeply honest and personal perspective.'*

— **Wayne Lynch, surfing legend**

'Owen Hargreaves *has written a cracking debut novel that succeeds in combining surf noir, a political thriller and an enigmatic love story with all elements melding and flowing into one another seamlessly, much like a well-shaped board. It's a slow burn that progressively draws you in as Hargreaves skilfully builds layers of intrigue that pull you deeper. The mystical Spanish rivermouth of the book's title looms as a central character, reflecting and fuelling the emotional journey of the young Australian surfer at the centre of the unfolding drama.'*

— **Tim Baker, former editor of *Tracks*, *Surfing Life* and *Slow Living* magazines, award-winning author, journalist and three-time winner of the Surfing Australia Hall of Fame Culture Award**

'Mundaca *captures the surfing zeitgeist of the '70s, nailing it on what it was like to be on the road, living the Kerouac dream with a surfboard. Any surfer from that era will relate, but the relationship with Maite is really the heart of the story for me ... the ending twist was a welcome surprise.'*

— **Kevin Naughton, journalist for** *Surfer,*
The Surfer's Journal, **The Surfer's Path,** *Surfline*
and *Travelers' Tales* **books; author of the**
surf novel *Trout Rising*

Mundaca

A Tale of Intrigue, Romance
and Surfing in Franco's Spain

Owen Hargreaves

UNBUCKLE & RUN PRESS

First published in 2021
by Unbuckle & Run Press
Melbourne, Australia
unbuckleandrun.com
unbuckleandrun@gmail.com

10 9 8 7 6 5 4 3 2 1

A catalogue record for this book is available from the National Library of Australia.
ISBN 978 0 6451 3480 3 (paperback)
ISBN 978 0 6451 3481 0 (ebook)

The author welcomes readers' feedback via the Mundaca page of unbuckleandrun.com

Cover design and typesetting: Luke Harris at WorkingType.
Editing: Clare Strahan and Dr Euan Mitchell.
Printed and bound by Ingram Spark.

The cover photo of the surf break at Mundaca, Spain, was first published by *Stab Magazine*, USA. All reasonable efforts were made by the author and Unbuckle & Run Press to identify the photographer and obtain authorisation. Any advice or claim concerning the copyright of the cover photo is welcomed.

Note: Mundaca is the Spanish language spelling for the Basque village of Mundaka in Viscaya, Spain. Basque language was suppressed during the Franco period, including 1975 when the story is set.

In tribute to George Steer and his book,
The Tree of Gernika.

Based on a true story

PROLOGUE

There are triggers of all kinds that send you scurrying. The trigger of a gun, of course. And you scurry fast. But there are other triggers. Ones that send you scurrying in a different direction — back to the distant past, to events you thought were well and truly buried.

A sight, a sound, a scent; a trigger can take any form. The trigger fires — like a gun — and your mind scurries. You are momentarily transfixed, transported. You live the memory again as if it were the first time. But it's not the first time. And the passage of time distorts things, plays tricks with your mind.

One memory might trigger another. And another. Fragments of events, not necessarily in sequence, the connections sometimes a mystery. You are left wondering what is the truth behind the memories. Did the event really unfold that way?

Sometimes the connections between real events are as tenuous as the memories themselves.

But it's a trigger that sets things off, jolts a memory, calls up the fragments, pulls the invisible threads that link them, conjures whole events, until a story — true or otherwise — grows and takes on a shape and life of its own.

Trigger, memory, event, story.

A red-checked tablecloth is one such trigger. It transports me to northern Spain, June 1975 ... the town of Guernica, deserted, midday hour. Arturo, his hand on my shoulder, urging me forward. A wide stone walkway, round tables, red-checked tablecloths.

A bar. An old man sitting in a corner reading a newspaper, red wine, black beret, thick-rimmed glasses.

Two middle-aged men standing, smoking, talking. Bartender wiping, listening. They study us — Arturo is one of *them*; me a foreigner, an *extranjero*. I squirm, look away. Dismissive grunt, they resume conversation.

Bartender sidles over. Arturo, arching thick black eyebrows, orders. San Miguel beer, two tall glasses. Froth surges up, subsides.

Small plates of *pinchos* atop the bar. Arturo passes a tortilla wedge. Warm, firm, juicy.

Sawdust floor: cigarette butts, toothpicks, crumpled serviettes.

Arturo chats with the bartender. A strange musical language. The two local men join in, frequently interrupting, hands moving fast. *Mundaca, Lequetio, Australiano.* They study me. Conversation halts abruptly. All eyes to the door.

Two men swagger in. Swarthy, moustachioed, rifles slung over shoulders. Heavy olive-green uniforms, black boots, belts, curious black hats. Patrons' faces hard-set, sullen. Transformation unnerving. I try to shrink.

The soldiers sit at a table, hanging their rifles over the backs of their chairs. The rifles sway backward and forward, the dark wooden butt of one grazing noisily against the chair leg, its long metal barrel pointing in a slow circling motion towards the ceiling.

'*Camarero!*' the heavier-set of the pair calls out impatiently.

The bartender regards them with a necessary politeness.

'*Dos vinos de marca ... y tráenos usted pinchos de atún y torti-lla,*' the soldier orders gruffly.

The bartender begins, unhurriedly, to prepare their drinks and food.

The soldier strums the tabletop with his fingertips and eyes each patron; and each, unflinchingly, turns his face. His eye catches mine. I shudder and look away. His contemptuous gaze moves on and I am drawn back to him in morbid fascination. Beyond the surly exterior something else lurks.

Arturo seems impatient to leave. He pays the bill in a business-like fashion, the bartender equally stern.

'*Adiós,*' Arturo calls out firmly.

'*Adiós,*' the locals reply, their focus shifting momentarily from the soldiers to us. Only the old man lost in his paper doesn't look up or speak.

'*Guardia Civil ... cabrones!*' Arturo almost spits when we reach the car. Civil guards ... 'the bastards'. From the same town? They couldn't be. Jeez, they wouldn't feel such hatred for their own kind. Would they? It seemed to come from both sides.

... How could I forget that first day in Spain? I haven't. I can't. And to think *she* came from that town. But that's not where this story begins. Not my version. It starts in South-West France, a few weeks later, when I met Greg.

CHAPTER 1

The Steakhouse sat atop the cliffs of the Côte des Basques, about a kilometre to the south of the glitzy centre of Biarritz. It was a low-budget night venue where the cool people, the more adventurous local girls and all the surfers went. There was a wood-panelled bar filled with foreigners, Aussie and American surfers noisily recounting their latest adventures. Bemused French surfers watched from the sidelines.

I went out to a verandah that overlooked the sea to get fresh air. A guy was leaning on the railing, gazing seaward into the darkness, tall and lean, with thin blond hair and the shoulders of a surfer. He shifted his weight from one foot to the other, restless. He turned my way and the moon lit his tortoise-shell glasses and carefully trimmed moustache. His slumped shoulders spoke of sadness, defeat.

'G'day,' I said tentatively, testing the waters.

He looked across, annoyed, as if I'd broken a spell, but his countenance softened. 'Howdy, amigo. Sorry, I was away with the birds.'

'Anything interesting out there?'

'The sea, the night sky. They're always interesting.'

'True. Although it's a bit hard to see the sea in the dark.'

'But you can hear it while you watch the stars. Truly soulful, man.'

I laughed. 'You must be a surfer.'

He grunted softly. 'Would anyone else come to a place like The Steakhouse?'

'I wouldn't know. It's my first time here.'

'Me too, but, man, it has that desperate surfer feel about it. Don't you think?'

'It's a surfer's haunt, for sure. But the French come too, girls included.'

'Not really my kind of place. What's your name?'

'Owen, from Melbourne.'

'Greg, Central Coast, California.'

'Been here long?'

'A few days. Flew in from the south of Spain.'

'Surfing?'

'No. I should have gone surfing. That was my mistake.'

'Mistake? How do you mean?'

Three or four beers later, I found out.

'Well, man, I wanted to travel and paint,' Greg said, after he'd drained his glass. 'So I went to Marrakesh, an amazing city, and headed up into the Atlas Mountains to this place called Ketama, where I heard they made hash. A local family invited me to stay. It was a fairly primitive farmhouse with a marijuana crop, but the scenery was beautiful and they seemed friendly enough, and I was able to paint. After four days I was ready to leave, but they wouldn't let me go. They made it pretty obvious that I risked my life if I tried to escape. Every day they'd have a family meeting to decide what to do with me — like they owned me!'

'Jesus! What did you do?'

'It was crazy, man!' He stole an anxious glance towards the sea. 'So I tore out the two main pages from my passport and put them, along with most of my travellers' cheques, in a plastic bag, which I stuck up ...' He made a face.

'Really? You did that?'

'It was the only thing I could think to do, man! And my instinct was right, because they went through all my stuff. They kept the cash in my wallet, which wasn't much, and I'd left a couple of travellers' cheques to keep them happy.'

'Then what happened?'

'The headman of the family "invited" me to help them build a mud-brick outbuilding. I couldn't refuse, but I took it real slow. They weren't too happy about that.' He grinned nervously and wiped the sweat from his forehead with the back of his hand, a silver sheen in the moonlight revealing a scar above his right eye.

'I was desperate.' His eyes grew large behind his glasses. 'I convinced them to let me go to the nearest town to cash the few travellers' cheques they'd kept and bring them back the money. But they'd only let me go with one of their goons.' He ran a hand through his hair. The moonlight caught his glasses and I couldn't see his eyes, but his voice was tight. 'We walked down through the valley to the main road and we met several other families along the way. The men all checked me out with the same conniving look. If I'd been alone, I wouldn't have got out of there.' His hand trembled.

'You poor bastard! How did you get away?'

'Thank God, the bank was closed for lunch, so we went to the market to wait. The *souk* was really crowded and I managed to give him the slip and got on a bus to Ceuta.' He drew a big breath of cool night air, then exhaled with a long, steady sound, like the wind, filled with emotion and relief. And when the breath escaped him, his shoulders relaxed.

I, on the other hand, was gripping the railing. 'Jeez, mate, what a lucky escape!'

'It was! I couldn't relax until I'd got out of Morocco. At the border I showed what remained of my passport, they shrugged, asked for a fee, and let me pass.' The edge in his voice petered out to a tired rasp. 'On the Spanish side, I convinced them I'd been abducted. They gave me a transit visa to get to the US embassy in Madrid to get a new passport. Then I came straight here. Arrived two days ago.' He dropped his hands to the rail and gazed out to the sea's gentle murmur.

'That's a wild story!' I let go of the rail. 'My heart's flying just listening!'

'Man, I was so relieved to get to Spain! My nerves are totally frazzled, though. I want to take it easy.' He leaned against the rail. 'And surf my brains out.'

'Makes sense,' I said. 'Surfing's good like that.'

A camping buddy passed by. 'Coming, Owen?' said the Kiwi.

'We're leaving.'

I turned to Greg. 'I better go, mate. Good to meet you. See you at the beach.'

'I'm there every day … and now you know why.'

§

In the heart of Biarritz, everything appeared remarkably new and clean, and somehow make-believe. The crisply dressed and manicured passers-by looked down their noses at me.

I headed down the broad terraced steps on the south side of the casino, along the elegant beachfront, to the beach.

The Grand Plage was like the stage in an amphitheatre — a groomed stretch of sand sat at the southern end of a bay, backed by steeply climbing hills and book-ended by rocky headlands to the north and south. The hills were strewn with magnificent villas and apartments, the foreshore dominated by the casino — an opulent but fading monument to the glory days of the 1920s and '30s.

The groomed section of the beach was organised with great élan. Umbrellas and deckchairs, all in tidy rows, could be rented at exorbitant prices, and rich beach-goers, mostly elderly, basked lazily in the sun in their skimpy swimwear. The ungroomed beach near the rocks was where the young people congregated. Long-haired youths in board shorts and bikini-clad girls sprawled on colourful towels, surfboards propped nearby, wetsuits drying in the sun. There was no order here, just disarray and a sense of anarchy. Beyond, in the cobalt blue sea, a disparate flock of surfers rode the meagre swell.

I found some vacant sand on the fringe of the ungroomed section, set down my board and wetsuit, and made myself comfortable. I watched the sea for a while, then got out my book, lay back, and tried to read. I soon dozed off.

I was lying on my towel, *The Tree of Gernika* open at the first page, when Greg approached. 'Hey, Owen.' He settled a beautiful long, blue surfboard on the sand, sat on his towel and flicked at the cover of my book. 'Guernica with a "k" and no "u",' he said.

I shook myself awake. 'Basque spelling.'

'Is that right?' He peered at me through the thick-lensed, tortoise-shell glasses with his pale blue eyes. 'I know the painting well, and that's spelt with a "c" and a "u" … probably because Picasso wasn't Basque. He was from Malaga. Well, he was born in Santiago de Compostela in Galicia, but raised in Malaga. He did the painting in Paris, for the World Fair. Then it toured all round the globe.'

'You seem to know a lot about Picasso.'

'Art college.' He brushed the sand off his hands. 'Guernica is one of the all-time great protest paintings and one of my personal favourites. But I've never heard of George Steer. Where did you get it?'

'From a girl in Mundaca.'

'Mundaca? The Spanish left-hander river-mouth wave?'

'That's right. A beautiful little fishing village.'

'And she gave you the book? That's curious. Didn't she want it back?'

'I don't think so. She said something about other copies.'

'Really? In English? That's strange.'

'I guess so,' I said. 'I wasn't thinking too clearly … if you know what I mean.'

Greg laughed. 'Oh! I get it! What's her name?'

'Maite.'

'My-tay. Never heard of that one.'

'Well, it's a Basque name.'

'Makes sense.'

'She's an artist too,' I added. 'Well, an art student at least. She studied in Dublin for a while.'

'Dublin?' He seemed surprised. 'Weird choice. Dublin's not famous for its art schools.'

'Maybe, but she has plenty of spectacular scenery to paint in the Basque country, Mundaca included.'

Greg's moustache twitched and one hand unconsciously moved towards it. 'Mundaca sounds inviting. Surf, a beautiful village, dramatic countryside, a great place to paint. It sounds more and more intriguing.' He smoothed his moustache from the middle out with a thumb and index finger. 'So does Maite.'

'She's more than intriguing.'

He laughed again. 'You're hooked!'

Greg stood, took off his shirt and picked up his board. 'Coming in?'

'Sure,' I said, strangling a yawn.

11

'Why so tired?'

'Hard ground and a snoring Kiwi. I'm camping with some guys from Down Under.'

He laughed at my nightly ritual — erecting the tent and bailing at dawn.

'You?'

'I live in a mansion.'

§

A few doors down from the Spanish consulate at the Côte des Basques was a magnificent four-storey stately villa in pale pink. A sign bearing a red skull and crossbones was the only clue that the rear of the ground floor had collapsed, falling a hundred metres to the sea below, leaving a gaping hole the width of the house. The remainder teetered on the edge of the cliff.

Inside was dusty. Pieces of broken ceiling plaster lay scattered on the floor, but the beautiful wide staircase leading to the upper floors was still intact and met the ground floor where the earth had subsided. Someone had put a board across from the nearest solid ground to the bottom of the stairs. By carefully 'walking the plank' you could reach the staircase and access the floors above.

Upstairs seemed safe enough, provided you stayed on the landward half.

Word had passed around and about fifteen itinerant travellers were now bedding down in this new-found luxury dormitory.

I set up my sleeping bag next to a French couple. The guy introduced himself. 'Marc,' he said. 'And this is Giselle.' I guessed Marc was in his late thirties by his wispy shoulder-length hair and matching grey beard, but I doubted Giselle was even twenty. Her sad eyes wandered past me.

They were an odd pair, not romantically linked, more like brother and sister. Marc spoke reasonable English, but not Giselle. She rarely conversed with the others and usually only through Marc. There was something beguiling in her fragile ways and she caught the attention of all the men. She, however, seemed oblivious, trapped in a sort of consuming depression. Mostly, she'd sit on her bed gazing vacantly into the distance, disconnected. Marc would occasionally whisper to her in French and bring her around. We never did learn precisely what had crushed this delicate woman's spirit, but at times you could sense the seeds of healing.

'What's your story?' asked one guy. She shrugged and look to Marc for assistance.

'She's had a difficult time,' said Marc gently. 'And she doesn't like to talk about it. So, please, don't pressure her.' He stroked her hair. Marc was a gentle soul, who'd left his native Paris to recover from drug addiction and become Giselle's saviour.

Marc had a wizardly aura. Much of the time, he too seemed lost in contemplation, drifting in another world. He was like an old sailor who'd travelled the world, returned, but told little of his adventures. When he did speak, we listened, like devotees of a mystical guru.

I talked to him about surfing, the exhilaration. 'That feeling's seductive,' he said. 'Takes a grip, you want more and more.' He stroked his beard. 'Take care to keep it in balance. It's an enlightening distraction, *mon ami*, not a destination.' I didn't know exactly what he meant. But it made me wonder.

Together, Marc and Giselle cast a soft ghostly shadow over our dark and dusty dormitory.

Greg had established himself on the other side of the room under a window, his drawing and painting tools in a satchel beside his sleeping bag.

I woke early the next morning and silently watched him propped against the wall sketching, using the shaft of dust-filled light that filtered through the broken shutters of the window above. He seemed right at home, natural, even in this strange abode. He laboured with a quiet controlled energy. There was a look in his eye that I caught from time to time, something from deep within warmed him, and drove him forward. He's lucky, I thought. He's found his purpose in life, his vocation, his passion. It made me a little jealous, a little sad. My path seemed so unclear. Was I really destined to become a doctor?

But Marc's caring for Giselle moved me too. His gentle way of looking after her was inspiring. He was part nurse, part counsellor, but mostly a devoted friend. Like Mum looking after my sister Louise, forever attentive, seeming to sense her needs before she realised them herself. Even the smallest things. Adjusting the makeshift pillow, helping her sit up, proffering a drink of water, wiping her brow, smoothing her hair, setting an errant wisp in place, a comforting look, a reassuring touch, a few whispered words. Just like Mum.

More like a nurse than a doctor.

Doctors and nurses both care for people, I supposed, in different ways. Nursing seemed more intimate. Could a doctor get that close? That intimate? I doubted it. They were men of science, preoccupied with rational thought. I'd seen them in the hospital, always in a hurry, passing from bed to bed, from patient to patient. Occasionally, they'd pause and then, for a brief moment, you might see that look in their eye, the one Greg had. But the glow didn't seem to last. Maybe it was buried too deep. Maybe they didn't give it time to burn, like Greg did.

The ancient ceiling was all cobwebs and dust and flaking paint. It needed care too. Incredibly grand in its heyday, I imagined, but now broken and crumbling and hanging on for dear life. A bit like Giselle.

And there we were, literally teetering on the brink. Mum would die if she could see me. She was a scaredy-cat at heart. Always worrying. Strange, I mused, that she allowed us boys to take such risks. That must have been hard. Perhaps she paired the risk with sport, and reconciled it that way. Sport was okay, and therefore risk in the name of sport was okay. So travelling, or anything else, in the name of surfing was okay too. Was that how she thought? I'd never asked.

I surveyed the room. This was a bit of grand old Europe.

Though not the kind my parents had in mind. Dad would have a field day in here. A fix-it man's heaven. He'd be at it from dusk until he fell into bed at night, distracted by his world of repair and renewal.

Giselle let out a muffled, hollow moan, like a cry from the bottom of the sea, and rolled over.

Repair and renewal. Humans needed that too. Maybe Mum was right. Maybe with her caring genes and Dad's fix-it genes, I could fix people. But a vocation should feel natural, shouldn't it? Surfing felt natural. And you should be passionate about what you do, shouldn't you?

Maite had lit up when she talked about her people, her heritage. Where was my glow? What made me burn inside?

Not much.

Maite. Mysterious Maite. I'd love to see her again. My feelings for her felt natural. Was she part of my destiny? But Maite meant Mundaca.

Mundaca. I felt natural there.

§

Every morning we surfed the Côte des Basques. In the afternoons, we'd hitch to the Grand Plage. Greg was keen to hear more about the waves in Mundaca. He'd heard about the mythical left-hander, and with his 'goofy foot' stance, the wave sounded especially appealing. He'd be facing into the wall of the fast-breaking wave, making it easier to ride. Between surfs, and sometimes out in the water, we continued our conversations. He talked less and less about Morocco, and more and more about finding good waves.

§

Well after midnight, Greg woke us up. 'There's someone downstairs,' he whispered loudly.

'Who?' I whispered back.

'Probably someone looking for a place to sleep,' he replied, yawning.

We listened. A few creaks, footsteps on the staircase. Then torches bounced off the ceiling in the landing. The door flung wide and torchlight filled the room. 'Attention! Attention!' a gruff voice shouted from behind the blinding light. 'Police!'

Everyone was suddenly awake.

Four heavy-booted gendarmes bustled into the room. 'Get up, all of you. *Allez! Vite!*'

'Okay, okay,' said Marc when a gendarme grabbed at his sleeping bag. '*Calmez-vous.*'

The gendarme started yelling. 'Everyone up. *Allez!* This house is condemned. You are illegal trespassers,' he boomed.

We were all dressing, packing our things, mutterings from the sleepiest heads, while the police hurried us along. The superior shone his torch at us. 'Passports, identity cards,' he called out sharply.

Silence. The shadows on the walls went still. A floorboard

creaked. We dropped what we were doing and fumbled to find our documents. One by one, they perused them. There was no escape. 'Get your things and come with us,' said the superior to one Spanish guy.

Jesus, I wonder what he'd done.

His face was all strangled grin. He shrugged and two gendarmes led him away while the rest of us were herded out of the building with a warning never to return.

'What a pain in the arse,' said Greg.

With our sleeping bags draped over our shoulders, we filed past the laughing guards outside the Spanish consulate to nearby bushes and bedded down on the uneven ground. I drifted off to the pitter-patter of light rain on my sleeping bag. Even the skies were spitting on us.

The following day, we snuck back into the mansion.

The Spanish man they had arrested reappeared late morning. 'They think I am Basque terrorist,' he mumbled. 'Me Basque, but not terrorist.'

Greg and I exchanged a vacant look.

'Basque terrorist not sleep here. Terrorist not stupid,' he added. 'Me? I look like terrorist?'

Greg gave him a bemused stare.

'Never met a terrorist, mate,' I said, shaking my head. 'Wouldn't know one if I fell over him.'

He laughed. 'Fall for terrorist? Not good idea.'

§

Greg and I hatched a plan to return to Mundaca. 'We'll have to camp out to begin with,' I told him, excited. 'It's summer and I reckon accommodation will be scarce.'

'I love camping!' He rubbed his hands on his thighs. 'Spain! I can't wait, man. Let's buy a car.'

I felt the smile slip from my face. 'I'm on a pretty tight budget, Greg. I don't have money for a car.'

He strummed his fingers on his thigh, as if weighing the risks. 'I tell you what,' he said. 'I'll buy us a car if you buy the camping equipment — tent, stove and cooking gear. And we can share the cost of petrol. How does that sound?'

'Perfect!' I felt like hugging him. 'Absolutely perfect!' Then a thought, my joy dissolving. 'But I can't drive.'

'I don't mind driving.' The moustache twitched. 'You'll be washing a lot of dishes.'

Greg already had his sights on an old grey Citroen Deux Chevaux, which he took me to check out. 'It's not powerful,' he said, 'but man, what it lacks in power it'll make up for in economy. It's stingy on the gas and fuel's going to be our biggest expense. How's this French gearstick?' He slid it in and out of a hole in the centre of the dashboard. 'I've never seen anything like it!'

We called by the mansion to collect our belongings. Marc was the only one there to bid us adieu. Giselle had been having a bad day and was sleeping.

'It's tragic, man,' said Greg, when we reached the car. 'Such a beautiful chick, but she looks like a ghost. I heard there was a suicide in her family.'

'Yeah, tragic alright,' I said, wondering why anyone would kill themselves. Could life get that bad?

CHAPTER 2

Greg guided the Citroen south, past The Steakhouse to the turn-off for Spain. His blue eyes gleamed behind his glasses and a grin was set firmly beneath his newly trimmed moustache. The little grey Citroen strained up the hills, laden with luggage and surfboards, but otherwise purred contentedly, heading south-west for the Spanish border.

Greg seemed to be purring too. He drove with his long limbs stretched out, left hand draped over the steering wheel.

I stretched and eased back against the seat. It felt good to be returning to Spain, as if I was back on track. And it was good for Greg too, one more step removed from the Morocco experience.

The hum of the motor and the sight of the distant Pyrenees sent me drifting back to that first journey.

§

My parents had sent me the few known details of my brother's whereabouts, the name of the town, and the bar where to ask for him. I'd studied a map of northern Spain in my London bed-sit, the route and the various turn-offs. It appeared straightforward enough. I was hoping he was still there.

He had to be. I'd worked hard for five months mopping the floor of a coffee factory and saving my precious pounds so I could make the trip. It was 1975, and anything seemed possible.

I was itching to head out into the world, but I left London later than planned and the journey through France was slow, marred by rain, interminable waits, an unpleasant night in a chicken coop with two Irishmen, and a long torturous walk out of Bordeaux.

Hitchhiking was certainly cheap, but it was so unreliable. At least the weather had fined up while I travelled further south, and when I crossed the border into Spain, it felt like the gates to summer had been opened.

I reached San Sebastian in the late afternoon, grubby, weary and hungry. I couldn't speak a word of Spanish and my schoolboy French was next to useless, but I found myself a hotel and before long I was under the shower. Running hot water — what a miracle!

In the evening I took a short walk along the seawall prom-enade and, as light faded into night, inhaled the salty breath of the Bay of Biscay for the first time. I felt an unexpected peace. In many ways, it was like breathing for the first time.

I slept well and before long was back on the road. A lucky ride had me at Amorebieta, the turn-off for Mundaca, an hour later.

§

Greg swerved around a pothole, rousing me momentarily, but I was soon drifting again, back to that road that climbs steadily out of the valley floor and into the hills.

The hills, paled by the strong sun, were a yellowy-green at that mid-morning hour. The early mist was gone, chased off by the sun's first rays. The sun, well clear of the mountains, pushed upwards.

I slung my backpack over my shoulders and looked behind. The car I'd hitched a lift with had disappeared, leaving the road deserted. I was alone.

Walking up the curving road, I began to unwind, a slow release from the grasp of the city and all things man-made. Each step took me higher above the town and deeper into the folding green hills of the Pyrenees. It was my first morning in Spain and I couldn't have felt better.

Hiking rhythmically up the cracked bitumen into the hills with the sun on my back, the road was deceptively steep, my thighs were straining and sweat trickled down my neck. I paused to rest. Gazing back, I was struck by the mountains. 'God! Look at that line of peaks,' I said to no-one. 'So mysterious, so silent.'

I was eighteen and venturing into a strange new land and, despite its foreignness to me, I felt quietly confident. I'd thumbed my way around, but that was only the beginning. A taste! I wanted to see more, experience more, like my brother, John. My surfing friends all had similar travel aspirations. We all had that longing, that dream to find perfection.

I loosened off my pack, took out a handkerchief and wiped the sweat from my face and neck. A hawk lifted from a nearby meadow, prey in its clutches, spiralling slowly upward to a carefree blue sky, drifting with the current across the valley until lost, a speck merging with nature.

Climbing the road again, the gentler foothills of the Pyrenees reminded me of Apollo Bay and the Otway Ranges along the Victorian coast, but the thick, long grass, wildflowers, low rough stone walls, the clay-tiled rooftops of the farmhouses — all set against a backdrop of pine forests, the Pyrenees and a pale blue sky — told me I was in Spain. I had a reason to feel that quiet pleasure.

One of those compact rounded Italian cars made in Spain snaked up the road, whining its way towards me. Instinctively, I stuck out my thumb.

'*Francés?*' the dark-haired driver asked when I opened the door.

'No,' I said. 'Australian.' I wondered if all young foreigners were French until proven otherwise.

'*Ahhh! Australiano!*' He sounded pleased. He ushered me in, sweeping the passenger seat forward with a sturdy tanned arm so I could stow my pack. '*A dónde va?*' he asked enthusiastically, easing the car back onto the road.

'Mundaca,' I replied.

'*Mundaca?*' he asked, his forehead knitted, his thick lips slightly open, a single gold tooth visible in a row of white. '*Lequetio.*' He pointed to himself, smiling broadly, glancing my way with a satisfied look. He spoke a few sentences in Spanish, finishing each with 'Guernica'.

I knew the name Guernica from the map, it was on my route.

'*Parlez-vous français?*' he asked, swivelling his muscular neck.

'*Un peu*,' I replied, a little nervously. It really was '*un peu*'. Three years of French at high school had left me with a minimum of conversational skill. Like my friends, I'd found learning a foreign language a compulsory torture.

'*Je m'appelle Arturo*,' he said, smiling gently and proffering his hand.

Big hands for a small man, I thought. 'Owen.' I returned his firm handshake. '*Je m'appelle Owen*.'

Arturo spoke only slightly more French than I did, which put me at ease, and we managed to conduct a primitive dialogue while we drove through the undulating hills. He seemed pleased. 'I don't get a chance to speak French too often,' he said, 'It's good to test my skill.'

It was a test for both of us. When the skill faltered our fumbling hands tried to do the talking, the pauses growing from hesitant silence to soft groans, head shakes, then laughter.

Guernica, more modern than old, was almost deserted at that midday hour. We pulled up at the town plaza, surrounded by older buildings. '*Manger*,' Arturo said, putting his fingers to his lips. He led me up a few steps to a wide stone walkway, and we made our way through the scattering of round tables covered with red-checked cloths that sat unoccupied outside several bars.

The bar Arturo chose was almost empty. An old man sat at a table reading the newspaper *El Correo* and sipping on a little glass of red wine, wearing a black beret and peering over his thick-rimmed glasses into the news of the day. Two middle-aged men stood at the long bar, smoking and talking intensely. The bartender hovered close by, wiping the bar and listening. They studied us when we entered, the long strap muscles in their necks standing out like palings in a fence. Arturo, short, stocky and wearing the same black beret as the old man, was one of them, but I was a foreigner, an *extranjero*. I squirmed and looked away. One grunted dismissively, and they resumed their conversation in muted tones.

The bartender sidled over. '*Qué quiere usted?*'

'*Bière?*' Arturo enquired, turning to me.

Wishing to be polite, I nodded. '*Oui.*'

The bartender whipped the caps off two bottles of San Miguel and poured them simultaneously into two tall glasses. The froth surged up, threatening to overflow, and subsided teasingly. I'd never seen drinks poured this way, and this would be the first beer I ever drank.

'*Salud! Santé!*' Arturo touched glasses with a reassuring smile.

'*Santé,*' I replied nervously and lifted the sweating glass to my lips. The bitter, fizzy taste was strangely refreshing, the sensation of delicate cold tentacles spreading through me, a revelation. So, that's why they drink it!

Arturo took a long draught, half-draining his glass. '*Pincho de tortilla?'* he asked, arching his thick black eyebrows. Small plates of *pinchos*, hors d'oeuvres impaled on wooden toothpicks, sat atop the bar. Arturo picked up a wedge of tortilla and handed it to me on a serviette. It was still warm. He took one for himself. Hungry, I attacked it in earnest, pausing only to sip the beer. 'Hmm-mm,' I purred between mouthfuls.

Arturo grinned, wiped his lips. *'Très bien, non?'*

'You bet ... I mean, *très délicieux!'*

He motioned to the *pinchos*, urging me on. *'Mange, mange.'* Another tortilla followed, firm but juicy.

It felt unnatural to drop my rubbish like Arturo did, but it was the custom and the sawdust floor was strewn with cigarette butts, toothpicks and crumpled serviettes.

Arturo chatted with the young bartender in a strange musical language. The two men along the bar joined in, frequently interrupting each other, their hands moving as fast as their tongues. Mundaca and Lequetio were the only words I recognised until they said *Australiano* and studied me in turn.

'What language is that?' I asked Arturo in French, but the conversation had halted abruptly, my question stranded, hanging mid-air.

Two men had swaggered into the bar. Swarthy and moustachioed, each with a rifle slung over his shoulder. By their heavy olive-green uniforms, black boots, belts and curious black hats, I guessed they were soldiers. The patrons' faces turned hard-set and sullen. The transformation was instant and unnerving. I tried to shrink.

The soldiers sat at a table, hanging their rifles over the backs of their chairs. The rifles swayed backward and forward, the dark wooden butt of one grazing noisily against the chair leg, its long metal barrel pointing in a slow circling motion towards the ceiling.

'*Camarero!*' the heavier-set of the pair called out impatiently.

The bartender regarded them with a necessary politeness.

'*Dos vinos de marca ... y tráenos usted pinchos de atún y tortilla,*' the soldier ordered gruffly.

The bartender began, unhurriedly, to prepare their drinks and food.

The soldier strummed the tabletop with his fingertips and eyed each patron and each, unflinchingly, turned his face. His eye caught mine, the cruel, dark look of the hunter, the lurking wolf that moves in packs. I shuddered and looked away. His contemptuous gaze moved on and I was drawn back to him in morbid fascination. Beyond the surly exterior something else lurked: the fear of the hunted.

Arturo seemed impatient to leave. He paid the bill in a business-like fashion, the bartender equally stern.

'*Adiós,*' Arturo called out firmly.

'*Adiós,*' the locals replied, their focus shifting momentarily from the soldiers to us. Only the old man lost in his paper didn't look up or speak.

'*Guardia Civil ... Cabrones!*' Arturo almost spat when we reached the car. I didn't have the nerve or command of French to ask him what it was all about, but there was no doubting the hostility of the patrons inside the bar. Civil guards … 'the bastards'. From the same town? They couldn't be. Jeez, they wouldn't feel such hatred for their own kind. Would they? It seemed to come from both sides.

Arturo hoisted my pack into the back seat again. 'I'll take you to Mundaca.'

'Are you sure?' I asked. 'It's out of your way.' Lequetio was on the coast, to the east of Guernica. Mundaca was on the road to Bermeo, almost due north.

'*Bien sûr*,' he replied, scowling slightly, almost offended. 'I'll take you to find your brother.' He waved away my thanks with his big broad hand, saying, 'No problem, I'm not in a hurry and it's a beautiful day for a drive.'

§

Arturo must have forgotten about the *Guardia Civil* because he soon began to whistle a tune. The road grew more winding. On one of the tight narrow turns, a passing truck brought us to a complete halt while it inched past. Arturo laughed. 'Don't worry,' he said, patting me on my tense, wincing shoulder, 'We're used to this!'

I was drawn by the widening river on our right as we continued, but the curves were making me sick and I had to focus on the road. At the summit of a hill, Arturo stopped so we could admire the view. I was glad to get out of the car and get a little fresh air, and my nausea was swept aside.

It was spectacularly beautiful. A river mouth about a kilo-metre wide heralded the deep blue waters of the Bay of Biscay. On either side, the Pyrenees tumbled dramatically into the ocean. Two or three kilometres out beyond the river mouth sat a solitary island. To my right, behind the first pine-treed head-land, a pale ochre cliff dropped violently into the sea. To the left, the hills rose steeply, turning rapidly into rolling moun-tains. In a nook, in the corner of the river mouth, protected by a sandbar, was a village, its church tower prominent. The full force of the sun at its zenith spread a powerful light over the whole scene. I was mesmerised.

'Wow!'

Arturo cocked an eyebrow.

'I mean ... *très belle!*'

'*Mundaca,*' Arturo said circumspectly, hands on hips. He, too, seemed bewitched by the panorama. '*Qué maravilloso!*' he said softly and slowly, as if recognising an old friend from afar.

So this was Mundaca. It was, as Arturo had said, 'marvel-lous'. I felt a thrill, a surge of energy pass through me.

We stood for a while, looking. A tiny wave broke down the length of a sandbar near the river mouth. Surf! Of course. Why else would John come here?

'*On y va,*' said Arturo, dragging me from my thoughts. 'We find your brother.'

'Yes, let's go.'

The road wound down from the hilltop into a narrow valley. We crossed a bridge and a pocket-size beach appeared between two rocky promontories. A group of children were playing in the shallows, watched by their chattering mothers.

The road climbed again into the village. Halfway up, a sign announced: *Mundaca*. My heart quickened. This is it, I've arrived! Near the top was a tiny old post office, with *Correos* above the door. That's where John would collect his mail.

We turned sharply into the main street. The road narrowed, bordered on both sides by tired but sturdy two-storey buildings, the ground floors housing shops, several banks and a number of bars. The street was almost deserted. Shopkeepers were locking their doors and closing their shutters, a few locals disappearing into the tenements.

'La siesta comienza,' Arturo declared. 'It doesn't matter. The bars stay open,' he said in French.

Good. If the bars were open, we should be able to find the one I needed. With a bit of luck, I'd soon be with John.

We turned down an even narrower street and into the shade of more tall dwellings. Bars, a bread shop marked *Panadería*, a glimpse of the plaza fronting the town hall, and the street opened up onto a large plaza or *paseo*. It was deathly quiet with no-one in the streets.

Behind the *paseo*, with its back to the sea, stood the imposing church and high bell tower that I'd seen from the lookout. Not particularly old, nor strikingly beautiful, it dominated its surroundings by virtue of its size. The *paseo* acted like a forecourt and was shaded by rows of tall plane trees, grand and lush like oaks, the paler, mottled trunks made them lighter on their feet.

31

Arturo turned into the car park behind the strange-looking, top-heavy, two-storey casino. We walked to the edge of the tiny port bounded by rocks on the far side. A cannon rusted on the low rear wall, and the port wall grew higher where it swung towards us. Between the port and the tenements was a broad cobbled path. A slipway intersected the path, behind it a wall, and above, several old buildings partly obscured by plane trees. All the walls were whitewashed, reflecting the bright early afternoon sun.

'Un-real,' I said slowly and softly. 'Just like a painting.'

'*Bonito, no?*' Arturo whispered. He raised a foot and leant on the low wall.

I followed suit, shading my eyes. Sweat trickled down my brow and I wiped it away.

A fleet of six wooden fishing boats sat calmly in the green-blue water. Tethered to iron rings set into the cobbled stone seawall, they were each painted in one vibrant colour: navy blue, blood red or emerald green. On the inner side of the larger seawall guarding the entrance, fishing nets were draped and a few fisherwomen were busy repairing holes. One saw us and murmured to the others. When they paused to look, Arturo tipped his hat and nodded. They smiled, nodded in reply, and chattering anew, returned to their nets.

'*Mira,*' said Arturo, pointing. A swallow darted across the port, a low-dipping flight, its wings just clearing the water.

The village grew up and out of the port, old buildings of three or four storeys with newer ones rising behind them.

32

Across the port a path led up to a smaller plaza. To our right, a naked headland overlooked the port entrance and sandbar. Between the headland and the church, shaded by rows of plane trees and bordered by elegant wrought-iron bench seats, was a much smaller rectangular *paseo* that overlooked the river mouth.

Arturo stirred me from a hazy half-dream. '*On y va*. We get your bag and find your brother.'

We headed to the sturdy old buildings above the slipway and reached a wide terrace shaded by smaller plane trees, whose lower trunks were painted white, highlighting their lush foliage. Raised above the port, the terrace had a perfect view.

'*Muy lindo, no?*' said Arturo.

I didn't understand the words, but knew what he meant. It was beautiful in every sense of the word, like an exotic illusion. I was besotted. Trust John to find the best places.

A couple of local fishermen emerged from a pair of ancient doors behind us. They wore black berets, navy shirts with the sleeves rolled up over stained white singlets, navy blue trousers and tattered espadrilles. They scrutinised us briefly, nodded and disappeared down a flight of stone steps at the port end of the terrace, close together, talking quietly.

We turned towards the dark doors, above which was the name of the bar, *Los Chopos*, carved in wood. Coming in from the bright sunlight, it felt like we had entered a cave and my eyes took time to adjust.

A barman was conversing with a lone customer who leant

on the bar, exploring his teeth with a toothpick. The dark wood and stone-wall interior was very dim and echoed the silent mood of the siesta hour.

'Carmen's place?' Arturo asked.

'No,' said the barman. He gestured with his head. 'Next door. *Bar El Puerto*.' Arturo nodded and the men watched in silence while we left.

Bar El Puerto was a corner building with thick stone walls and commanded an impressive view of the port. The stone stairway led up from the path surrounding the tiny harbour and straight to its narrow wooden doors, and I guessed it must have been the original bar of the village. We entered through the salt-bleached doors into a surprisingly light-filled bar. The windows were open to the port to catch the available breeze.

'*Buenas tardes*,' Arturo began, wiping his brow with a handkerchief.

The barkeeper, a short thick-set woman of late middle-age with dark auburn hair, lifted her gaze. Her dulled brown eyes emerging from the shadows of dark rings, she exhaled audibly, continuing to dry a line of *tinto* glasses with a red-checked tea towel. '*Buenas tardes*.'

She was in no hurry. Did this tired soul know my brother? I hoped so.

She dried the last glass and set aside her tea towel. '*Qué quiere ustedes?*' she asked wearily.

Arturo ordered two beers. '*Se llama Carmen?*' he asked while she poured them. She nodded.

I smiled, and her eyes came to life. '*Y qué?*' she asked.

'*Buscamos el hermano de éste chico.* We're looking for this boy's brother, John,' said Arturo.

'John?' she repeated, thoughtfully. '*No, no recuerdo a ningún* "John".' With a glint in her eye and the beginnings of a smile, she pronounced it in the French way, '*Quizás Jean.*' And, her smile broadening, '*Sí, un Jean.*'

My brother had made an impact, you could tell. John had that way about him.

'An Australian was here in the village with two Americans,' Arturo translated for me. She hadn't seen them for three or four weeks. '*Muchachos simpáticos,*' she said. 'And *Jean*, the Australian, he resembles you. Your brother, for sure.'

They were here, but had gone! My chest emptied of air with a low groan.

Arturo grimaced, patted me on the back. '*Mala suerte, chico!*'

Bad luck or blind stupidity? I knew deep down the odds were against me, but I couldn't help build on that faint hope.

Arturo checked his watch and spoke with the woman. 'I must go to Lequetio,' he said, looking defeated. He drained his glass. 'Sorry we didn't find your brother. This lady, *Señora Carmen*, she will find you accommodation for tonight. *Ça va?*' He looked inquiringly across to Carmen.

She studied me for a moment, twitched slightly, and sighed maternally. A warm inner glow seemed to have chased the dullness from her eyes.

'The rest is up to you my friend … *Bonne chance et au*

revoir!' Arturo shook my hand heartily and wished me good luck.

I watched him go. My shoulders dropped, the breath pushing out of me. I looked down at the floor and the crushed cigarette butts scattered about. All his efforts had come to naught and here I was ... alone in a strange, if beautiful, little village in rural Spain. Jesus! What to do?

CHAPTER 3

Greg woke me at the border where the French, bored and uninterested, waved us through dismissively.

The Spanish side was another story and altogether different from my first crossing. A haughty immigration official, mood as dark as a storm, questioned us while he thumbed, meticulously, through each passport. His expression suggested we'd committed a crime that we ought to confess. I squirmed, even though I was innocent. Greg remained calm and we weathered the storm. At last, he stamped our passports and tossed them back at us, but the motor had barely turned over when two heavily armed *Guardia Civil* directed Greg to pull over.

'Out,' said one, motioning with his machine gun. 'Open the boot,' he said in heavily accented English.

Greg lifted the boot lid.

The *Guardia* peered in. It was crammed with our gear. 'Everything out.'

'Everything?'

'Everything,' said the *Guardia*, 'back seat too.'

Greg groaned. 'Come on, *amigo*, unpack.'

We emptied the car.

'Stand over there,' said the *Guardia*, pointing ten metres

away. We watched them poke and nose their way around the vehicle.

'Searching for drugs?' I whispered to Greg.

'I guess,' he replied, with a look of resignation.

They didn't find anything suspicious and gave up, leaving a surly guard to watch us re-load our scattered possessions. We got back in the car and the *Guardia* motioned us on with his gun.

I felt somehow violated but Greg wasn't bothered. 'You should see the *Federales* in Mexico! Man, they're way scarier and totally corrupt. A bribe is normal, but occasionally foreigners get arrested for possessing drugs planted by the *Federales* when they're searching the vehicle. Once you're in jail you, or your family, have to pay hefty bribes to get you out.'

'Well, I guess the *Guardia* aren't so corrupt,' I said. 'But they look nasty. I suppose they have to contend with Basque resistance fighters. I told you about that *Guardia* being assassinated in Guernica.'

'When you were with that guy Arturo?'

'No. I didn't learn about it until later, at the fiesta, with the French guys.'

'Oh, the French guys. You haven't told me much about them.'

'I met them that first day, after Arturo left me with Carmen in *Bar El Puerto*.'

§

We were alone with no common language, and neither of us spoke while Carmen continued her minor chores. I watched the bubbles rise from the bottom of the glass. It soon ran out of fizz.

When I finished the beer, Carmen took off her apron and plucked a large key from a hook on the wall. 'Ven, *muchacho*. Come, my boy,' she said.

The village was beginning to stir from its slumber. She locked the weathered door of the bar and led me down the stone steps to the cobbled path that skirted the port. She didn't rush, and I could feel the heat of the late afternoon sun reflected off the paint-chipped walls and the cobbles.

In the heart of the village we came to a modern apartment building. There was no elevator and we took the stairs to the third floor. Carmen pressed a buzzer and a black-garbed woman opened the nearest door. She was plain-looking, with a welcoming smile, and smelt of fish, garlic and perfume. She held out a large, rough hand. I shook it firmly, but couldn't match her powerful grip.

'*Australiano*,' Carmen said, introducing me. 'Owen.'

'Maria,' the woman said softly.

They talked briefly and Carmen said goodbye. The tired lines of her handsome face softened, like calm restored to a windswept sea. There was a lightness in her step when she descended the stairs, reminding me of home, of my own mother.

Mum. She'd be disappointed I missed the rendezvous with John. But, hell, John was elusive, and she knew that.

Maria and I stood regarding each other in the wood-panelled living room with its dining area and large window that overlooked the port. Under it sat a dark wooden table and chairs and, nearer me, a formal lounge suite with crimson cushions. Jesus wearing a crown of thorns hung on the wall and there was a crucifix above the door. She was calm, almost angelic, while she studied her new charge.

Maria then ushered me into an adjacent room where there was an untouched single bed near the door. The bed looked neat and clean. There were three other single beds in the room, all unmade. Three surfboards stood upright against the far wall. The whole room seemed fairly well ordered.

'*Dos cientas pesetas al noche.* Two hundred pesetas a night. Okay?' she said.

My thoughts were still mostly with John, so I nodded absently. 'Okay.' I was in the hands of others and had to trust them.

I dropped my dirty backpack beside the offered, untouched bed, glad to be relieved of the thing. Almost as soon as my backpack hit the floor, three guys filed into the room and Maria began introducing me to the owners of the three surfboards.

Dark-eyed Luc wore a winning grin. Jean-Louis nodded shyly, a leaner, taller, studious type with sandy hair and steel-rimmed glasses, and Michel, who gave me the once-over. I returned the scrutiny. He was a little older than me — tall and slim with brown hair, steady brown eyes and a fine wispy moustache. The three of them greeted me with the same brief, loose-grip handshake, one with more style than substance. A handshake that never really got going.

'They speak English,' Michel said. 'But not so good like me.' He smiled and the room felt instantly lighter. 'Come,' he beckoned me with a forefinger. 'We make a little tour.'

Michel, with due Gallic gravity, carefully explained the details of the domestic arrangements. The white-tiled bathroom and kitchen were scrubbed meticulously clean. Michel turned his back on Maria who hovered not so discreetly in the background, touched his nose and winced. 'Maria's husband, Adolfo, is a fisherman,' he whispered. 'She try hard to keep the stink of fish out of the apartment.'

But I could smell it everywhere. I could imagine Maria with the other fishwives I'd seen repairing nets down at the seawall, bringing home the catch when the boats came in, cleaning and scaling the fish. Over time, the smell must have become ingrained into her tough leathery skin.

Back in the bedroom, Luc and Jean-Louis were reclining on their beds under the crucifix, reading surfing magazines. They observed me over their pages, Jean-Louis discreetly, Luc less so.

'You come from where?' asked Michel coolly, eyebrows rising.

'London.' I was a little taken aback by his tone. 'I hitched.'

'Hitched?' His demeanour changed. He seemed impressed. The others too.

'I like hitching,' I said. 'I've hitched all over the place. Since I was thirteen.'

'Really?'

I told them how I'd started off hitching with a group of mates from Melbourne to the coast.

'Your parents, they do not mind?' asked Michel.

'At the beginning, but everybody hitches, especially surfers. "Safety in numbers," Mum always said. Besides, my brother made it easy for me.'

John had fought the heated battles about hitching years ahead of me; I'd merely watched anxiously from the sidelines as the arguments unfolded. Eventually, the folks gave up. John became too big and strong and I don't think Dad was the fighting kind. When my turn arrived, I quietly followed in my brother's footsteps.

'They'd seen that John had come to no harm hitchhiking,' I added. 'Although I'm sure he didn't tell them everything that happened. Mind you, neither did I.'

'*Did* anything happen?' Jean-Louis asked.

'Well, occasionally you'd get separated on the road, and end up in a car alone. On one of my earlier rides, an old codger put his hand on my knee. I screamed. He panicked and jammed on the brakes, wanting me out as quickly as I wanted to get out.'

They all laughed.

'I was more wary after that, but there was no way I was telling the folks. That would have put a stop to my weekend surfing trips away with my mates.'

'*J'imagine.*' Michel tapped his chin with his finger.

'Go anywhere interesting?' asked Luc, setting his magazine aside.

'When I was sixteen, I flew to New Zealand for my first overseas rendezvous with John. He was living and working there. We hitched from Auckland down the east coast to Gisborne, and then on to Mahia to go surfing. Six months ago I hitched to London from my aunt's in Genoa.'

'Genoa?' said Jean-Louis, frowning.

'I was glad to get out of that place. Poor aunty was struggling.'

'Why?' he asked.

'It's complicated,' I said. I didn't tell them how she'd gone a little crazy living there, divorced, with a young child to bring up. She tried hard for twenty years, but remained forever an outsider. Not even a passion for opera and the violin could break down the local prejudices. It finally got to her. I'd seen her rage against the world and it wasn't pretty. I had to escape. 'I was lucky,' I added. 'One long ride with two chirpy Canadians, the whole length of France, all the way from Nice to Lille. It must have been some kind of record.'

'A long ride, but Lille?' Jean-Louis frowned again. 'You finish in Lille?'

'We picked up a medical student on the outskirts of Paris. He was hitching to university in Lille. We got talking and he invited me to stay. It was a cramped apartment, so I spent a few nights on the floor amongst scattered anatomy and physiology books on a stained mattress that a mate and his girlfriend occasionally used.'

'An *intimate* encounter with French anatomy and physiology, *n'est-ce pas?'* Jean-Louis mused. The others laughed and I joined in.

'Anyway, he took me under his wing and we visited his various girlfriends. He was a real charmer, the girls seemed to love him.' I was silent for a moment, reflecting. 'A good guy, shared what he had. Thoughtful too, he seemed interested in my prospects.'

Michel digested the anecdote. Then he shrugged. 'Hitch anywhere else, anywhere *interesting?'*

'Mostly the local coast of Victoria. The surfing brotherhood in Australia are an adventurous lot, you know.' I felt proud telling them about exploring for surf breaks, the never-ending obsession fuelled by surf magazines and the promise of uncrowded perfect waves. 'Dad used to say when he drove us along the coast, "You boys always think the waves will be better at the next spot around the next corner." My father had his limits, that's for sure.'

'And you?' asked Michel.

'Limits? Not really. I nearly drowned once and got chased out of the water by a shark at Yallingup, but other than that, no. Not me. Not yet.'

'And so, what now?' he asked, hands on hips.

'I came to find my brother. He was here, but he's gone. I don't know where.' I shrugged. 'I guess I'll go travelling.'

'In London, you did what?'

Michel's English, although slightly comical, was pretty good. His forthright manner, however, was off-putting. I glanced at the others. Luc rolled his eyes, Jean-Louis sighed and stretched out his arms, mirroring the crucified Christ above.

I launched into the part of my story that began in London and they listened, nodding, looking me over. In London I'd focused on survival and saving money so I could meet up with John. My back-up plan if I didn't find him was to travel around Europe and see the sights.

'*Et voilà!*' Michel said, with a grand sweep of his right arm, when the interrogation was over. His theatrics made me laugh. I wondered what they'd make of him back home.

'What about you guys?' I asked.

'University students from Paris,' he said, puffing out his chest. 'But the study year is finished and it's time for *le surf.*' The detached look deserted him momentarily. '*Le surf* is important for us. Also, there is fiesta,' he said. 'It begin in a few days.'

The Frenchmen intrigued me. These guys had learnt the basic skills, bought the latest equipment and adopted many of the ways of the beach culture, but they hadn't dropped out or let surfing dominate their lives. After all, they were Parisians and *le surf* was only really possible in holidays, mostly in summer. The rest of the time they studied hard, preparing for their careers. They were well-groomed for surfers, their hair relatively short, their clothes casual, yet well-tailored. Their gestures were refined and even their excitement when discussing *le surf*, restrained. I'd never seen such an enthusiastic yet stylish approach to the sport. It was like Paris at the beach.

'I haven't surfed for seven months,' I confessed. But now,

faced by three keen surfers, I felt a rush of blood through the veins, a familiar tingle in the skin.

Luc sat forward on the edge of his bed, a little fire in his eyes. 'You want to surf! I can see it. Good!' He gave an excited glance to Jean-Louis.

Jean-Louis pushed his glasses high on his long narrow nose and ran his left hand through his thick sandy hair. Something about his hands made me wonder if he played the piano. 'Where is your board, your wetsuit?' he asked in meticulous English. The parlour cat was as capable and accomplished as he was reserved — you could tell, he only had to stretch.

'In Australia.'

Luc checked his watch. A hungry light prowled in the depths of his eyes. Panther-like, he sprang to his feet. 'Mes amis, it's time,' he said. 'Allez!'

Michel beckoned me with a wave of his hand. 'You want to come and watch?'

Thoughts of John were swept aside by talk of the sea, he barely need ask. The reply shot out. 'You bet!'

'On y va!'

§

Greg grinned. 'Man, you must have been excited! Seven months without waves. I can't imagine it. How did you feel when they were suiting up, grabbing their boards?'

'It was like my blood was flowing again! I was hot on their

46

heels from then on.'

'What happened next?'

§

I stood beside the cannon while the Frenchmen cautiously descended a short flight of moss-covered steps to a patch of sand exposed by the low tide. They negotiated the taut slimy ropes that cross-tethered several grounded fishing boats to the walls, waded into the murky green water and paddled to where the port opened to the sea.

What a sight! Surfers slipping across the silent waters of this tiny ancient harbour. In the distance, framed by the seawalls, waves were breaking in the river mouth, and beyond, the mountains and that huge cliff. This was surfing like I'd never seen or imagined. When I thought of surf, I thought of bush, coastal hills and wild, wide, open beaches that stretched for miles. This was bizarre — surf in a medieval setting.

I followed the path around the port, taking my gaze from the surfers only to prevent a fall into the oily water. Out of the port, the surfers paddled into a channel that narrowed between the sandbar and a rocky outcropping. Beyond the breakers, they paddled parallel to the waves around to the edge of the sandbar to sit on their boards to wait.

The swell was modest and inconsistent. A gentle breeze flitted down the river, smoothing the sea and momentarily holding up the waves when they peaked. Arriving in sets of three or four, the swells rose precipitously and broke with a sharp cracking sound on the shallow sandbar, a well-delineated triangle at this low tide, running from the rocky outcrop into the river mouth and away from the shoreline. I could see a weathered old chapel on the point beyond the rocks.

A set approached and the surfers paddled for the first wave. Luc caught it, but was barely upright before the wave broke around him, throwing him forward and off his board. The others tried their luck with the swells that followed, but all were tossed aside and left flailing in the sandy whitewash, no doubt slightly stunned.

As waves go, these were challenging. They were fast and powerful. You'd need excellent technique. Today's waves were too small and too fast to ride properly, but I could see the potential of this perfect set-up with the long, shallow sandbank abutting the deep ocean. In certain respects the wave was safe because it ran down into the river, but the out-flowing channel was dangerous. It allowed easy access from the port to the break, but it could also suck you well out to sea if you lost your board.

At sunset, they emerged from the water looking frustrated. Luc was crestfallen and silent. Jean-Louis put his arm around him, like a big brother would. 'Ça va, Luc. Ça va. It's okay.'

§

'Poor Luc!' said Greg. 'He must have been bummed.'
'He was, and Michel rubbed it in. He didn't let up.'

48

'That's harsh, man. Sounds like a critical wave. Any surfer could get rolled there.'

'It is critical. The locals have a healthy respect for it.'

'Local surfers?'

'No. There aren't any. The fishermen I mean. The landlord told us that night.'

§

We joined Maria and her husband — the wiry, diminutive Adolfo — and their two watchful children, for dinner.

'You boys love the sea, don't you?' said Adolfo. 'We fishermen do, too. It's our livelihood. But we also fear it.' He took a sip of red wine. 'Most of us can't swim, or not well.' He leant forward, still clutching the glass. Half his little finger was missing. 'The waves are our enemy. We can't leave the port if there are waves. In the summer it's not a problem, but in autumn and winter, when the waves are big, we stay at home.'

He put down his glass and ran a hand through his cropped greying hair. 'When we see you boys paddling out in the big waves, we think you're crazy.' He grimaced and scratched his scalp. 'Don't get me wrong, we know you're brave, and that you understand the sea, and the winds, the tides and the currents. We can see that.' He picked up a piece of crusty bread and snapped it in two. 'But still we think you're mad.' He waved one of the pieces. 'All I can say is that it must feel damn good to ride those wretched waves and take such risks.' Adolfo shook his head. 'I take my hat off to you … but still think you're crazy … *locos!*' He took a bite and began chewing.

§

'Adolfo sounds like quite a character,' said Greg.

'He is. He doesn't hold back. You should have heard what he said the next night about surfers.'

§

We were sitting around the dining table waiting for Maria to bring the meal. She was singing quietly as she cooked, her gentle melody battling with the spit of the fry-pan. The aroma of fried fish preceded her, stealing in on the breeze from the kitchen window.

Adolfo was hungry. He kept glancing towards the kitchen door and playing with his cutlery. The backs of his hands were covered in linear scars, presumably where the hand lines had bitten deep when they fished. 'Well, the villagers think surfers are eccentrics,' Adolfo observed with a glint in his eye. He seemed determined to share his insider knowledge. 'And a little bit like gypsies, only fairer.' He rolled up his sleeves and leant forward as if about to tell a secret. 'Gypsies, you know, have a bad reputation in Spain. They pass through,' he made a sweeping motion of his scarred hand, 'never stay long, and get up to mischief.' He scowled. 'They're often dirty, lazy and thieving.' He jabbed the air with his finger. 'And not to be trusted.'

He sat back hard against his seat, crossed his arms and examined our blank faces. 'The surfers aren't thieves, don't get me wrong,' he clarified, uncrossing his arms and offering up his calloused palms. 'But a number are scruffy and they do come and go like gypsies. The villagers are naturally suspicious.' He raised his palms, shrugging, bringing deep creases to the weather-beaten skin of his neck.

He leaned towards us again, another secret to share. 'The villagers work hard. When they see the foreigners hanging about doing nothing, they think they're lazy.' His face hardened, as if feeling a sudden tug on his hand-line. 'And we don't tolerate laziness. No, no, not at all. Never!' He threw back his shoulders, laughing, and showed his palms again. 'So that's what you're up against!'

§

The road began to climb. I took a long deep breath and let it out, releasing the tension.

'Well, surfers are accustomed to those kinds of sentiments,' said Greg. 'We battle a similar denigration back home.'

'Yeah, in Australia, we're depicted like hippies or dropouts or fringe-dwellers, living on the edge of society,' I said.

'Same in America, man. They say we're a subversive influence with nothing valuable to contribute.'

'I reckon the allure of surfing has always been hard to explain to those that don't surf.'

'Exactly. Why would it be any different here?'

I took another big breath and surveyed the peaceful countryside.

'So, did you get to ride Mundaca?' asked Greg.

'We waited for it.'

§

Over the following days the weather was near perfect. It was a time to relax, to rejuvenate, to stretch the limbs. And the Frenchmen and I did just that.

The village readied itself for the coming fiesta and we idled, spending long intervals sunbaking on the seawalls. From there we could observe the villagers at work: fishermen making minor repairs or painting their boats; fisherwomen patching nets on the walls below us, rarely silent; bartenders tidying their bars in the quiet of the morning; villagers white-washing everything that didn't move, including the lower trunks of every plane tree. Steadily, the village was renewed.

Body pressed against the hot cement atop the seawall, closed eyes to the sky, I could let my thoughts go. The sun on the skin, the slight taste of salt, a lick of sea breeze and the lap of the water against the seawalls proved an intoxicating combination. Sometimes, like today, it felt good to laze.

When I sat up from time to time, I saw that the preparations for the fiesta continued, conducted in a steady, almost mechanical, fashion — each chore presumably passed down over time from father to son and mother to daughter.

We weren't alone on the seawalls. School was out and the local children gravitated there to sunbake and jump or dive into the port to swim. The water, a fusion of seawater, boat engine oil and fish remnants, was uninviting for us, but didn't seem to bother them.

We stationed ourselves at a polite distance. The local children seemed intrigued by our foreign ways, and watched when we sunbaked, swam, climbed the rusty ladder, read, chatted and snoozed. They took it all in.

'Look,' said Michel. 'They talk about us.'

The girls our age gazed discreetly, when they thought we wouldn't notice. But they seemed glad if we did, covering their smiles with their hands when they turned away. They teased each other and soon grew bolder, stealing longer glances.

Michel smiled openly, encouraging them.

'*Extranjeros*,' the local boys reminded the girls. Foreigners. Off limits. We heard that word, *extranjeros*, a lot, and wondered how far off limits we really were. Michel was keen to find out, Luc too, but Jean-Louis reminded them that Mundaca was, after all, a tight-knit fishing village and the customs were strict. 'It's Spain,' he said. 'Not France.'

§

'So you just hung out?' said Greg.

'Not exactly. The swell was dropping and there was no surf at Mundaca. The Frenchmen wanted to try another spot they thought might have waves and invited me along. We headed out after lunch, towards Bermeo.'

§

Bermeo was a thriving fishing town of about 20,000 people. Its port boasted a large harbour, protected by a long phalanx-like seawall stretching 300 metres out to sea, home to a sizeable fishing fleet. The vessels were ocean-going trawlers of unique design — sturdy, with rounded bow and stern, and painted in the same vibrant blue, red or green, with white Plimsoll lines, neatly berthed in rows across the harbour, resting. You could smell the fish a good distance away.

We traversed Bermeo, quiet now in its siesta lull, via a narrow winding thoroughfare that ran between the many apartment buildings. Shutters were drawn against the strong afternoon heat; the townsfolk bunkered within, to eat and sleep.

The road widened and climbed at the outskirts of the town. Buildings gave way to a patchwork of fields, the shapely haystacks resting, new-cut hay shining bright beside the faded yellow bundles of the previous day's labours. A shifting breeze created swirling patterns in the remaining uncut grass. We crossed the fields, climbing steadily to a ridge beyond the town where the road twisted and I could glimpse back to see Bermeo, its port, the island of Izaro and, away in the distance, the pale gold cliff of Laga.

'Wow!' I said, unable to contain myself. 'Look at that!'

'The Basque country,' said Michel. *'C'est magnifique, n'est-ce pas?'*

Magnificent it was. But there was something else, a magnetic power, and I could feel it drawing me in. For some strange reason I felt right at home.

On the ridge, the road wandered through pine woods, skirting the coast, past the cape, Cabo Machichaco, before regaining the steep coastal edge where the forest thins. The road flattened and descended, always in curves, past a spectacular rugged island that lay close to the shore. A hand-hewn path zigzagged up from its base at the beach to the chapel atop the island's precarious peak. A large bell sat silent in the bell tower, circled by marauding gulls when they spiralled up from the ocean below.

Baquio sat in a break in the mountain chain on a coastal plain abutting the sea. Its broad beach stretched between rocky headlands from which grew hills that rose to mountains. The village itself was rather dispersed, with the main road running parallel to the beach, but separated from it by a row of modern high-rise holiday apartments. I couldn't believe it. Another sleepy coastal retreat wrecked by thoughtless development.

A dirt track off the main road led to the beach. We parked near the sand under the shade of a two-storey condominium.

The Frenchmen gazed in earnest at the meagre swell, gauging the possibilities. The wind was offshore, the beach deserted, no humans in sight. A set of waves arrived and broke in acceptable patterns.

'*Bonnes vagues!*' said Luc, his brown eyes almost leaping out of his tanned face. He was in his element now, soon to be freed from his cage, restless, ready to pounce.

'Good waves,' I agreed. 'Definitely rideable.'

'*On y va!*' said Michel, throwing the car door open. Feverishly they converged on the boot, climbed into wetsuits and freed their tethered surfboards from the roof. '*Tiens!* Take these!' said Michel, throwing the keys at me before they sprinted to the water's edge and catapulted themselves into the sea.

'Lucky bastards,' I said to myself.

I stood watching while they launched over the shore-break and paddled rhythmically over the gleaming undulations, out to the farthest reaches of the sandbar. I longed to go with them, to feel the sand around my feet, the invigorating plunge of my head through the first breaking wave, to feel awakened and refreshed on the other side, to feel the stealth of cool water into my wetsuit — that first flush that washed away the clammy half-sweat, then the feel of the gentler, softer water, soft because the skin grows accustomed to the sea's initial chill. I wanted that baptismal experience, that cool salty submersion that strips away the imperceptible layers of terrestrial life, like the shedding of a reptile's skin.

'Oh, God!' I whispered to the winds.

I longed to be surfing, stroking through the water, the ocean slipping between the splayed fingers of my hands; to feel the rise and fall of the surfboard when it climbs each swell and dips on the other side; to feel the ocean's rhythm when I glide across its surface. I longed to feel my muscles working and straining. To taste the salt and the breeze, eyes wide open, mind alert, the sound of the wind and the water's movement, to feel all the senses at work.

And to sit and wait — that simple aesthetic of witnessing and appreciating the natural elements of sea and sky, a time to relax, unwind, reflect, be silent, humble; to feel at one with nature, to feel spiritual.

I felt a prisoner on the beach. I stripped to my shorts and plunged into the sea. The water was brisk and numbing with the bite of the residual winter chill. I couldn't stay in long, despite the call of the waves. I was skinny and the cold penetrated straight to my bones.

I retreated to the warm sand, sat on my towel and watched. Before long, Jean-Louis gave up and joined me. He was shivering but seemed to sense my frustration immediately. 'You want to try? Take my board ... and, if you want, my wetsuit too.'

He helped me to peel on his dripping suit. I picked up the board and leapt into the sea. Aaaaah! There it was — that wonderful feeling — exhilaration and peace — all in the same moment! Nothing had changed! God, I loved surfing!

I took a few strokes. Something wasn't quite right. Jean-Louis's surfboard was so different from mine, the wetsuit was a little too large and my shoulders were weak from prolonged inactivity. I struggled to move the board. Gradually, I gained rhythm and momentum. Before long I was stroking across the water towards the sandbank. Liberated. 'Unnn-reeeal!' It was a loud, long holler.

Paddling was one thing but catching a wave was another. I made several attempts, all disastrous. I could see the French-men, all on the beach now, chuckling away. 'Come on, Owen,' I urged myself. 'Get into it.' Finally I got one, a long one too, right to the shore.

'You make us laugh in the beginning!' said Michel, a broad grin beneath his damp moustache. 'But the last wave ... *pas mal.*'

'Well, you know, I like to entertain,' I said.

They laughed and even if they were laughing at me, I didn't care. I'd been surfing!

§

'You must have been stoked, man!' said Greg.

'I was! I beamed all the way back to Mundaca ... until we reached Bermeo, that is.'

§

'What does "GORA ETA" mean?' I asked Michel, as we passed graffiti splashed in red paint on one of the tenement building walls on the outskirts of the town.

'GORA, I don't know this word, but *ETA* … you know … the Basque resistance, the guerrillas fighting against General Franco. Ask Jean-Louis. He is our Basque man.'

Jean-Louis grunted softly and examined his hands. 'GORA means *Vive* … so in English it means something like "Long live *ETA*!"'

'I've never heard of *ETA*,' I said.

Michel was incredulous. 'Really? *C'est incroyable!*'

Jean-Louis stared at me. '*Euskadi Ta Askatasuna.*'

'What does it mean?'

'Basque Homeland and Freedom.'

'That sounds straightforward.'

'The concept is. In Spain, the Basques suffer too much because of Franco. Not everyone agrees with *ETA* methods — bombs, assassinations, extortion — but still, *ETA* fights against Franco, against the fascists. Don't you learn about this in Australia, about the Spanish Civil War?'

'No,' I confessed. 'We don't study the Spanish Civil War. I did mostly science, and the history I learnt was Australian and British.'

'But surely you read the newspapers?' said Jean-Louis with a tone of disbelief.

'Only the sports section. Politics, it's always about the same things: Vietnam, apartheid and the Whitlam government.' My father watched the news every night on TV, scouring the papers and discussing it with the neighbour who joined us in the car on the way to work. Gough Whitlam, they said, was turning Australia upside down with reform after reform — Indigenous rights, women's rights, free university education, health care. He was doing it all, no expense spared.

'But politics is vitally important.' There was an edge to Jean-Louis's voice of unqualified disapproval.

I felt eyes boring into me. 'Maybe,' I said defensively. 'But Australia's a long way from anywhere and, except for Vietnam perhaps, it doesn't seem relevant … My neighbour was killed in Vietnam, you know. Eighteen years old, and ambushed by the Viet Cong. The curtains next door were drawn for years and his parents turned to ghosts. That was surreal … It's different in Europe, history's visible all around you. Australia isn't the same. No castles. No signs of war to speak of. The Indigenous history is invisibly woven into nature. Most people don't know about that and it's certainly not taught in schools.'

'Okay.' He sounded exasperated. 'But the Spanish Civil War was extremely important. A watershed in history. And for us Basques, a festering wound.'

'But it finished so long ago,' I said, half-turning towards him.

'True.' Jean-Louis's voice faltered. 'But you must understand, the Basques here in Spain have been suffering ever since Franco won the Civil War — since 1939. And, of course, Guernica suffered badly. Bombed to oblivion. That's a terribly sad story … but everybody knows about Guernica, thanks to Picasso.'

His words rang through me. I didn't know a bloody thing about Guernica except what I'd seen with my own eyes. Was the famous painting about *that* little town? It seemed unlikely, but it must be true.

§

Greg shook his head. 'Man, I can't believe you didn't know about Guernica.'

'Well, I knew nothing about the history, only my impressions from that first day with Arturo. But it soon took on new meaning.'

'How so?' asked Greg.

'When I met her.'

'When was that?'

'That night. After the Baquio surf. After dinner with Maria and Adolfo.'

§

The Frenchmen led me out of the apartment and into the streets. 'Come on,' said Michel. 'We take you on a *vuelta*.'

'What's that?'

'We make a tour of the bars, Spanish style! There are twelve in the village, most in the main street and near the port, others scattered about.'

We started at *Bar El Puerto*. It was curious to watch the locals come and go in groups and take their shots, standing almost nervously at the bar while Carmen poured one long sweep into a line of glasses, rarely spilling a single red drop. The men threw the wine back in one or two draughts, leaving a little in the bottom, and banged down the glasses with a thud. And they didn't hang about. A minute or two and they were off to the next bar. The fishermen were the quickest, and the quietest, but they had their reasons, not least the early morning rise. Silent and gruff, they dispatched their *tintos* as if the sea was bearing down on them and this might be their last drink.

'These fishermen are part of a long and proud Basque tradition of brave, hardy seafarers and navigators,' said Jean-Louis proudly. 'Their ancestors fished the seas for centuries, even millennia. They hunted whales in the Bay of Biscay, venturing further and further north for their diminishing prey, even establishing a colony on the Labrador coast of North America.'

'They got to America?' I asked, incredulous.

'Possibly even the United States, and the Caribbean too.'

'Really? In little boats?'

'Of course.'

While we watched them, the locals watched us. They gave no outward sign of approval or disapproval, rather a kind of benign curiosity. You could guess when they were talking about us from their quieter tones and awkward gaze.

'Look at this one!' said Michel, nudging me, and grinning wickedly. 'Raul. He look like a turtle.'

Indeed, his limbs hung loose and floppy from his stout trunk, his gait slow and tortuous. His forward-thrust head bobbled on a long, thick neck. He had a bulbous nose, goggle eyes, and guzzled his *tinto* through thick lips.

They said that Raul was a fixture on the *vuelta*, circulated alone, and drank with dedication and regularity in every bar. He was mostly quiet and inoffensive, but not this night. He burst into song, or something resembling it, at the top of his voice.

The response was swift. '*Cállate, Raul! Cállate!*' they yelled. Raul, momentarily hushed, receded into his shell for a bit but it wasn't long before he was at it again and everyone joined the chorus, '*Cállate, Raul! Cállate!*'

He stopped singing, swayed, appeared as if he might fall over, and staggered out of the bar, hurling slurred insults to one and all. It was hard not to laugh.

We followed a group out of *Bar El Puerto* to the casino. The cobbled streets were busy with groups of people coming and going, talking loudly.

From the street side, the casino appeared sturdy but on the three sides facing the port, estuary and *paseo* in turn, a wooden balcony enclosed by tall elegant windows had been constructed on the upper floor, making the building seem top-heavy. But the windows with their white-painted frames lightened the upper level.

'Iconic,' said Michel reassuringly.

An icon alright. It had drawn my eye ever since arriving with Arturo.

A dark oak staircase climbed to a landing that led to a long high-ceilinged room enclosed by a second wall of glass. Inside sat a dozen or so round tables with pristine white tablecloths, each with half a dozen handsome chairs and a long polished table for formal gatherings. The floor-to-ceiling drapes were tied back to allow entrance to the enclosed balcony through the inner glass doors where light streamed in. Here were smaller tables, where you could sit and enjoy the sun, or view the port, the river mouth, the church and the *paseo*.

The atmosphere was quieter, and more refined. The Frenchmen were right at home. 'So,' said Michel with a cheeky grin. 'Did you enjoy making *le surf* today?'

'Of course,' I replied coolly. I could see where this was going.

'It was interesting to watch you,' said Michel, his grin widening. 'At first I say to Luc, "My mother can surf better than him!"'

Here we go, I thought.

'And Luc said that his *grand-mère* could surf better than you!'

They laughed and I chewed on a smile.

'And you caught that last wave and we say, "*Now* he begins!"'

A group of girls caught our eye. They watched us, talking rapidly and smiling. The Frenchmen puffed out their chests and, almost in a blink, Michel was by their sides, chatting in Spanish. Luc and Jean-Louis followed, but I stood slightly adrift, watching on.

The girls were mostly dark-haired, dark-eyed, and vivacious. Once they got going, I began to appreciate Spanish women's reputation for fire and passion. I was drawn in, irresistibly.

Their eyes, mouths, faces, hands, mannerisms, postures were a whirl of movement. Everything sizzled.

One girl, fairer and quieter than the others, turned my way. She had a shapely mouth, a slightly upturned nose and captivating, light-filled, sea-green eyes. 'What's your name?' she asked cautiously.

I was taken aback, not expecting to hear English. 'Owen. And yours?'

'Maite.' She smiled gently, then looked away, smoothing back her long brown hair with slim delicate hands, revealing two large gold earrings.

'My ... tay,' I repeated. 'That's an unusual name. Is it Spanish?'

She turned back, her reserve cast aside. 'It's a traditional name,' she said proudly.

'Oh, I see. I'm afraid I haven't been here long.'

She appeared bemused.

'But I love what I've seen so far,' I continued. 'This village, the coast, the countryside. It's incredibly beautiful. The people seem so friendly. And the Basque culture and history, what I know of it, are fascinating.'

'It *is* beautiful,' she said, a smile playing at the corners of her mouth. 'And we Basques are proud of our country, our tradition.'

'You're Basque!'

'Yes. Where are you from?'

'Australia,' I replied. 'Melbourne.'

She nodded.

'Where did you learn your English?' I asked.

'Dublin. I was there six months, studying. I'm an art student.'

'Painting?'

'Drawing, sketching, painting. You have to learn to draw and sketch before you can paint properly.'

'True. My brother is talented and did a number of good abstract paintings. He began with drawing.'

'You don't paint?'

'No. I don't have the talent.'

'How do you know? Have you tried?'

'A little at school … I was better at science than art.'

'Maybe you should try one day.'

'Maybe.'

Her eyes fixed on mine … soft, warm, intense. Two deep green pools that you could swim in forever. I caught my breath and began to tingle all over. She blushed and reached to smooth her hair again.

'How long are you staying in Mundaca?' she asked.

'I'm not sure. I came to find my brother, but he's gone.' I sighed. 'I miss him.'

'When did you last see him?'

'Three years ago. He left home when he was seventeen.'

'Seventeen, that's pretty young! Where did he go?' Maite's brow furrowed.

'He and a mate dropped out of school and went surfing in the South Pacific. He was bursting to leave home,' I said,

66

recalling the arguments with my parents. 'He didn't even finish his last year at school. Mum and Dad were upset about that.'

'I can imagine.' A worried look crossed her face. 'Then what?'

'He was in the Pacific islands for a while, worked for a year in New Zealand, then California, before heading south on a surfing trip to Mexico and Central America. After that, he came to Europe, worked in Italy and then headed to Biarritz to go surfing. He came here with friends, stayed for a while, before heading off. South, towards Morocco, I think.'

'And now that you've missed him?'

'I'll probably go travelling, see the sights like my parents wanted. Although my friends are trying to persuade me to go with them back to Biarritz. I'm tempted.'

'A dilemma.'

'Yes … my head says go travelling. My heart says go surfing.'

She laughed. 'I think I know what you'll decide.'

'Do you?'

We smiled at each other. Hers, a warm, mysterious, elusive smile that first encircled and then enveloped me. I felt a shiver deep within.

'And after travelling or surfing? Then what?'

'I'm going to university next year to study medicine,' I said. 'Well, that's the plan.'

'Oh!' Her eyes filled with light. She studied me afresh, more seriously, seemingly surprised by my revelation. 'That's an honour.'

'An honour? I hadn't thought of it like that … Do you live in Mundaca?' I asked.

'Guernica.'

'Guernica!' The mere mention of the name conjured up contradictory images of the sleepy rural town I'd encountered, the menacing *Guardia Civil* in the bar, the infamous bombing during the Civil War that I could only imagine, and Picasso's painting, full of rage.

'Yes, Guernica.' She stared at me curiously. 'Have you been there?'

'I passed through on the way here. It made an impression. Jean-Louis is French Basque, he knows a lot about Basque history and politics.'

Her eyes narrowed when I said the word politics. She tensed and briefly scanned the room. 'Politics are complicated in this part of the world, and dangerous.'

'I'm beginning to appreciate that,' I said quietly.

She softened again and leant back. 'You have a lot to learn.'

'I'm a good student,' I said. 'With the right teacher.'

She studied me again. 'If you are really interested in the Basques, I have a book, in English, you could read.'

'I'd like that.'

'I'll bring it tomorrow.'

'Tomorrow?' My heart began to sprint. 'Wonderful!'

The others had drifted away from us. '*Oye chicas!*' she called out. '*Bego y Ines,*' she said, introducing them. We shook hands. '*Otro bar?*' Maite asked the girls.

'*Por supuesto,*' Ines replied. 'I'll round up the others.'

They ferried us to the next crowded noisy bar and plied us with drinks. And so it went on. We passed Adolfo in the street amid a group of hardy blue-garbed fishermen, flush with *tinto.* '*Adiós, muchachos! Agur!*' he cried.

'*Los extranjeros,*' his comrades called out. '*Adiós!*'

We returned the salute, '*Adiós, Adolfo! Adiós, señores!*'

The girls led us from bar to bar around the village. Each bar seemed a little crazier than the one before, warming up for the fiesta beginning the following day. Could it get any better?

Only when we returned (yet again) to *Bar El Puerto*, under the watchful eye of Carmen, was there a hint of reproach. She had raised an eyebrow affectionately on my first pass through, but by the third, when the drink took hold, she was scowling. But it was too late. We were off to the next bar.

By the end, Ines was finding it difficult to fend off Michel and signalled to Maite, pointing to her watch. It was well after midnight.

Maite shrugged her shoulders. 'We have to go.'

'Yes, of course.' A sigh escaped, betraying me.

A light flickered in her eyes, her lips parted. '*Hasta mañana, Doctor.*'

I touched her arm. 'Don't forget the book.'

'I won't.'

Michel urged the girls to stay, but to no avail. We followed them while they negotiated their way to the door through several groups of men.

'Guernica girls,' said one man derisively.

'Out-of-towners,' said another.

'Shameful hanging out with foreigners,' muttered a third.

But I didn't take in their words or their tone. I was drifting on a different current. Only later, back at the apartment, did Michel translate what they'd said.

Why 'shameful'? I wondered, as I lay in bed. Nothing shameful about Maite. On the contrary.

§

'I see what you mean,' said Greg. 'Man! So she's from Guernica.'

'You bet.'

'What happened the next day?'

'We went looking for them.'

§

'*On y va*,' said Luc.

We were about to leave Maria's when suddenly a noise, a drum roll and a loud voice in the street below drew me to the window.

'Check this out,' I said, motioning to the others. A thin elderly man with a kettle drum stood at a nearby corner giving a speech. When he'd finished, he walked to the next corner, stopped, performed another short drum roll and repeated the speech.

'What's he selling?' I asked Jean-Louis.

'Nothing. He tells the news.'

'A town crier!' I said. 'Who would have thought?' My eyes followed the man as he turned the corner. 'Such a wonderful old custom.'

'Old is right. How about something new?' said Michel impatiently. 'Let's go.'

I stood listening until the drum roll and speech was lost in the alleyways. The old man's voice echoed the fading of a bygone era.

'Owen!' Jean-Louis called from the open door. '*On y va!*' Michel and Luc were already halfway down the stairs.

The main *paseo* in front of the church was heaving to new life, transformed into a fun fair with colourful stalls and noisy rides. A rusting Ferris wheel rotated wearily to the strains of a worn soundtrack. A dodgem-car arena, its cars silent, sat waiting for the evening's thrill-seekers. The machinery was sturdy but old and in need of a coat of paint. The operators, gypsies from the south, were much the same. Each stood at his post, plying his trade with practised congeniality. I thought the friendly veneer belied a chronic fatigue wrought by perpetual struggle. The local children rushed around in bands, feasting on *churros*.

Michel spied the girls on the far side of the *pelota* court and we headed to them, but the village's best young men, dressed all in white, save for a red scarf at the waist, were warming up for a match of *pelota a mano* and a crowd was quickly gathering to watch this handball contest. *'Allons-y!'* Michel hurried us impatiently, but the girls were surrounded before we could reach them, disappearing from view, and we were forced to stay put.

The players took turns to swipe the grapefruit-sized metal ball with a cupped hand into the front wall. 'See there.' Jean-Louis pointed with a bony finger. 'If the ball hits below that metre-high line on the front wall, or bounces outside the marked perimeter of the court, or bounces twice, the point is lost.' He pushed his glasses up his nose. 'Watch. They play in teams of two, taking turns to hit the ball, either hand. The ball is allowed to bounce off the left-hand side wall, but not that rear wall.'

The players, calloused palms readied, took up their positions. It was an intense affair, no player giving an inch. The onlookers applauded, cheered or groaned at the combinations of brute strength, technique and ball placement.

'Pégalo fuerte!' the man beside me kept yelling and motioning. 'Hit it hard!'

He almost hit me.

The spectators, urging their team on, worked themselves into a frenzy. *'Anda! Corre!* Go! Run!' Finally the winning blow was struck. The man beside me groaned, *'La hostia!'* He took his beret from his head and mopped his brow with a bright red handkerchief. *'Juegan, pero no como en nuestro día,'* he muttered.

Jean-Louis grunted softly.

'What did he say?' I asked.

'They can play, but not like in our day.'

'I guess every generation says that.'

72

By the time the court cleared, the girls were drifting with the crowd to an alfresco bar that had been set up near the port.

The early evening sun drifted lazily down to the horizon. It too was in fiesta mood, the sunset a feast of iridescent pinks and purples. With the diminishing light, we became less conspicuous and I began to lower my guard. Perpetual scrutiny by the locals didn't seem to bother the Frenchmen, but I found it tiring.

Bego saw us and beckoned us to join them. '*Hola, muchachos!* Did you watch the game? Ines's cousin was playing,' she said. Maite didn't seem to be with them. My heart sank like an anchor.

Ines patted my arm. 'Maite had to go somewhere with her brother.' She reached in to her handbag. 'But she asked me to give you this.' She handed me a brown paper parcel.

'Thank you.' The book was inside. *The Tree of Gernika*, by a war correspondent called George Steer.

I thumbed through. It appeared interesting enough, about the Basques and the Spanish Civil War. Several photos showed Guernica in ruins. Gee ... the place I'd driven through the other day, bombed to smithereens! Well, it was a war, I supposed, and places got bombed in wars, but the Guernica in the photos was totally destroyed. No wonder the town was such a strange mix of old and new. It appeared peaceful enough the other day, at least until those *Guardia Civil* came into the bar. You could feel a kind of instant hatred. What was that about? The Spanish Civil War finished a long time ago.

73

The girls bought a jug of *sangría*. Ines, their ringleader, poured us each a tall glass. 'Owen,' she said, laughing, 'you can read the book later. Put it away … your sad face too! Have a drink.'

The *sangria* was tasty, but deceptively potent. After the first sip, I hesitated. It was too strong.

'Come on, you must try,' implored Ines. 'This is the tradition. It's fiesta time — time to have fun! *Bébelo!* Drink up!'

Michel was again holding court. I watched from the sidelines, my spirits dampened, unable to communicate. I wished I spoke Spanish, or even half-decent French for that matter.

I sipped my *sangría*. The Frenchmen drank with gusto and grew increasingly confident. Jean-Louis struck up a conversation with Miren. Things were loosening up.

We progressed to another bar, and another, and another. And so began the long *vuelta*, a night filled with swirling colour, raucous music, delicious aromas, exuberant song and unrestrained laughter — all in the company of our beautiful hostesses.

I wished to God that Maite was there. When we passed through *Bar El Puerto*, Carmen gazed at me across the crowd. I attempted a smile. She raised her eyebrows but didn't smile back as if aware of my feelings. Just like Mum.

Michel and Luc battled it out for Ines's affections. Michel seemed to hold the upper hand, but Luc would find a way to muscle in. For his part, Michel appeared to be enjoying the contest as much as the potential prize. He kept up a sideline of running commentary on the status of their battle and Luc's impossible task.

Meanwhile, Jean-Louis, through sheer willpower, gradually won over Miren and by the end of the night they were locked arm in arm. She rested her head on his shoulder.

'Bravo!' said Michel. 'Bravo, Jean-Louis!'

I had to laugh. Jean-Louis had upstaged the other two and couldn't let the moment pass without a victory lap. Basque heritage perhaps, but he was still French.

Things were getting blurry and the toll of crowds, dance, sweat, drink and sustained exhilaration began to take its toll. I steered a wayward course for Maria's apartment.

§

'So, she didn't show,' said Greg.

'No.'

'Did you see her again?'

'I kept looking.'

§

The fiesta lasted for three days. I kept my eyes peeled at the boat races in the river mouth, the pelota matches and, of course, the endless rounds of the bars, willing Maite to appear.

We came across folk dancing at the *paseo* outside the town hall, a variety of intricate dances to the haunting tunes of the Basque flute. Boys wore white trousers; girls, bright skirts. All wore a white shirt, a coloured vest, a beret, and soft leather slippers with leather laces that criss-crossed over long white socks to the knee. Hands above their heads, they clicked their fingers to the music, while they danced a series of unique Basque steps.

'Have a try!' said one of the villagers. So we joined the shy local girls our age and clumsily tried to learn the steps of a dance. The older women, dressed in black, watched warily from the fringes, intent on overseeing their blossoming maidens. The girls, all too aware, were at pains to keep apart from us, to avoid physical contact, but their eyes sparkled. We gave up in the end and stood back amongst the onlookers to watch the younger dancers in the next performance.

A jeep full of *Guardia Civil*, all heavily armed, cruised down the street on the far side of the *paseo* and disappeared from view.

'*Cabrones!*' spat out an old man. '*Mira. Todavía buscan los de ETA que mataron a ése teniente en Guernica el mes pasado.*' He eyed us narrowly and turned away with a grunt.

'What did he say?' I asked Jean-Louis.

'He said those *Guardia Civil* bastards are still looking for the ETA men who killed one of their lieutenants in Guernica last month.'

Now I understood the tense atmosphere in the bar in Guernica. I felt my throat tightening.

'We read about it in Paris,' said Jean-Louis, grimly. 'Those things happen from time to time.'

§

'A *Guardia* killed, assassinated … not far from Mundaca!' said Greg.

'Yeah. Things were happening that I didn't understand.'

'Is the situation so desperate?'

'It doesn't look that way on the surface — not at all.'

'Jeez, man, it's deceptive.' Greg stretched his neck. 'So, did you find Maite?'

'I thought she'd show on the last night.'

§

The final night was the climax of the festivities; the young men carried an effigy of a witch on a platform above their heads around the village, stopping at all the bars along the way, followed by a drunken brass band and a large excited crowd. They finally bore the witch to a bonfire on the headland overlooking the river mouth. The effigy was hoisted to the top, and the bonfire set alight.

The young folk danced around the bonfire to the strains of the band, flames leaping skyward, while the rest of the crowd watched on with glee. When the flames reached the witch at the apex, I thought I heard a muffled scream. It was probably someone in the crowd, but it made me wonder. 'Poor wretch,' I said under my breath.

Jean-Louis leaned towards me. 'Those poor witches were mostly innocent herbalists and traditional healers,' he said in my ear. 'The ritual stretches back centuries to the time of the religious persecutions throughout Europe and the infamous Spanish inquisition.'

I winced when she was engulfed by fire. Healing was a risky business in those days.

Jean-Louis gestured to the bonfire. 'There were serious witch-hunts in this region in the late sixteenth and early seventeenth centuries. Thousands confessed under inquisitor torture, but later recanted. A few maintained their confessions and were put to the torch. It became known as The Basque Witch-Hunt.'

Death by fire. What a terrible way to go. I presumed that in modern times the pyre had lost its significance and was simply a fiery entertainment. You couldn't really tell for sure. But every summer solstice the ritual was repeated, reproducing the same powerful image of black night, raging bonfire, burning witch and dancing youths. When I think of it, I can still hear that muffled cry.

§

Greg chuckled. 'No girl, just *Guardia Civil* and witches, hey?'

'That's right. Bullets and bonfires, but no Maite.'

'You could have stayed, waited, or gone looking for her.'

'I suppose,' I sighed. 'I wasn't sure what to do. I was still thinking about John and what my folks had in mind.'

§

The following morning, our bags packed, we bid our farewells to Maria and the children. Adolfo had woken much earlier and gone out fishing. The boys were returning to Biarritz and I was heading south by train into the heart of Spain.

'So,' Luc said, raising his dark eyebrows, 'why don't you come back to Biarritz with us?'

Michel folded his arms, his chin set high. 'Luc is right. It's a good idea.'

'No, no,' I resisted. 'I have to see the rest of Europe while I'm here. Who knows if I'll ever be back again?'

'You are crazy!' said Michel. 'What are you going to see? Cathedrals? Churches? Castles? Museums? You can see those things later, *mon ami!* It's summer, the time for the beach, for *le surf! Allez!* Don't be *stupide!*'

I bit the inside of my lip while I digested his words. 'Perhaps.'

Jean-Louis glared at me over the top of his glasses. 'Michel is right. It's summer. The rest can wait. Not forever, but for now, yes, it can wait.'

'You are a surfer, no?' Michel raised his eyebrows and threw up his hands. '*Mon dieu! On y va!*'

'Come with us, *mon ami!* We have room in the car,' said Luc. 'We fit you in. No problem. Don't be crazy! Come to Biarritz! It's summer. You must return to *le surf!*'

Glancing across the quiet port and through the seawalls, I spied a wave in the river mouth. The offshore breeze had caught the top of it, sending a gentle spume of spray airborne. The wave feathered teasingly, broke with a sharp crack, and rolled out of sight. I looked at the Frenchmen's faces and the surfboards stowed atop the car. Something moved inside me.

'Okay!' I said and pushed out a breath. 'You win.'

'*Bravo!*' Luc grabbed my backpack and put it in the boot before I could change my mind. '*Vite! Allez!*'

We stopped in Guernica on the way through. 'Jean-Louis wants to show you something,' Michel said dismissively.

In the *paseo* outside the town hall was a fairly ordinary-looking oak tree surrounded by a low metal fence. 'This,' said Jean-Louis proudly, 'is the tree of Guernica. The symbol of the Basque people since the Middle Ages.'

We didn't hang around long. The tree was unremarkable and Michel was itching to leave. While we motored out of Guernica, I looked everywhere for Maite.

At least I had the book, I consoled myself. The tree's namesake. For the moment, that would have to suffice.

CHAPTER 4

'How sweet is this?' said Greg when we passed into the foothills of the Pyrenees. He put his hand out the open window as if reaching out to the landscape. The scent of hay, wildflowers and herbs rushed in, answering his call.

The Pyrenees grew around us when we approached San Sebastian. A massive black bull glared at us from a billboard in a cornfield, reminding me of the fascist menace. It was advertising a liquor. Greg saw it and shuddered too.

A signpost. Amorebieta left. San Sebastian right. 'Which way, man?'

I pointed left.

'Through the tunnel?'

'Yes.'

We emerged in the floor of the long valley that stretches to Bilbao, dwarfed on either side by high peaks. Greg whistled. 'This is beautiful, dramatic,' he said, 'like Switzerland.'

'Welcome to the Basque country,' I said with a sweep of my arm, and with the same feeling of relief and awe I'd felt that first time.

'I think I'm gonna like it here. Look at these mountains, the hills, the patchwork of little farms, the haystacks, the meadows, the stone walls. Look at the way the farmhouses are built, the lines, the symmetry, the colours, the terracotta tiles. It's an artist's paradise!'

'Wait till you see the Pyrenees tumble into the ocean.'

He drank it in. 'I'll need to get more art supplies,' he murmured to himself. He strummed the steering wheel, his fingers singing a happy tune.

We drove through Amorebieta. 'Go right here,' I said, and we turned into the steep road I'd hiked up that first day. It slithered silver up through the green fields.

'Oh! What a vista!' Greg slowed the car to a crawl. 'It's waiting to be painted.'

'Are landscapes your favourite?'

'Not necessarily. It's whatever inspires me, moves me, drives me.'

'Like good waves.'

'Same feeling.'

'No wonder you paint.'

Greg rounded a curve. Two tethered goats were munching grass by the side of the road. 'I can show you how to draw, if you like?' he said.

Maite's words came to me and a warm feeling spread from my chest out to my limbs. 'Alright,' I said. 'I don't think I'm naturally talented, but I'll have a go.'

He gazed to where the far hills gathered themselves, grew into mountains and reached to the skies. 'No shortage of inspiration here.'

We passed through a hamlet, a few houses snoozing in the siesta hour, a half-built stone wall. Greg's face hardened.

'Spain,' I said soothingly, 'will be better than Morocco.'

Greg studied me briefly. 'So, are you close to your brother?'

'Yes and no,' I said. 'He dropped out of school and went surfing in the South Pacific.'

'Are the rumours true? Did they find good waves?'

I stretched my shoulders and neck, the muscles tight from surfing, and eased back against the seat. 'No, nothing spectacular.'

'That's a drag! Then what did he do?'

'Travelled, worked, surfed — New Zealand, California, Mexico, Central America. Then Europe. And, well, you know the rest.'

'Man, I thought I'd travelled a lot!'

'Surfers thought he was a real hero, but not the teachers or the other parents. They thought he was a bad influence, a villain. But I was proud of him.'

'I can tell. You've followed in his footsteps.'

'Nothing wrong with that, is there?'

'No. But one day you'll have to find your own path.'

'I suppose.' But what was my own path?

'Got any other brothers or sisters?'

Memories flooded in. 'My little sister's only four, really cute.'

'You must miss her.'

'I do ... I felt bad leaving her. Still do.' I stretched out my legs as far as they'd go. Not far enough. 'My other little sister —' I swallowed hard. 'My other sister died, six years ago.'

Greg's voice was low, hesitant. 'How old was she?'

'Ten.'

'What did she die from, man?'

'She'd been sick since she was a baby,' I said quietly, a flurry of memories crashing in uninvited. Louise standing in front of the heater in the living room in her favourite nightie — stunted, limbs slender, belly distended by a swollen liver, skin and eyes tinged golden yellow, her body — but not her temperament — overloaded with bile, scratching herself. Always scratching herself. They said it was the bile salts that made her scratch. She never complained, not even when her nose bled for hours, the white bath towel draped over her chest and lap blotched with crimson, her yellow fingers clamped firmly on her nose. Not even when she had to go back to hospital, again.

I swallowed back tears. 'Something to do with her liver.'

Greg stole a glance. 'Sorry to hear that, man. It must have had a big effect on your family.'

'I suppose so. At the time it certainly did.' I gathered myself. 'But that was six years ago … and then my baby sister was born. And well, you know … life goes on.' I turned to the side window to look for that circling hawk, but all I could see was smudged glass.

§

It was siesta in Guernica and the streets were deserted. 'So this is it,' said Greg, looking about. 'I imagined something different. I'm not sure what exactly. I guess the painting gave me ideas.'

The photos in George's book had transformed my perception and with the *ETA* killing of that *Guardia Civil*, the town had seemed full of violence and ghosts and shadows, but when we drove through, the reality was different again. Here was a peaceful, modest, rural town, almost asleep. Was Maite sleeping too?

We got out, stretched and went to look at the famous tree. 'There it is, the tree of Guernica, the symbol of the Basque people,' I said, parroting Jean-Louis.

'Huh,' said Greg, 'just a regular-looking oak tree.'

Déjà vu! 'Apparently the Spanish kings came here to pledge to uphold ancient Basque rights. Is it in Picasso's painting?'

Greg frowned and ran his fingers through his damp hair. 'The painting's full of symbols, but I don't remember a tree.'

We drove on. My eyes roamed the streets and houses, wondering where Maite might live, until, too soon, the town gave way to fields.

'George says they bombed Guernica because it was the centre of Basque culture. To break the morale of the Basques,' I said.

'I guess it worked,' said Greg.

'I've only read bits and pieces of the book, but you'd have to think so.'

§

Greg, too, was speechless at the first sight of Mundaca. At the lookout, we took in the view. 'It's an artist's dream!'

The surf was modest, but there was sufficient swell on this low tide to demonstrate the long left break. Greg licked his lips and smiled a big goofy smile. His eyes danced along the sandbar while he followed a larger wave. 'Man, it's stunning!'

'I knew you'd love it.'

The sleepy fishing village was alive with people, the streets busy, shops and bars overflowing, the port and beach host to myriad holiday folk. I was right, despite Carmen and Maria being happy to see me, there was no accommodation anywhere.

We retreated along the coast to Baquio and found a primitive camping ground alongside the beach. It bordered on a cornfield, the corn almost ready for harvest, and the ground was hard and uneven. There was no shade, unless you counted the tent, and the sun was fierce. The ocean was our refuge.

Quiet solitude had been replaced by the noisy energy of a thousand vacationers. Umbrellas, deckchairs, towels, beach balls, and people of all ages, shapes and sizes — sat, lay, swam, walked, talked, read, slept, ate and drank. Greg and I found a quieter spot on the beach and in the water found our peace, for by and large, the Spanish had not yet discovered surfing.

Our lives took on a hypnotic quality. One day blended into another. Endless blue skies, searing heat, and the sea restrained and playful. Our routine changed little, dictated as it was by the water, the tides and the wind. We whiled away our time surfing the gentle glassy waves.

Greg had great style — relaxed, polished. He manoeuvred his long blue board rhythmically across the arcing green waves with deceptive ease, always matching the wave's power, blending his ride smoothly with the wave's unfolding. He had that artful stance — poised, limbs loose and graceful.

'You surf like Gerry Lopez,' I told him. 'You make it look so easy.'

But it wasn't easy, and he taught me his underlying technique: how to turn the board, thrust the ankles, use the power in your legs, shift weight, position yourself, watch the wave's movement, sense its energy, time the moves, anticipate, react, balance, and string it all together in a seamless flow of motion, like a dancer.

We slipped deep into summer, and my surfing improved. Gradually, wave by wave.

§

On a bigger day we ventured to Mundaca to try the sandbar. Greg had first taste. He paddled back to the take-off area, beaming. 'Man, what a freight train!' said Greg. 'I can't wait to ride it on a decent swell.'

'Me too! How big do you reckon it can hold?'

'No idea, eight, maybe ten feet. Imagine it at that size! I can't wait until September.'

'Four to six feet will do me fine!' I said. The adrenaline surged through me thinking about it.

On my third wave, the lip hit my head and I wiped out. Sharp pain pierced my backside, but it eased and I kept surfing. In the car park, I stripped my wetsuit to the waist. 'Hey, Greg, is there much of a bruise?'

He screwed up his face like he'd seen something dead. 'Man, that's horrible!'

I twisted my neck, managing a glimpse. The fin had ripped through the wetsuit and I could see muscle. Suddenly, I couldn't move.

'We better get you to a doctor.' Greg tried not to look at the wound, but couldn't resist. Again, the screwed-up face. 'Pull up your wetsuit, man, or I'll faint!'

I did what he said and leant on the car, not daring to move, while Greg dressed and ran to find a doctor. Five minutes later he came rushing back.

'There's a doc at the nursing home,' he panted.

'Where's that?'

'Near the bridge where you come in from Guernica. It's that big old stone place on the corner. Hurry up, *amigo*! Get in the car.' Greg jumped into the driver's seat. He was on a mission.

I leant over and scowled at him through the window.

He laughed. 'Sorry, man!' He jumped back out and supported me while I eased into the front seat, still dripping, my wetsuit at half-mast.

'Don't forget the boards!' I said, when he jumped in again.

'Man, I nearly forgot!' He jumped out, tied the boards

on the roof, and jumped back in. He grinned, all teeth.

'*Vámanos?*'

'*Vámanos!*'

§

The plane tree-lined street beyond the boat-building yard climbed gently up to the main road near the post office. From there, we descended in the shade of the buildings, almost to the bridge. The nursing home — half-fortress, half-manor house — sat comfortably perched on the corner and overlooked the gully, the bridge, and an inlet that reduced at low tide to a beach the breadth of the river.

The nurse eyed Greg and then me. She lowered her scrutiny from my wet hair, to my bare chest, to wetsuit at half-mast, its vacant arms hanging at my side, to wet, sandy feet, to the pavement I was standing on, pooled with seawater. I shivered.

'*Qué pasó?*' she asked.

Greg explained in Spanish.

She nodded curtly and said, 'Wait here.' Moments later she reappeared with crutches, motioning for us to stay put, then went off again.

Greg took the crutches while I leaned against the door jamb. 'I broke my leg once. I'll give you a demo.' He took off down the pavement. 'Watch this.'

The nurse, returning with a dressing gown, barked, '*Qué hace usted?*'

Greg sheepishly tried to explain himself and it was my turn to laugh.

She scowled. '*Déme éstos.*' Taking them and growling instructions, she herded us down several corridors to a consulting room. She glared at Greg. '*Abra la puerta.*'

He opened the door.

The room was empty. A floor-to-ceiling bookcase occupied the far wall. In front of it was an old, leather-top desk and a wooden chair, a stethoscope dangling from it.

'*Adelante.*' She engineered me towards an examination couch. '*Espere.*' She parked me, still dripping, beside it. There was a trail of bloody water on the parquetry floor, back to the door. '*Trae una toalla!*' she barked at Greg, who took off, almost running. She shook her head. A faint smile crossed her face, vanishing when Greg returned with my beach towel and clothes. She pointed to the floor, glaring again. '*Seca.*'

I moved aside and Greg sank to his knees and rubbed the floor with my towel. He chuckled while he dried. It was a nervous habit I'd seen before. The nurse watched him, unamused. When he was finished, I stood on the towel and Greg helped me out of the wetsuit. The nurse supported me. Greg's chuckling intensified.

The nurse couldn't see the humour. '*Qué pasa?*' she demanded.

That only made things worse. Greg's chuckling increased. The nurse, face on fire, went at him in rapid Spanish.

'Greg, you're not helping the situation,' I pleaded, as I lay down on the couch.

'I can't help it, man.' He tried to contain himself.

The nurse pointed at the wetsuit. '*Fuera!*'

Greg, shoulders convulsing, left the room with the wet gear. He was still quaking when he returned.

The smell of tobacco and mint followed the doctor through the door. Slightly stooped with thin grey hair, a silver beard and spectacles, he wore a white coat over a crumpled suit. The nurse scowled. He raised his hands in protest, face etched with mischief. 'Yes, I know, I promised, *Begoña*. I'll give up soon.' When he closed the door, his hand trembled.

'Who have we here?' he asked in English and approached the couch. 'What's happened, *muchachos?*'

Greg explained, beginning in English and then switching to Spanish. The doctor listened, lifting the gown to examine the wound. 'Hmmm.' He bent down to look at me, face to face. '*Chico*, this will hurt a bit. Be brave.' He patted me on the shoulder and stood up.

'Take a seat over there,' he instructed Greg. 'We don't want a second patient. I've seen a few faint over the years, bang their heads.'

The nurse returned with a tray laden with metal instruments. I turned away while they prepared the equipment. 'Ready?' he asked. I heard Greg squirm. 'Here goes.' The needle went in, deep, searing. I jumped. 'Hold still,' he said firmly. Pressure, painful pressure, progressed down one side of the wound. Then, momentary relief. The needle bit again on the other side. 'That will numb it.'

He chatted with Greg in Spanish while he waited for the anaesthetic to work. 'Let's see.' He prodded the wound. 'Sharp?'

I shook my head. 'No.'

'I can sew.' I felt the needle push and the stitch pull. He worked rapidly, chatting with Greg while he sewed.

My eyes roamed the spines on the bookcase, starting with the lower shelf. Medical books. I recognised a few of the technical words, similar to the English. The books on the top shelf were smaller, more like novels. One resembled *The Tree of Gernika*.

'Your friend says you are going to be a doctor, too, one day,' the doctor said warmly. 'Last stitch.'

'I'm not sure,' I said.

'Who is sure of anything at your age?' he said softly, a tinge of melancholy to his voice. The nurse cut the thread and he patted me on the back. 'All done. Come back in a week. I'll remove the stitches.' He turned to Greg. 'You must get tetanus at the pharmacy and give him a jab. I'll give you a script.'

'Sure,' said Greg. 'No problem.'

'And bring your paintings,' he added in Spanish, while the nurse helped me from the couch. 'I'm sure we can come to an arrangement to cover the fee.' The nurse scowled again. The doctor smiled at her and shook his head. '*Señora*, you forget how it is to be young.'

At the door, he turned to study me. 'It's a good profession, you know. Because of the Civil War, I started late. I was a medic in those days. I saw terrible things, but I was able to help. Eventually I became a doctor. It wasn't straightforward.'

§

Greg had never given an injection before.

The pharmacy supplied the vaccine, needle and syringe but they couldn't administer it. Against the rules. They offered us a cubicle with a hospital bed where they also stored cartons of supplies.

Greg recalled that you should slap the skin before you put the needle in, that this somehow made it easier. I wasn't so sure, but deferred to his age and experience. Seven years seems a lot older when you're eighteen.

I glanced over my shoulder. Greg, a distinct gleam in his eye, held the needle and syringe like a dart in his left hand, as if he were aiming for a bull's eye.

'Ready?' he asked. The nervous chuckle began, infectious like always.

I buried my face in the pillow, which smelled of cardboard and dust. He slapped me. I laughed and tensed. 'Ouch!' The needle bit but didn't penetrate.

'Relax, man! Your arse is like a brick.' The chuckle intensified.

I laughed again, but this was serious. 'Hurry up!'

He slapped again. I broke into laughter. 'Ouch!' Same result, the needle bounced.

He laughed too. 'Man! This ain't so easy.' He stepped back

to reassess.

'It might help if you stopped laughing! Get it over with. Push harder.'

'Alrighty! You asked for it.' The chuckle was building again.

I buried my face. 'Jesus! That hurts like hell.'

'There you go!' He laughed heartily.

The pharmacist, curious, perplexed, raised an eyebrow when we left. He must have heard the laughter and probably the slaps.

CHAPTER 5

A week later we were back in Mundaca waiting for the tide to drop so Greg could surf. 'I'm going to check for mail,' I said.

There was a sign on one of the little cubicles behind the post office counter, *Correos Listos*. The post office lady glared at me, pulled out a bundle of letters and thumbed slowly through them. Midway, she pursed her lips and extracted one with a pincer grip, as if it contained the plague. She glared at the letter when she handed it to me. It was from home. There was also one for Greg.

At the river mouth, we retired to the ornate park benches under the plane trees, to read them.

They were missing me, especially my little sister, Rosie. Mum wanted to know why they hadn't had a letter since I left London and if I'd met up with John. She hadn't heard from him, or me, for months.

Obviously, she hadn't received my postcard. The Frenchmen told me the Spanish post was slow. If I'd known I was going back to Biarritz, I'd have posted it from there.

Larry had been chasing cars again with Brandy. I could see the dogs right now, lying under that bush in the neighbour's front yard across the road, tongues out, plotting, waiting for the next car to run the gauntlet, ambush it, legs flying, tails aloft, barking. Mum said he'd nearly been killed by a stationwagon.

I missed Larry.

Mum had had a letter from the medical faculty. My place was confirmed. Just a couple of forms I had to complete. She'd arranged to do it on my behalf.

A delicate breeze teased the waves approaching the sandbar. What was Maite doing at this moment? I watched a gull swoop low across the sea and I followed the expanse of dark blue out to that line where it met the endless light blue. I wasn't too sure about the whole doctor thing. Mum thought the world of doctors. I suppose it was to be expected after what happened with Louise. With all that time in hospital, Mum got to know doctors pretty well. John and I had played outside mostly when we visited, supervised by Dad, but we saw enough to scare us. You can't forget those sights or smells. Sometimes Mum would sleep overnight beside Louise's bed, when things were really bad. She didn't want her to be alone. My sister never complained.

I looked up from the page to the river mouth through the wrought-iron fence. My eyes fixed on the vertical bars, the background a blur.

Mum was worried about John. He was always on the move, and didn't write much. Where was he? He'd escaped somewhere. Morocco probably. Nothing I could do now. She was afraid I'd wander too. Afraid I'd be lost. Afraid I might not return to study medicine.

Was John really running, anyway? He seemed to follow his instincts. If there was a deeper meaning to his travels, it wasn't clear to me.

And *I* wasn't lost. True, I wasn't sure of my path. But I was open to possibilities. Open in a good way, a positive way. Shouldn't I let life happen, come what may, trust my instincts, have faith that they would lead me to the right decisions, the right path, *my* path?

God, I missed them all! Especially little Rosie. I stowed the letter in my shirt pocket and hung my head, examining the cracks in the cement between my feet.

'You okay, man?' asked Greg.

I sat back and inhaled the salty air. The beautiful panorama before me came into focus: the river flowing into the sea, the pines on the far headland stirring with the breeze, gulls winging towards the distant cliff, the ocean, its waves a pulse, a heartbeat.

'Bugger this,' I said. 'Let's go for a surf.'

'You can't surf yet.'

'I can paddle.'

The first wave washed away my lingering thoughts of home, and John. Thank God for surfing!

§

The local artist, Javier, had set his easel up near the port, boats in the foreground. Middle-aged and balding, he wore a loose-fitting beige shirt, baggy white trousers and espadrilles. Greg and I stood at a distance, watching him work. His brush was a flurry, moving from palette to canvas, his eyes darting from scene to palette to easel. Greg couldn't contain himself and edged closer. The canvas was awash with colour, alive with movement. He set down his brush, wiped his face with a flamboyant handkerchief and reached for a bottle of water. Seizing the moment, Greg greeted him in Spanish and introduced himself as a fellow artist.

'I found out where to get art supplies,' he said, when the artist returned to his canvas. 'Guernica.'

'Guernica,' I repeated, my thoughts racing at the thought of maybe finding Maite. She'd be pleased to know I was reading the book, even if I was dipping in at random.

§

Greg bought his art supplies in a musty backstreet stationers while Guernica was winding down for the siesta. When we passed the main *paseo* heading out of town, I spied a girl disappearing into a narrow street. 'Stop the car!' I said. 'I saw her.'

'Are you sure?'

I scampered across the *paseo* and into the narrow street. Empty. I walked its length, but nothing. All was quiet, only the sound of my own footsteps.

'No luck,' I said, hopping back in the car.

Greg laughed. '*Amigo*, in this life, you make your own luck.'

§

A group of surfers had discovered our stretch of water at Baquio. I wasn't supposed to surf with the stitches in, but I couldn't resist. I wasn't out there long.

One of the new guys left the water too. He was tall and lean with shoulder-length blond hair and a crooked grin. He put on steel-rimmed glasses. 'Short sighted,' he said with an American accent. 'It's a bit hard out in the surf.'

'I bet.'

'I'm starving,' he said. 'Want to get something to eat?'

'Sure. There's a bar over there.'

We introduced ourselves over a cold beer and watched the surf through the window. 'Fun waves out there,' said Jock. He swept his long hair behind his ears while he examined me with a curious expression. 'Man, you look familiar,' he said. 'What's your story?'

'I came to Mundaca looking for my brother. He was there for a few months, Biarritz before that. He ...'

'Biarritz?' He pointed at me. '*Jean!*'

'John. My brother's name is John.'

Jock shook his head in wonder. 'I was with *Jean* last September! What a character! He tells the best stories — adventures in the South Pacific, Mexico, Central America.'

'Sounds like John, alright.'

'He said he had a little brother that surfed.'

'Did he? What were his plans? Did he say?'

'Spain and Morocco and all the new surf spots they were going to find.'

'And after that? Did he give you any clues?'

'Nothing definite.'

'Mum's worried about him.'

'All moms worry, man.'

'Still, I'd like to catch up with him.'

He tucked his hair behind an ear. '*Jean* headed off with my buddy from home. Cal's got to go back to school in September. Who knows what *Jean* will do?'

'Maybe *he* doesn't even know.'

'What about you?'

'I'm supposed to go to uni next year. Medicine.'

'Cool.' Jock made a clicking sound with his mouth. 'A doctor, really cool.'

'You think so? I'm not so sure.'

'Beats banging nails.'

'I guess. Not sure it's really me.'

'My cousin's doing Med. He says it's like an apprenticeship. You study the theory, but mostly you learn on the job — by doing.'

'I hadn't thought of it like that.'

'It's a vocation, man, a practical profession.'

A good set rolled in. We watched it wash through the surfers, all caught out of position, and chuckled.

A vocation, I thought. Learn by doing.

The barman approached. I turned to Jock. 'Another beer?'

'Why not? I'm thirsty.'

'*Dos más, señor.*'

The barman ambled away. I sat back and took in the vista. The surfers were coming in. One by one, they straggled up the sand.

§

A week later, we returned to the nursing home to get my stitches out, Greg bearing a selection of his artwork. The nurse greeted us curtly, eyed the canvases dismissively, and escorted us with the same confected hostility as the week before. She cast Greg a malevolent glance that sent the grin scurrying from his face.

'Wait here.'

There was a ladder at the bottom of the bookcase, the type you find in libraries. I was about to hoist myself up to check out the doc's copy of George's book when the nurse blustered in.

She frowned at me. 'The doctor's busy at the moment.' She motioned me impatiently to the examination couch. 'I'll take out the sutures.' Her eyes dropped to the paintings. 'He wants to see those. End of the corridor and turn left.'

Greg smiled sweetly and left.

She pulled down my pants and set to work with tweezers

and scissors. She counted as each stitch came out. '*Uno.*' It didn't hurt. '*Due.*' That one did and so did the rest.

'*Siete.*' She applied a dressing. 'You can go.' She ushered me out and pointed down the corridor. 'That way.'

'*Gracias Señora.*' What a battle-axe.

She nodded back with a hint of a smile. A battle-axe with a soft centre.

Large glass doors gave way to a sunny stone-paved patio that overlooked the little beach. The courtyard was fenced with stylish black wrought iron, a climbing rose woven through the intricate curving design; the patio strewn with flower pots of geraniums, red and white. A number of elderly patients, strategically parked in old-fashioned cane wheelchairs, were warming their bones.

Greg, his back to me, was admiring the view from an unfenced wall where you could look down to the beach. The doctor was talking to an older patient who sat in a wheelchair on the patio in the shade of a palm. They were examining Greg's paintings. The doctor acknowledged me and resumed his discussions.

Greg lifted his eyes from the beach and the incoming sea. 'All done?'

'Stitches out. Still feels strange, but Battle-axe seems to think it's okay.'

Greg grimaced. 'She's a piece of work.'

'What's happening?'

'The doc's going to take a painting for payment. His friend is helping him choose.'

The doctor smoked and carefully examined Greg's promised offerings. His friend, a shock of white hair perched on a tanned forehead, scanned the paintings through narrowed eyes. He held several up with large disfigured hands, pursed his lips and commented to the doctor. I caught his eye. A steely look from steel-blue eyes. I was forced to look away.

With a nod of assent from the older man, they reached a decision. The doctor stubbed his cigarette. 'This one,' he said to Greg, beaming. It was a coloured sketch of the Mundaca bridge. He studied it once more, tapping the edge with a finger. 'I like it.'

'It's yours.'

'I might be interested in other paintings of the region.'

'I'll keep that in mind.'

'Yes do, please do.' He paused. 'And both of you feel free to visit any time. You can sit out here on the patio, admire the view, read, paint, talk to the patients.'

He shook our hands. '*Adiós, muchachos.*' Then added eagerly to me, 'You won't forget what I said about doctoring?'

'No, sir, I won't.'

He pointed to my backside. 'The scar will be a permanent reminder!'

Greg and I laughed.

'*Adiós*, Doctor!'

The courtyard gate hinge was a slow groan behind us. When we reached the car, a jeep full of *Guardia Civil* came down the slope heading towards Guernica. It slowed to a crawl when it passed, the occupants in the back, heavily armed, giving us the once-over.

'*Extranjeros*,' one called out to the driver. '*Vamos!*'

The jeep sped up, rounded the curve, crossed the bridge and disappeared.

§

We waited for a decent swell with a growing restlessness. September seemed a long way off. We were beginning to itch. The holiday season drew to an end and almost overnight everyone decamped, returning to the city, their homes, their work and their schools, but against the tide, two British surfers arrived in a van.

I was disturbed from my book by a lean man with thick blond hair, dark brown eyes and a wizened salt-and-pepper beard saying, 'Are we disturbing you?'

'Not really.'

'Must be gripping,' said the taller one. He had fine dark hair to the shoulders and matching moustache and goatee. Both surfers were burnished to a chestnut brown.

'I'm having trouble putting it down,' I said, rising to my feet. 'It's about the Spanish Civil War.'

'We passed through Guernica this afternoon,' said the bearded one. He extended a hand, one of the hairiest I'd ever seen. 'Jim.'

'Owen,' I said. We shook.

'How's the surf been?' he asked.

'Well, we've been waiting a week for Mundaca to break, but so far *nada*. There are plenty of waves *here*, though.'

Dave's hand was less hairy. 'Suits us,' he said. 'We prefer the gentler stuff. Mundaca sounds pretty heavy.'

Greg arrived bearing ingredients for the evening meal. 'Greeting, *amigos*. Hungry?'

'A bit peckish,' said Jim.

'Pull up some dirt,' I said.

Dave cast a discerning eye over the ground and took off towards the van. 'Get those olives,' Jim called after him.

He returned with two decrepit camp seats and the olives. Greg brought out cheese, chilli peppers and crusty bread. 'Watch the *guindillas*,' he cautioned. 'You only need a tiny bit.'

'First time here?' I asked.

'We surfed Baquio last year,' Dave said, reaching for a chilli. 'On our way back from Portugal.' He loaded a *guindilla* onto a piece of bread. 'We had quite a time there, didn't we, Jim?' He bit down, and almost instantly started cursing, tears streaming down his face.

'Aye, we did,' said Jim, laughing. 'He told you to go easy on the chillies!'

'Dusk's approaching.' Greg grinned mischievously. '*Tinto* time!'

Greg had bought a large flagon of *vino tinto* — sixteen litres of rough red for 240 *pesetas*. It was a steal! Feeling victorious, he'd hauled the flagon back to the car and lodged it proudly in the boot.

We heaved the flagon out. I grabbed the empty regular-size wine bottle and the funnel. Greg lifted the flagon, half-grunting, half-laughing, and poured. I steadied the smaller bottle and the funnel. A thick layer of dregs was beginning to surface and the operation required delicacy.

I started chuckling and shaking. Greg, laughing too, knocked the funnel with the mouth of the flagon and wine spilled. 'Shit, man!' he said. 'Hold it still!'

'I'm trying!' I said. 'Hurry up!'

We were laughing uncontrollably. Greg put the flagon down and I let go of the still upright smaller bottle, the funnel lolling in its neck. Greg wiped the back of his hand across his face. His toothy wine-stained grin made me laugh harder.

We regrouped. 'Ah! Victory!' I exclaimed when the wine gurgled to the top.

Greg replaced the giant cork. 'That's quite a flagon,' said Jim, accepting his glass.

The sun dipped below the horizon, the sky darkening from rose through crimson to purple. A rustling breeze wandered through the cornfield.

'How sweet is life?' said Dave, sipping the wine.

'To the simple life,' we replied, returning the salute.

'I like that flagon,' mused Dave. The moon was rising behind him, floating above the foothills into a purple-blue sky. A warm breeze from the interior herded a few wispy clouds towards the sea. The clouds lingered above the shoreline as if afraid to get their feet wet.

'Yeah, man,' said Greg. 'There's something about its size and shape and the sailors cord coiled around the lower half. Such a squat vessel.'

'Artful,' said Dave.

'It amuses us plenty,' I said.

'The quality of the wine seems somehow less important.' Greg examined the contents of his glass, delicately removed a few dregs and flicked them into the dirt.

I raised my glass to it. 'A trophy for a bargain well struck.'

Greg chuckled. He picked up a stone and lobbed it casually into the corn field.

'Greg haggled hard.'

'Yep,' said Greg. 'I did. In fact, it's more than a trophy. It's a symbol of our new-found Spanish lifestyle.' He raised his glass to the flagon in salute.

We lapsed into silence and watched the sky. 'Tell us the Portugal story,' I said.

'Our first morning in Lisbon,' said Jim, setting his wine down on the ground beside him. 'There we were, wandering about thinking what a lovely city, when — bam! — army tanks roll through. Guns going off, bullets ricocheting, people running!'

'A shopkeeper ran out and pulled us into his store.' Dave motioned with his hands, the red wine rocked in his glass. A few drops escaped and trickled down the outside. 'Our first day in Lisbon and we walk straight into a military coup!' He shifted the glass to the other hand and licked his fingers.

Jim stroked his beard. 'We'd arrived just in time for an

uprising by a leftist faction of the military. The Carnation Revolution. What a name!'

'We took off at dusk and drove out fast,' added Dave, his face flushing. 'We got through the military roadblocks, but it was scary!'

'Sounds heavy, man!' said Greg, as he topped up our glasses.

'You must have been glad to find somewhere peaceful,' I said. 'A beach like this.'

Jim sighed. 'Too right.'

Dave studied the flagon where it sat bathed in moonlight. 'It's got personality,' he said. 'It's sort of womanly too.' He outlined the shape in the air in front of him with two rough hands.

'Yes,' said Jim. 'It is a bit.' He rubbed his chin. 'Actually, it reminds me of that girl Margie you used to go out with.' He looked mischievously towards Dave. 'Remember Margie, all hips and no chest!'

'Leave off!' said Dave. He flushed. 'She might have been a bit broad in the beam, but she was no pirate's dream!'

'Dave, she was flat,' retorted Jim. He ran a hand parallel with the horizon, now drowning in the black, sea-whispering night beyond the shoreline.

'Well,' Dave replied, quick to counter, 'if I turned that flagon upside down, it would look like your old girlfriend Paula. She was all chest and no hips!'

'Oh, I don't mind a big chest,' said Jim slowly. You could see him digesting the thought. 'Lads, it's been a while since we had any female company.' He raised his glass to his sunburnt lips and took a long draught. 'I tell you, I wouldn't mind meeting a nice *señorita*.'

A wave broke close to shore and washed up the sand, its frothy fingers reaching towards us. Greg stood up. 'Well, you guys can dream on! I'm putting this little baby to bed.' He lugged the flagon back to its resting place in the boot and sat back down.

'We saw a few gorgeous girls in Guernica today,' Jim mused, a far-off look in his eye.

I lurched forward. 'In Guernica?' Was Maite one of those gorgeous girls?

Greg grunted, stretched. 'Speaking of Guernica, Owen, how's your book going?'

'Oh, the book.' I sighed, settled in my seat, and looked skyward, imagining the aircraft. 'There was an arms factory on the outskirts of Guernica, but they didn't even bomb that. They firebombed the centre of the town and strafed all the people fleeing into the fields. Killed women and children and old people! Can you believe it?'

'After Portugal, I believe it.' Dave drew his knees up to his chest and clasped his hands around them, as if protecting himself. 'They wouldn't have known what hit them.'

'And it was the bloody Nazis that did it, not even Franco's air force.' I gazed up to the stars. 'It was *George* that discovered that. He alerted the world through his newspaper articles, telling how he found German shells and unexploded incendiary bombs.' I took a long breath and let the air drain out, imagining him wandering around the charred, smoking town. 'He interviewed eyewitnesses who verified the types of planes — *all* German. The Nazis were helping out Franco, and practising their *Blitzkrieg* strategy.'

A wave cracked on the shore, followed by another. Jim jumped out of his skin, and we all laughed.

'We all know *now* what the Nazis were capable of,' said Dave. He stretched out his arms and grimaced. 'Those bastards were warming up.'

'Yeah, but it was so blatant!' I accidentally kicked over the empty glass at my feet. 'It broke all the rules.'

'And got Picasso painting.' Greg emptied his glass, licked the last drops from his lips and set the glass down.

'And Franco lives on.' Dave sighed.

'Yes, and all his henchmen.' Greg shook his head. 'How about those *Guardia?*'

'Strange-looking characters.' Jim threw the dregs of his glass to the dirt. 'I wouldn't want to cross them.'

'One was killed in Guernica in May by *ETA*.' I sat forward again. 'So a few of the Basques are still fighting Franco. And from what I've seen, I'd say the Basques hate him and his regime.'

'You wouldn't really know it driving around.' Greg surveyed the camping ground, the beach and the hinterland. He swept an arm across the panorama. 'It seems peaceful enough.'

The breeze caught the flap of the tent.

'Appearances can be deceptive,' said Jim. 'It's a dictatorship and the Basques are under the thumb. No doubt about that ... But they're not the only ones, it's the same for the Catalans,' he continued. 'It's been this way for a long time, but Franco's on his last legs. It will all change.'

'You think so?' I asked.

'Absolutely.' He scratched at his beard. 'I read in the paper it'll go back to being a kingdom.'

'A kingdom, really?' I sat back and my shirt stuck to the salty damp of my back. 'That's not what *ETA* wants. This French Basque guy I met said the Basques want independence.'

'*ETA*'s a radical communist group,' said Jim dismissively. 'They're not only fighting Franco. They want an independent Basque Marxist state that includes the French Basques.'

'Really, I didn't know they were Marxist.' I reached back to free my shirt. 'I thought they wanted to get rid of Franco.'

I thought of Maite. I wondered if she supported *ETA*. Was she a Marxist?

'That's why it's complicated.' Jim wagged his finger again. 'You can imagine *all* the Basques are anti-Franco, and perhaps a lot want to be independent, but how many would want to live in a Marxist state? Not too many, I wouldn't think.'

'Spanish politics is complicated, mate. There were so many parties and factions fighting during the Civil War — socialists, communists, Trotskyists and anarchists. And there were the regional groups — Basques, Catalans and others. And foreigners got involved. It's hard to get your head around. And that was only the Republican side.'

'You've learnt a lot from that book, Owen,' said Greg.

'Maybe,' said Dave, who'd gone quiet. 'But you came here to surf, didn't you?'

'I did, but …'

'I wouldn't get too concerned about the politics.' Dave yawned. 'That's for the locals to worry about. Go surfing. Give the book a rest.'

'Perhaps. But I want to understand how the place ticks.'

Dave turned away and busied himself with the wine bottle.

'Besides, there isn't any really decent surf.' I looked towards the sleeping sea. 'We're ready for a few serious waves, though. Aren't we, Greg?'

Greg rubbed his eyes and revived himself. 'We sure are, *amigo*. These beach breaks are fun enough, but bring on Mundaca. I can't wait for those autumn swells!'

'Me neither.' I gazed at the dark ocean, imagining the waves steaming down the sandbar.

'Listen, if you lads get tired of no waves, you can come and visit us in Manchester,' said Jim. 'We'll take you surfing in Wales.'

We thanked him, but I wasn't keen to head back to the UK. I liked it here. I wanted to stay.

§

The next morning Jim wandered over with an English

newspaper he'd come across while cleaning out the van. There was a short article he thought might be of interest, on page three.

I read it aloud while Greg brushed his teeth. 'A policeman was killed by *ETA* in San Sebastian on March 30, another in Algorta on April 22. A serious clash between police and *ETA* militants erupted on April 24 with one *ETA* militant killed. On April 25, the Franco Government declared a state of emergency in the Basque Provinces of Guipúzcoa and Vizcaya. But that has done nothing to halt the violence. On May 6 another policeman was killed in Guernica and a further clash occurred on May 14 with three *ETA* militants and one policeman killed.'

'No wonder the *Guardia Civil* look so edgy,' said Greg, his lips flecked with paste. 'It's like a guerrilla war.'

'The last paragraph says the government lifted the state of emergency in July.'

'Even so, all these killings put a different slant on things, don't they?'

'Well, I knew there were killings, but Guernica ... so close to Mundaca. That brings it home. We'll have to keep our eyes open. They're not interested in foreigners, are they?'

'Man, I can't imagine they would be, especially not surfers. No-one but surfers are interested in surfers.' Greg laughed. 'Except the girls.'

§

With the end of the tourist season and the visitors leaving, accommodation would be available in Mundaca, so we packed up our tent and camping gear, the flagon on the back seat. I surveyed the empty campsite: the hard beaten ground where the tent had been, a few flattened tufts of parched grass, a pair of worn-out espadrilles, the dying cornfield, the deserted beach, a windswept swell. Life seemed to be a series of brief chapters. I wasn't sure how they should hang together. I was hoping my instincts would take care of that.

A wave broke and we followed its path. A smile formed briefly at the corners of Greg's mouth, dissolving when the wave petered out. 'Let's go,' he said. He fired up the little Citroen and we laboured up the hill out of Baquio to San Juan de Gaztelugatxe. Flocks of birds seemed to be the only visitors to this lonely island. The familiar scent of pine resin filled the car when we traversed the forest at Cabo Machichaco before descending down through the farmlands to Bermeo and on to Mundaca.

CHAPTER 6

The village was calm again, the bustle over and order restored, the villagers wearied by the summer onslaught.

At Adolfo's place, Maria welcomed me back with a warm glint in her eye. There was something comforting about returning to familiar people and surroundings. It was like coming home.

Greg chatted with her in Spanish.

'You speak with a Latin American accent,' she said softly.

'Señora, I've travelled to Mexico, Costa Rica and other places, surfing,' he replied. 'And there are a lot of Mexicans in California.'

Maria showed us to the same room I'd shared with the Frenchmen. I wondered what they were doing. Heading back to Paris, I supposed.

After a month in a tent, Maria's place seemed a haven of singular luxury. It felt so good to shed that second skin.

Maria poked at our mountain of washing with both disgust and relish. She shook her head, grunted, and began to wash. 'Peor que pescado,' she murmured, loud enough for us to hear. Huh! Worse than fish? I doubted that.

§

At the river mouth waves were beginning to break on the sand-bank. Two swallows dipped over the crest of one and winged into the port where a few older fishermen were pottering. On a whim, we headed over the railway line, and up the steep hill that formed the backdrop to the village, laboured up a narrow track to the edge of a meadow, and lay back, resting on elbows in the sun-warmed grass to take in the panorama — a tapestry of variegated green mountains, deep-sea blues, pale cliff face and sandy gold, all delicately veiled by a light ocean mist. We breathed it in. It felt good to be back in Mundaca.

Cicadas broke the silence. Further up the hill, two sturdy middle-aged farm women cut the waist-high grass with long scythes. When the breeze stilled, I could hear the blades whiz-zing. They stopped every so often to mop their brows with bright handkerchiefs and lean on the long wooden handles. They spoke little until they spied us, and I could almost hear them say: 'Look at those lucky souls, lazing away while we break our backs.' They saluted us from a distance with their scythes, and we responded with a sleepy wave. Re-establishing their rhythm, the grass fell about them in an age-old pattern. A dog barked, far off, but enough to rouse us and we retraced our path down to the village.

Jim and Dave's van sat in the main street, deserted, and so we set out to look for them.

§

The main room of the casino was an inner sanctum of sorts, where the town's veterans gathered to chat, play cards, drink coffee and wine, or enjoy an aperitif. It had an air of stately elegance, attracting the well-to-do and a few fawning aspirants. Perhaps even one or two of Franco's men — spies or informants, anti-communists or sympathisers — sat amongst them.

The mayor and businessmen and professionals on the town council sat at the long table, enjoying a leisurely lunch followed by a cigar, holding court like in any old drawing room of the established gentry.

At the other tables, they were playing cards, the women finely dressed and carefully groomed, their faces painted to varying degrees — subtly highlighting their fading beauty, or more garishly disguising what used to be. They chatted at pace while the games unfolded and the scores were tallied. The men sat at their own tables, strategically distant from the womenfolk. They smoked and joked, but played their hands with due gravity.

The very elderly sat out on the balcony fast asleep. From beneath their berets came a variety of irregular snores, purrs and wheezes. Occasionally the breathing stopped altogether, only to recommence with a sudden smacking of lips and the rushed in-draw of breath.

Reaching the bar meant running the gauntlet of scrutiny by the town's finer citizens.

We braved it and found Jim and Dave there enjoying a beer. A number of the village men were glued to the TV. 'In the

117

nick of time, lads!' Jim raised his glass. 'Barcelona versus Real Sociedad, any minute.'

The weather girl appeared with her map. She moved her pointer to a low-pressure system that sat in the North Sea, the number 994 in its centre. 'Not a major low,' said Greg. 'We need less than 980 and closer to Iceland, for a decent swell.'

'Mate, you've done your homework,' I said with a nod of approval.

'Got to keep your finger on the pulse, man. You should know that.' He was right.

I carefully studied the configuration before it was overtaken by the football.

'Oh no, not soccer!' said Greg, scowling. 'I'm out of here.'

All the major games were televised. The locals supported the Athletic Club of Bilbao, but no team could match Barcelona with its Dutch imports and its game of total football. After ten minutes, the bar erupted in a crescendo of 'ooohs' and 'ahhhs' when a magical goal was scored. Even the parochial Basques could only shake their heads in disbelief at the sublime artistry of Johan Cruyff. '*Es increíble!*'

There was a news flash before I left. Two *ETA* militants had been sentenced to death for murdering a policeman. 'Jeez,' I whispered to myself. 'It'll never end.'

§

The back road near the fish factory wound into the hills, into the hinterland behind Bermeo that grew into Mount Sollube. The Citroen strained and whined up the tight curves. Engine heat and oil fumes filled the cabin making me sicker than usual. We wound down the windows.

Greg grimaced. 'She's threatening to quit.'

'Go easy on the pedal, mate.'

On the plateau, the Citroen caught its breath and purred again. The fumes dissipated, swept away by a gentle mountain breeze. We passed a hamlet, and another. No-one to be seen. Siesta time.

Halfway along a dirt road that led to an old farmhouse, a grassy slope covered in wildflowers sat below the edge of a dense wood. A perfect vantage point to look back at the coast. 'There's a spot,' said Greg.

We lugged our gear to the top of the slope. The scent of pine and wild thyme and sunflowers enveloped us. In the foreground, the grass, long and lazy, bent with the breeze, forming a moving sea of yellowy green. The dotted wildflowers tilted and rode like flotsam. The old stone farmhouse with its ramshackle terracotta roof sat in the middle ground, in the distance, the Bay of Biscay.

We set to work. 'Structure first,' Greg said. 'Proportions. Everything in scale.'

How thinly blue the sky appeared against the dark green pines. The hills too, where they rolled sleepily to meet that same blue, and in the distance ran the edge of the earth, the line where the sky's light blue met the deep dark of the ocean.

A car edged from behind the farmhouse and wound towards us. A girl got out and started up the slope towards us, wading through the long grass. 'It's her,' I whispered, my mouth almost too dry to speak.

Halfway up she picked a wildflower, a red one, and put it in the pocket of her white shirt. The wind caught her hair, revealing her large gold earring. She reached with a hand to set her hair straight. 'Ah! So it *is* you. The Australian. I thought so. We saw you with binoculars from the house.' She laughed. 'We don't get many visitors here. Especially cars with foreign plates. We were curious.'

'Are we intruding?' asked Greg.

'Yes. It's my uncle's property. But you are forgiven. When I saw you both sketching, I convinced my uncle you were artists, harmless. But I'm afraid you will have to leave.' She reached out her slender arm and grazed mine with a fingertip. 'So you came back?'

My heart skipped a beat. I smiled. 'Yes ... yes, I did.'

'And you like art, after all?'

'Greg's teaching me.' I motioned a hand towards him, unable to really believe Maite was standing there, in front of me. 'This is Greg.'

She extended a delicate hand for Greg to shake. 'Maite.'

'I've heard about you.'

She blushed. 'A fellow artist?'

'Commercial,' Greg clarified. 'This is for fun.'

Maite leaned forward to look at his sketch. *'Muy bien.'*

'Thank you.'

'She's an art student,' I said.

'Yes, you told me.' Greg smiled at her. 'A few times.'

Maite flushed. A hand appeared from the far side of the car, beckoning her.

'I better go. And you should too. My cousin's not the patient type.'

We shook hands. 'Thanks for the book,' I said, her hand in mine.

'Have you read it?'

'Parts of it.'

'*Muy bien.*' Her grip tightened. 'Read it all.' Her voice took on a harder edge. 'Then you will understand.'

The car's horn sounded in two sharp trills. Her grip dissolved, but she caught me with her eyes. 'We'll meet again.'

'How will I contact you?'

'Not here, please, you'll get into trouble if you trespass again. I'll come to Mundaca, to the bars, one Friday or Saturday night.'

'When?'

'I'm not sure.' Her cousin stood, half out of the car. 'Soon.' She set off down the slope through the swirling sea of grass.

§

We arrived back in Mundaca an hour before dark. The surf was good, but the tide was dropping fast. Jim and Dave had had their fill and were getting out via the port wall steps while we were entering the water near the cannon. The sun was sinking behind the hills and the light beginning to fade.

'Do you think it's a bit late?' I asked, as we stroked across the port's calm waters.

'Come on, man. We handled it well the last time. A piece of cake.'

'But the tide was coming in that day.'

'I think we've got it wired. That session has given me wings. What would George do? And your brother?'

I knew what George would do, and John. 'Alright,' I said, still on a high from seeing Maite. 'But be careful.'

We paddled out, the channel a torrent where the sea tried to empty itself from the river mouth. Before we knew it, we'd been carried out beyond the break and had to circle around, paddling furiously against the outgoing tide to reach the take-off area. The wind had lightened, making the drop easier, and before long we'd both snared two silky long rides on glass-smooth waves.

'One for the road,' said Greg.

We sat waiting for the next set, the sun well gone and darkness closing in.

'Man, I can't see a thing!' Greg was squinting out to sea.

'Mate, here comes a set.'

'Hell!'

Greg dropped late. His board shot up and disappeared. He resurfaced, yelled, 'Shit, leg rope's broken.' He duck-dived under the second wave. I took the drop to the bottom and straightened out, abandoning the ride. I lay down, bouncing along, waiting for the wave's power to dissipate, angling towards the channel, pushing hard and fast in towards the headland, now a black silhouette against the indigo sky.

As luck would have it, Greg's board was moving steadily in front of me on its way out to sea. I secured the trailing leg rope to mine and paddled hard. But where the hell was Greg?

I spotted Jim on the headland. 'Have you seen Greg?' I yelled, paddling closer to shore. 'I've found his surfboard, but not him!'

'No!' he yelled back, clearly distressed. 'I saw him fall, but lost sight of him in the whitewater.'

I cleared the channel and reached the still waters of the port. Save for the dull amber light cast by the port lamps over the swaying boats, it was pitch-dark. I paddled swiftly to the steps on the port wall where Jim was waiting.

'Leave the boards here, mate!'

We scampered along the seawall and ran as fast as we could around the edge of the port, up the street to Plaza Santa Catalina and along the narrow, walled-in dirt path to the other port wall. Bare-footed, the rocky path slowed me down. Jim, shoes on, arrived there first. 'Greg!' he screamed repeatedly towards the shadows of the rocky point. I joined in and we battled the crash and roar of the breaking waves. Our shouts grew more desperate.

'Jesus!' Jim screamed at me. 'Where the hell is he?'

'I don't know. I think he's been carried out to sea! What'll we do?'

'I don't know! You lads are bloody idiots, why didn't you come in earlier?'

'We should have, but it got dark so quickly!'

'Crazy fools!'

We were close to giving up and running to raise the alarm when Greg, crab-like in the dim amber light, came clambering over the rocks beyond the foot of the port wall. Jim and I jumped up and down, hugging. Tears streamed down my face.

'Greg! Are you okay, mate?' I yelled.

His reply was muffled by the breaking waves.

We scampered down the narrow steps cut into the ocean side and helped him to the top of the port wall. He lay for a few minutes and sat up, gasping. 'I got caught in the damn channel and was heading out to sea,' he said between breaths. 'I knew I couldn't fight the current, so I swam towards the rocks and when I reached the passage, I managed to grab the *last* rock on the point and pull myself on to it. I thought I was a goner! I nearly missed it!' He took a long slow breath. 'I could see the port lights … but it's dark out there. Those rocks are sharp, man!'

His feet were a bloody mess and his hands not much better.

'Could you hear us?' asked Jim.

'I couldn't hear anything, man, except the surf. Once I hit land, I headed to the port lights. But I kept slipping over.'

'We thought you'd drowned!' I said, my voice hoarse. 'I shouldn't have rushed you into taking that wave.'

'Not your fault, man. I should have made the drop.'

We nursed him back to the *piso* and I went to collect the boards.

'You found it!' Greg was happy to see his beloved board again.

'Yeah. It popped up in front of me.'

But it was a minor detail. He'd had a brush with death.

'Luck's a fortune,' I added, glancing at Jim, silent beside him, a stony look in his eye.

In our own way, Jim and I had felt the grasping pull of the current, the stinging sharpness of the rocks with that last desperate lunge, the tenuous grip on life, straining to hold on, reeling one's self in, the pounding of the surf on clambering shoreward, like a drum beat, a portent of our ultimate fate. For Jim and I it was in the all-too-real imagining, for Greg it was palpable. He'd felt the tentacles of death wrapped around his legs.

Is that how soldiers felt — out of their depth, out of control, fearing death? Fighting the elements to survive made sense to me. Fighting other humans didn't. What drove those soldiers to fight and kill? Did they have a choice, a real choice? Do any of us have a real choice in life?

§

With the rising swell, vanloads of surfers snuck into Mundaca overnight and set up camp in the car park. They surfed with us across the morning, and the following days, until the swell died. Greg's feet and hands were sore but he was determined to surf and, ignoring the pain, managed some of the best rides.

Finally, we could experience the beautiful waves we had dreamt so long about. We surfed each day until we could paddle no more. One speeding ride after another, a blur of endless, silky pleasure. At night, sated, we floated around the bars with our surfing brethren, chatting, reliving the day, before collapsing into an unshakeable sleep.

News among the surfers was that the *Guardia Civil* had killed two *ETA* militants, one in Madrid and one in Barcelona and an *ETA* militant had been sentenced to death for murdering a *Guardia* in Barcelona. The surfers were edgy talking about it, the news delivered in low voices away from the bars. And there was more. The day I'd seen Maite, the Spanish government had executed two *ETA* militants.

When the weekend came, I looked for her in the bars, but she didn't show. 'Where the hell is she? Why hasn't she come?' I muttered, while I dragged through the village laneways on one last round.

§

The swell diminished substantially and then was gone. It was difficult to comprehend the rapid transition from towering waves to a tame, still ocean. With the lake-like serenity, began the exodus. One by one the surfers' vans, entrails retracted, departed the car park. Jim and Dave headed north back to

France and the UK, and others south to Morocco to escape the winter.

Greg was the last to go. He planned to sell the car back to the same dealer in Biarritz, fly to Madrid, and on to California. My mate packed his belongings into the boot of our little Citroen. We stared at each other long and hard, embraced and shook hands.

The motor spluttered, and died. He paused, head down, and took a big breath. The motor kicked alive and held. He edged away from the port wall and the window went down. He was grinning, all bravado. 'Be seeing you, Owen! *Adiós, mi amigo!*'

'See you, mate.' My voice sounded distant, strangled. 'Take care, buddy.' My smile died when he departed up the cobblestone street and out of Mundaca, back to France. I watched until he drove out of sight, an empty feeling in my chest. Another brother lost. My real brother seemed more mythical than real. Greg was the brother that loves you more, because they don't have to. A knot tied in common thread. It seemed the thread was unravelling. No friends. No Maite.

Perhaps my parents were right, and I should have stuck with the original plan.

I missed them. Home. Louise's ghost standing in front of the heater. A boat strained on its mooring behind me and a seagull angled on the breeze across the little port and flew off into the empty sky. I looked around. Nobody. Only the hard stone walls and cobbled streets.

§

The sudden quiet of our room at Maria's was depressing. Alone, I felt deflated, isolated, bereft. I tried to study Spanish with the well-thumbed text Greg had left behind but couldn't concentrate. 'Jesus!' I picked up George's book but couldn't focus. 'Bugger this!'

My thoughts turned to John. Following him to Morocco was tempting, but Agadir was so far away. Chasing after him was a wild goose chase. What if I got there and he'd moved on? Too risky. And after Greg's experience, I was even less tempted.

The room felt suffocating. I had to get out and not just for a few hours. I had to find another place to stay, my own place, where I could spread out. Somewhere I might even invite Maite.

Maria appeared from the kitchen when I neared the front door. 'Where are you off to, *muchacho*?'

'A long walk.'

'Alone?'

'Yes.'

She studied me. 'You look sad. Time you found a new friend … a girlfriend perhaps.'

I frowned. 'A girlfriend?'

'Why not? Only, take care. A girl's honour is important. To be shamed in a village like Mundaca is a lifelong curse. Not many girls would risk that.'

'I guess not.' I tried to smile and went out.

I circled around the village and up the hill behind Mundaca.

Near the summit I gazed back down on the village and the estuary. It seemed unbearably calm and quiet. I lay back in the grass and for a long while watched the clouds change shape as they drifted by.

§

Carmen's son-in-law nodded sleepily when I took up a stool at the far end of the wooden bar at *Bar El Puerto*. I couldn't face returning to Maria and Adolfo's *piso*. It was Friday night, but not yet dark. Maybe this would be the night Maite turned up.

'*Qué quieres? Vino?*' the bartender asked languidly, still rousing from his snooze.

'*Una cerveza.*'

I'd confined myself to beer since a horrible experience with the dregs of the giant wine flagon. I thumbed through *El Correo*, turning the newsprint pages slowly, perusing the articles, studying the photographs. A double-page article detailed an *ETA* car bombing from two years earlier, with photos of the burnt-out vehicle and several dead bodies. *ETA* suspects had been arrested near the French border; photos showed two bearded men and a slim woman, hands cuffed, being escorted by *Guardia Civil* into a police van. The men appeared sullen and resigned while they bent to get in, but the woman, gazing straight into the camera, appeared distraught, as if she didn't belong there. Maite! But no, the girl in the newspaper was clearly older. Did Maite have a sister? If so, with *ETA*? Surely not.

'*Pepe!*'

The call stirred the bartender from his half-sleep. '*Ah, Manolo!*'

Manolo took his place behind the bar, removed his *boina*, the Basque beret, to reveal thick brown hair tinged with grey at the temples, and rolled up the sleeves of his pressed white shirt. He saw my glass was empty and approached, tea towel in hand. '*Otra cerveza, muchacho?*' His lively eyes were surprisingly blue and sat deep below the arches of his neat dark eyebrows. He had large ears, a large fleshy nose and a muscular neck, but you could see the resemblance to Carmen. 'Another beer?'

'*Sí, gracias,*' I replied.

'Speak English?' he asked with an American accent.

'Yes.' I was taken aback by his brusque manner.

'Australian!' he said with a sudden spark in his eye. '*Muchacho*, I worked in Queensland cutting cane for a year.' He smiled warmly, his broad shoulders relaxing when he leant on the bar. 'Which part are you from?'

'Melbourne.'

'I never went there.' He rubbed his strong hands together, the network of veins on the back of them prominent. 'But I did visit Sydney. What a beautiful city! *Magnífico!* And what brings you to Mundaca?'

'Well, I'm here by accident, really.'

He grinned. 'Life is like that, *muchacho*. The unexpected adventures are always the best! So what will you do?'

'I'm going to surf!' I said, almost defensively.

'Ah, of course, the surfing!' he said. 'I saw them in Queensland, on the Gold Coast, beautiful to watch! Never tried it myself. I didn't have time, in the end. I had to go back to the States to sort out my divorce.'

'Shame,' I said. With his physique, he would have made a good surfer.

'Do you know *jai alai*?'

'Yes.' I'd seen the Basque game *jai alai* on TV at the casino. I patted the newspaper. 'There are photos in here of yesterday's game. So fast.' Much faster than the *pelota* I'd watched at the fiesta, because the players used a wicker hurling device called a *cesta* inside a walled court.

'It's a big gambling sport in parts of America. A lot of Basques emigrated there. South America too, especially Chile. Anyway, I played professionally over there for a few years. I did okay, but I got injured. Because it's incredibly fast, you need to be fit!' He surveyed his hands and forearms, and shook his head. 'Sometimes you have to re-invent yourself, *muchacho*! These days I teach history to university students. Not much older than you.' He picked up the tea towel. 'But today I'm here, helping out. My nephew Pepe, the sleepy one, works the bar with my sister. He and his wife Rosa have a new baby and they're exhausted. Carmen's there now, minding the grand-daughter.'

That explained his less than professional beer pouring skills.

'I love it here in Spain,' I said, gazing out the window across the port to the river mouth.

131

He lowered his voice. 'Not Spain, *muchacho*. This is the Basque country! We are not Spanish.' He shook his upraised finger in the way many locals did, signifying, *no, no, no!* 'Look, *muchacho*.' He leaned across the bar. 'Basque people are proud. You must understand their situation.'

'Yes, of course,' I said. 'I know a little. I've been reading about the Civil War and talking to others.'

'Civil War?' He checked to see if anyone had come into the bar unnoticed. 'What about it? Be careful who you talk to about these things. It might be history, but it's also political, and you best not get mixed up in politics around here. It's ruthless. And there are spies.'

'Really?'

He frowned. 'Franco has his ways. He rules with an iron fist. He's repressed all potential threats to his regime.'

'And to his vision of Spain?'

'Yes, fascism, that's what it is!'

'He called it National Socialism.'

'So did Hitler.'

'Franco didn't kill Jews though, did he?' I said.

'No. He wasn't mad. More cunning, calculated.'

'And staunchly Catholic, isn't he?'

Manolo snorted. 'We all were. Well, most of us. Even the anarchists, who said they weren't. Catholics, deep down.'

'The Catholic Church sided with the fascists during the Civil War. True?'

'They did!' He made as if to spit, but thought better of it.

'They deserted us.' He took a deep breath and exhaled through his nostrils. 'Officially, we aren't allowed to speak Basque, you know.' He swivelled around again, as if someone might be listening. 'ETA wants an independent Basque state based on Marxism.' He threw his hands up. 'Most people want democracy. Who will accept a communist state?'

I shrugged.

'Not many.' He leaned towards me again. 'But because they're Basque and against Franco, they've had support.' His thick black eyebrows arched upward. 'You might be surprised, but across the border in France, our Basque brothers have helped ETA too. Many activists have taken refuge there.'

'I heard that.'

'The border is easy to cross in certain parts and Franco can't control it. He even asked the French government to help catch the ETA activists.' Manolo smiled wryly and wagged his finger. 'But the French have never been a friend of Franco and, despite the rhetoric, they've been content to do nothing.'

'Sounds like Franco will do anything to stop Basque independence and ETA will do anything to achieve it.'

His eyes narrowed. 'That's right. It's a kind of war. The Basque Provinces have always been prosperous. We have natural resources, industries and commerce.'

I shook my head. 'Franco could never let them go.'

'No. Unthinkable from his point of view. It would devastate the Spanish economy.'

'And if the Basques were allowed independence, what about

133

the Catalans and other regions?'

'Exactly. It will never happen. Autonomy is the best we can hope for.'

'ETA won't accept that, will they?'

'No. Like many repressed minority populations, we're desperate. But such violent methods are wrong.' He flung down his tea towel. 'The terrorist tactics apply pressure but they won't bring independence.'

'Is there any other way?'

He picked up his tea towel again. 'Of course. All Basques are proud of their history and culture, passionately so. We were never going to take this lying down. Many Basques have resisted, in a pacifist way. We have to be patient.'

'Until Franco dies?'

'That's not far away. And, with luck, democracy will be restored.' Manolo's shoulders sank. 'It's been a long road. Thirty-six years under the thumb. I was only young when Franco won the war.'

'The book I'm reading gives an insight. A personal account by the journalist, George Steer.'

'A foreigner's account.' He motioned with his hand as if to brush it way. 'I've never heard of this George Steer.'

'He was the war correspondent who told the world about the Nazi bombing of Guernica.'

'Guernica! My father evacuated us from Lequetio and we passed through Guernica on the day after the bombing. I was ten years old. Guernica was rubble, all black and smoking, people wandering around … dead bodies on the side of the road. Horrible! My father told me not to look, but I saw it out of the window of the truck.'

Two local fishermen came in for a drink. Manolo collected himself. 'Come again, *muchacho*. We can talk more. I'll be here every Thursday, sometimes Fridays. You can tell me about your book.'

I finished my beer. Manolo, his face set, nodded goodbye, the message clear enough: *Remember, not a word to anyone.*

Night had settled on the village without me noticing. Noisy groups had begun their *vuelta*. I wanted to find Maite but strolled out to the headland to look at the sea and order my thoughts. The sea was flat and grey like my mood. Maite's cousin had seemed menacing enough to be a terrorist, but not the girl in the photo.

Manolo was intense, passionate, a link between my world and theirs. Could I trust him? I needed a friend. And there was George Steer. He would have been a true friend — loyal, committed, passionate, fearless — a great man to have by your side. A real brother-in-arms.

I thought of John, my own brother, my blood brother. And where was he?

§

The next morning Carmen was busy serving. When my turn came she stopped to inspect me, all motherly, nodding her head as if to say you've come a long way since that first day. 'Any news of *Jean, muchacho?*'

'I'm afraid not.'

'Your friends?'

'All gone.'

'*Ah! Estás solito.*' She looked bemused. 'Don't worry, you won't be alone for long. Things will happen. It's good to be on your own for a bit, especially now your Spanish has improved.'

'Greg taught me a lot and I've been studying hard and practising.'

'There you are. A chance to become a real man.'

A real man. What was that?

She looked at me sweetly and sighed. '*Muchacho,* can I help in any way?'

'Actually, *Señora,* you can. I want my own place. Something cheap.'

'I'll see what I can do.'

A group of fishermen breezed in. It was as if each wore an invisible cloak of fish scales — you could smell them before you saw them. They nodded, hearty but grim. Soldiers of the sea. I nodded back.

Carmen poured them a line of *tintos.* '*Muchacho,* come by tomorrow. I may have news.'

I took a long walk into the hills to stretch my legs. It was evening when I returned, the streets alive with groups — each with their own agenda, their own energy and rhythm. I wandered through them to a bar called *Bodegon,* under the casino, ordered a beer and some *pinchos* and watched out for Maite.

The crowd were dressed in their finest. It was the women's make-up that grabbed me — modest and discreet for the young ladies; in the older women, it took on a life of its own.

I then headed to *Los Chopos*, where things were livening up. The music caught my ear. The Greek singer was unique and the songs, mostly in English, were strangely alluring, several quite haunting.

A surge of heat radiated through me. Maite was standing at the bar on the other side of the room with Ines, ordering drinks. When she saw me, she smiled shyly and a warm flush filled her cheeks. Her eyes seemed to penetrate me, to my very being. She leant forward and whispered to Ines, who gazed at me across the bar.

'*Con permiso*,' I said firmly, but politely, as I pressed past one group after another to where they stood waiting. '*Qué tal?*' I asked, shaking her hand.

'*Bien*. Do you remember my friend Ines?'

'Of course.' I shook Ines's hand. Her dark hair matched her eyes, with full red lips and pale white skin. She was big-boned, strong and handsome.

'*Estás solo?*' she asked.

'Yes. The others have all left.'

'*Oh! Qué pena!*'

'Yes, a pity. I'm on my own,' I said, but I guessed she was disappointed for other reasons.

'*Salud!*' I said, raising the glass, my attention on Maite.

Maite smiled, her eyes two peridots flickering in the half-light. The photo of the girl in the newspaper had to be her sister! But, what did it matter what her sister did?

'*Salud!*'

Ines raised her eyebrows. 'What are you going to do here alone?'

'Surf,' I said.

'Surf. That's all?'

'Well, and study Spanish.' Turning to Maite. 'I've been reading that book.'

She smiled again, but said nothing.

'And I was hoping to learn to paint.'

'I can help you with that,' said Maite.

'You don't have to work?' Ines asked, frowning.

'Not yet. I saved money for travelling before I came. Next year, I'll return to study medicine.'

'You're going to be a doctor?' Her mouth hung open for a moment.

'Apparently.'

'Apparently?' The corner of her mouth twitched. 'You're not sure?'

'No.'

She peered at me. 'Why not?'

'I don't know if it's right for me ... if I'm right for it.'

'But it's such an opportunity, an honour.'

'So people keep saying. But how do you know if something's

138

right for you?'

'Give it a try, of course. Find out.' She made it sound so simple.

'You're a student, aren't you?' I asked.

'Social work.'

'How did you choose?'

'My mother's a social worker.'

'Family tradition, hey? On that basis I should become an engineer.'

Ines pouted. 'It seemed natural for me.'

'That's what *I* want!' I said. 'For it to feel natural.'

'Oh, I see!' She flashed a grin at Maite. 'A natural feeling.'

Maite flushed.

'Yes.' I laughed. 'Nothing wrong with natural feelings, is there?'

'Not at all!' Ines laughed too. 'They're fine. But I'm not sure they're what you should base a career on.'

'Probably not, but isn't instinct important?'

'I suppose, to a degree.'

'What about you?' I asked Maite. 'What made you choose art? A natural feeling, instinct, or is your father an artist?'

'Art?' She pushed a lock of hair behind her ear. 'My father's not an artist. I didn't have to think too much. I had a certain talent, teachers encouraged me, it grew into a passion. A natural progression, I'd say. Now I'm committed.'

Those words again. Passion, commitment. 'You're lucky,' I said.

'It's not luck.' Her cheeks began to colour. 'You make a choice. We all have to make choices. Don't you feel passionate about anything? Like, helping people?'

'I've had a few inklings about doctoring, but hardly passionate.'

'Don't you have a cause?'

'Surfing.'

'That's not a cause! Don't you believe in anything?'

'Of course I do.' I could have said the obvious things — antiwar, peace in Vietnam, an end to apartheid in South Africa, land rights, social justice for all ... but it somehow didn't ring true here. There was only one issue that mattered in the Basque country. 'The book, George's, it's a real insight.'

'I told you it was important.'

'Yes, I can see it is. But more important than art?'

'Our whole culture is under threat.'

'But you continue to paint.'

She drew her lips in, minced for a moment. 'We all contribute in our own way.' She said it as if she was letting me in on a secret.

'Have you been painting much lately?' I asked.

'No ... I've had family matters to attend to.'

'Anything important?'

'Serious issues,' she said, crossing her arms brusquely, a signal there would be no further details.

'So, no time for teaching me painting?'

She laughed, relaxing, and returned my smile. I felt a warm

tingle spread through me. The pale freckles on her cheeks and nose fascinated me and I couldn't help but stare. She blushed but swept the hair back from her face and the gold earrings appeared. 'I'm sure I can find time,' she said. 'But you must promise to read the whole book. We can talk about it when we paint.'

'I promise.'

Ines was getting restless. 'Shall we go to another bar?'

A group of young locals muttered when we negotiated past, their knifing eyes in my back. The girls lowered their gaze and I put away my smile.

In the warm late-September night, the stars lit up a sky of unbroken Prussian blue, a crescent moon in the south. A gentle breeze stirred the leaves of the plane trees. In the port, fishing boats rocked, water gently lapping at their timbers, and salt and fish and seaweed spiced the air. All this and Maite by my side.

We strolled the short distance to *Bar El Puerto*, our steps a quiet patter on the terrace paving.

'*Hola, muchacho!*' Manolo called out, a broad grin matching the keen light in his eyes. 'How are you, my surfing friend?' The patrons turned to look at me, at the girls, and back to me. The third degree.

'*Hola, Manolo.*'

His boyish enthusiasm tickled me. The girls, however, appeared uncomfortable. 'I'm here with friends.'

'So I see. Can I get you all a drink?'

I ordered two *mostos* and a beer, and the girls headed off to a quiet corner of the bar.

'The fairer one,' he said, glancing at Maite and Ines, out of earshot, 'she's familiar.'

'Maite?'

'What's her surname?'

'I don't know. She's from Guernica.'

'It'll come to me.' A new group of patrons called for drinks. '*Vengo!* I'm coming!' Manolo called out. 'It's Saturday night … look after your lady friends!' He winked and tipped his head towards Maite and Ines.

'He's a character!' said Ines, eyebrows raised. 'How do you know him?'

'He is quite a character,' I admitted. 'I met him here in the bar. He lived in America a long time, so he speaks excellent English. I'm not sure what to make of him … but he seems harmless enough. I think his heart's in the right place.'

Ines glanced towards the bar. 'An extrovert.'

'Undoubtedly.' My focus shifted to Maite. 'But let's forget about him.'

'Yes, let's!' Maite laughed.

I raised my glass. '*Salud!*'

'*Ondo ibili!*' said Maite, and clinked it with hers.

'*On-do-i –?*'

'*Ondo ibili!* … Basque.'

I only knew *Agur*, the Basque greeting, meaning goodbye, used on passing in the street. '*On-do-i-bi-li,*' I repeated.

Maite made a clicking sound of approval with her teeth. 'It literally means "go well".'

'I don't know any Basque,' I said. 'I'm busy learning Spanish.'

Maite suddenly turned serious. 'You must learn Basque too! This is the Basque country, not Spain.' She turned, quickly scanning the room. 'But this is not the time,' she said quietly. 'Speaking Basque is forbidden. You can't splash it about where the *Guardia*, or spies, might be listening!'

'Go easy,' said Ines. 'He's a foreigner, he doesn't understand. And there are no *Guardia* here.'

Maite shrugged. 'Spies perhaps.'

Ines reassured her. 'No-one can hear us over here.'

Maite whispered to me eagerly. 'You want to learn about the Basques, learn our language, don't you?'

'I do,' I said. 'But be patient with me!'

They laughed when I tried to get my tongue around a few words. The language bore no resemblance to the Latin languages I was more familiar with: French, Spanish and Italian.

A group of men descended on the bar. Manolo stood, arms wide, as if ready to embrace them all in one great swoop. '*Hombres!* It's been a long time.' He poured a long line of *tintos*.

Maite gasped, raised her hand to her face and turned to Ines. 'Look who's here!'

'We have to leave,' said Ines, collecting herself. She beckoned me to follow them and we sidled out. The large group, busy talking to Manolo, didn't seem to notice us.

'What's the matter?' I asked, in the quiet of the street.

'A friend of my elder brother is with those men. If he sees me with you, a foreigner, he would tell him and that would make things difficult for me. You understand?' Maite pleaded.

'What does it matter?'

'It matters!' Maite insisted. 'Please understand.'

'Let's go somewhere more discreet,' said Ines firmly, taking Maite's arm.

§

We arrived at a hole-in-the-wall place where Greg had bought the flagon. A fishermen's bar that few people bothered with.

'I'm a harmless Aussie, you know,' I said to Maite. 'Neutral, no axe to grind.'

She passed me a beer. 'Neutral?'

'Well, not exactly neutral. I love it here. Isn't it obvious?'

'It's impossible to be neutral in these times.'

'The more I read and learn and understand the Basques, the more I support their cause. A bit like George.'

Her face softened, the steel dissolving. She was even lovelier with her guard down. I felt like I could see her real self. Somehow vulnerable.

'Can I trust you?' she asked. She took a breath, the tension fell away like sails collapsing when the wind dies off. 'I went to visit my brother yesterday, in prison.'

'Prison!' I was surprised by my own voice. 'Prison?' I repeated in a whisper.

She lowered her voice to match my whisper. 'They say he is a terrorist, but he's not! He's innocent.' She bit her lip. 'He didn't do anything bad.'

I understood her caution. It wasn't wise to talk openly, not even here in the heart of the Basque country. She had said there were spies. You never knew who might inform.

'What did he do?' I was still stunned at the real possibility of her being connected to terrorists.

'They said he was involved in *ETA* — but it's not true! Anyway,' she examined me, her voice softer, calmer, 'you're a foreigner, you can't fully understand. You have to know what Franco has done to us. Not only what happened in the Civil War, but since. My brother, in his own way, was helping the Basque cause. Somebody has to.' Her shoulders slumped. 'In the end, it doesn't matter. He was sentenced to seven years.'

'Seven years!' The words flew out of me and the bartender stirred in our direction, before his lids closed again. I was reeling. Had he killed someone? No, he'd get more than seven years for that, perhaps even execution. A bombing, perhaps?

Maite was watching my face. 'I know what you're thinking. I can't tell you what happened, but it was nothing really bad.'

'How long has he been in prison?'

'Six months. My mother's devastated, my father too. The whole family is suffering. And they don't allow many visits.'

'How's he coping?'

'He's not strong like the others are.' Her voice caught. 'They get badly treated.' A tear ran down her cheek. 'Most have been tortured.'

I didn't know anyone who'd been to prison, let alone tortured. I didn't know what to say. 'It sounds terrible,' I managed.

She took a mouthful of wine before wiping her eyes with the back of her hand and collecting herself, 'Do you have brothers and sisters?'

'I came to Mundaca looking for my brother, John, remember?' I passed her a photo from my wallet, which she held to the light. 'And that's my little sister, Rosie.'

'How cute! *Y qué rubia!*'

'Yes, they love the blondes in Italy. Every place we went, the women pinched her cheeks and ran their hands through her hair.'

'I don't blame them! *Qué muñeca!* What a doll!' She returned the photo and stared at me, her lips parting. Her hand was soft and warm when it found mine and she leaned into me gently.

'I'm tired,' said Ines. 'Can we go?'

'Of course,' said Maite. '*Vámanos.*'

'Where's your car?' I asked.

'Near the church.'

'I'll walk you there.'

At the car, Maite offered her cheek. '*Agur,*' she said softly. I drew her to me. Her hands on my arms were gentle, reassuring.

'*Agur,*' I said. My mouth was dry, the beat of my heart in my ears. 'When will I see you again?'

146

'Next week.' She kissed me on the cheek and got into the car. She wound down the window. 'We'll go painting in the countryside. Okay?' She smiled mischievously.

'Okay.' A surge of energy rose up in me. 'Next week!'

'*Ondo ibili!*' she said, laughing, while they inched away.

'*Ondo ibili!*' I called out, and waved goodbye.

The car took off into the night. I followed its tail-lights until they disappeared around the curve near the boat builder's yard. She was gone and I was alone again but a thrilling flush washed through me. I raised my face to the sky and laughed out loud. 'Thank you, whoever you are up there!' What an intriguing, beautiful girl! I couldn't believe my luck. I floated back to the apartment on a tide of joy.

But later, when I lay in my bed and re-traced the events of the night, I couldn't help wondering why she wouldn't tell me what her brother had done. And what was that intense streak whenever we touched on anything vaguely political? She became almost hostile. There was a lingering uncertainty and the more I thought about it, the less sure I felt. But when I remembered her gentle side, that beguiling smile and the soft light in her eyes, I was filled with a warmth and energy that I'd never felt before. I hoped she felt the same way I did.

Hours later, drifting off, I imagined huge seas, the calm of the ocean depths and a mermaid beckoning me to an underwater world.

§

The next morning, with the high tide, the river mouth was calm, save for the faint rhythmic undulations of a tiny swell. I watched a fishing boat, still a distance out to sea, steadily motoring back to port and breathed in the vista — the restive sea, the sleeping river, the imposing mountains, the nestled village and the tucked-in little port. I hadn't lied to Maite, I really did love this place. It was hard to imagine leaving.

Carmen stood in her usual spot, drying glasses. She gave me the once-over, as if making sure I'd dressed properly, brushed my teeth. '*Café?*' she asked, seemingly satisfied all was in order.

'Please.' I looked through the window to the sandbar. 'Mmmm,' a purr of satisfaction escaped me.

Carmen followed my gaze. '*Oye, muchacho*, Mundaca is certainly beautiful, and we are proud. But one has to work and every day starts to look the same. It becomes monotonous.'

'But look at the view,' I said, with a sweep of my arm. 'It's magnificent!'

'*Sí*. It's beautiful. But I grew up here.' She dismissed the view with a wave of her hand. 'I'm used to it.' She set her tea towel aside and stood silent, her posture sagging. 'One day you'll understand.' The corners of her mouth quivered. 'My options were limited, *muchacho*, like for most women here. Marriage, work, children, work, grandchildren, work. Cooking, cleaning, tending to sick kids … it soon wears you down. Only yesterday we had the doctor come to the *piso* to see my grand-daughter — my poor Rosa's Arantza.'

'The doc from the nursing home?'

'Yes, of course. There's only one in the village. Dr Arriaza. We're fortunate he's so devoted. The last one wouldn't visit, wouldn't leave his office.'

I nodded politely. The nursing home. Greg and I hadn't been back to visit, but I was sure the doctor's offer was still good.

'Anyway, listen, *muchacho*, men have it different. Look at my brother. Manolo took off, travelled the world, worked in foreign places, had adventures, two careers … some difficulties too, a divorce, it's true … but opportunities no less. Opportunities to test himself, grow. Life soon passes you by … you'll see.'

Carmen seemed hostage to an endless routine from which there was only one escape. Does age and death creep up so fast? It didn't feel that way. She must be mistaken.

'And what are you going to do with your life?' she asked, composing herself.

'I'm going to study medicine,' I parroted.

'Medicine!' she exclaimed. 'So you are smart?'

'Smart enough, I suppose. But not the smartest. Not even close.'

'When do you start, *muchacho*?'

'March, next year.' Saying it aloud somehow made it concrete.

Carmen pushed out a breath and examined the swollen joints of her fingers. 'Youth, time on your hands and a laudable career ahead — you're a lucky boy.' I felt so moved by her. Like the door of her tavern, she was worn and weather-beaten. Would I look like that one day? I bit my lip and turned away.

For a while we were silent, each lost in our thoughts.

She sighed, packed away her longing, and picked up a glass to dry. 'I have found a place for you, *muchacho*. An old house, but spacious and cheap.'

'Sounds perfect!'

Carmen chuckled and shook her head. 'Far from perfect, believe me.' She set down the glass and picked up another. 'You can meet the owner, Ignacia, tomorrow. Santa Catalina Plaza at ten.' Her gaze narrowed slightly. 'Don't be late.'

'I won't.' There were words I wanted to say, but they caught in my throat.

Carmen hung up her tea towel and began pouring a line of *tintos* for the incoming men.

CHAPTER 7

gnacia turned an ornate old key in the large rusting lock of the paired portico doors with a sallow crinkle-skin hand and pushed. The top hinge was loose and the door wedged on the uneven cement floor. She regarded me through a confusion of wrinkles, her eyes like two lights hidden in the crevices of a gnarled old tree.

'*Por favor,*' she said, with a sweeping gesture of her black-cardiganed arm and trembling hand.

'*Por supuesto,*' I said, and gave the old wooden door a solid nudge with hip and shoulder. It gave way with a jerk and struck the portico wall with a ricocheting bang.

'*Basta, basta!*' She moved past me into the portico where she gradually leant down and secured the open door's foot bolt into a hole in the floor. Then, reeling herself upright, she reached up and unbolted the other door and motioned to me to secure it like the other.

She flicked a switch and the portico light revealed a flight of dusty wooden steps. '*Sucio, sucio,*' she said, gradually mounting the stairs.

Dusty was an understatement.

At the top of the stairs, she reached into the deep pocket of her crow-black dress and withdrew another large, impressive key. This door opened with ease. The bulb's pale glow revealed the peeling paint of the upper walls of a dim hallway but barely penetrated to the floor. Musty. Dark and musty.

'*Venga, venga*,' she said, motioning for me to come along. She brushed aside loose strands of silver hair that had escaped from her tight bun. '*La cocina*.'

The kitchen was ancient and looked like it hadn't been used in years. Alongside the blackened wood stove was a gas stove, which apparently worked. She said I would need to buy *butano* and re-fill the gas bottle. She threw back the kitchen curtains with all the force she could muster and opened the full-length windows and shutters to reveal a little balcony. The strong morning light stole in as if invading a long-sealed tomb.

Ignacia beckoned me to the balcony, which sagged noticeably. I advanced warily and grasped the heavily rusted wrought-iron rail. Ignacia eyed me curiously. '*Fuerte, fuerte!*' she said, reassuring me of its strength and gripping the rail like she was ready to jump up and down.

The balcony overlooked a large walled garden with a chicken coop and rows of well-tended vegetables, plants and flowers, like a miniature farm and orchard, a large fig tree in the far corner. Set into the mortar of the high, roughly rendered stone walls were shards of broken glass of amber, emerald green, and untinted glass, weathered opaque. Along its outside length ran the path from Plaza Santa Catalina to the west side of the port. Beyond the secret garden and its wall was the port and to the left, the harbour entrance between the seawalls, with the river mouth behind. What a view! You could see the surf from here!

Ignacia's sea of wrinkles was momentarily at a standstill. *'Bonito, no?'*

'Sí, magnífico!' I acknowledged, my gaze fixed on the narrow view of the sandbar.

'Vamos! Vamos!' she said, urging me from the balcony to resume the tour of the house.

The light may have been better, with the strong light penetrating from the kitchen, but the mustiness intensified when we reached the corner of the L-shaped hallway. Ignacia flicked on the bathroom light. Old and damp, but with curtains and window opened, it was partially resurrected by the bright morning sun and transformed to marginally habitable.

There were four bedrooms — one with a window overlooking the Plaza Santa Catalina. All were brought tenuously to life with a combination of air and light.

The hall opened into a large lounge and dining room with windows on both sides and four old lounge chairs. The good-sized dining table had eight chairs. Double doors — the top halves were glass and covered by miniature curtains — opened onto another balcony. This balcony was larger and sturdier, with a wide view through the port walls to the sandbar and the waves.

The house leaned a little, creaking, deprived of oxygen and light, but I could see the potential. The location was near perfect.

Ignacia, not too old to mistake my enthusiasm, led me back

to the front door. '*Quinientas pesetas a la semana. Vale?*' The rent was ridiculously low and I could have it straight away.

'*Vale!*' I accepted without hesitation.

§

Two days after I'd settled in at Ignacia's, I walked around to the nursing home with my book and a sketchpad. I stopped at the gate to the quiet courtyard garden, as I often had on my walks around the village, and peered through the scrolls of the black wrought-iron fence and its climbing roses, to discreetly watch the veterans of the community, chair-bound in their cloistered solitude.

Inside the gate, I crossed the patio and sat on a bench seat in a protected corner that overlooked the river and gave a clear view of the patio and the patients, shaded by a plane tree. The patients appeared lost in slumber, lost in their weary dreams, perhaps? Lost in memories, in hopes and imaginings, in aspirations fulfilled and those left wanting; in a reckoning of a past now fading and clouding over. I wanted to capture that gentle confusion of reality and illusion in my drawings.

A number must have fought in the war, and all of them had lived through it. What memories must haunt them now? Violence and death, fear, hunger, hope, betrayal, grief, despondency, outrage, hatred, revenge.

I set to work, drawing as Greg had taught me.

The doctor saw me on the bench seat and approached. 'Ah!

Finally, you've come to visit.' He shook my hand. 'How's the backside?'

I patted it. 'Seems good as new.'

'Glad to hear. Where's your friend, the artist?'

'Gone home. Back to the States.'

'A great shame.' He glanced at my sketches. 'So, now you're the artist?'

'Not really. I'm dabbling. Greg taught me a little.'

He swivelled his head to better see the pad. 'Not bad ... I thought you were going to study medicine?'

'University doesn't begin until March. I've got plenty of time yet. I want to stick around, ride the big swells.'

'That's all?'

I shrugged. 'I'm trying new things ... whatever life brings.'

'Such luxury of time.' He sighed. 'What it is to be young!'

He noticed the book and frowned. 'Where did you get that?'

'A friend,' I said.

He grunted softly and studied me. 'Interesting?'

'Absolutely.'

His face was strangely impassive. 'I'm glad.' He reached for his pocket and pulled out a packet of cigarettes. He scanned the terrace while he took one out. 'A quick smoke before I get back to work ... I'll duck around the corner in case Begoña is watching.' He took a few steps, then turned. '*Muchacho*, come as often as you like.' He paused. 'You never know what life may bring.'

§

155

The following days brought the end of summer. Early mornings and late evenings turned cool, contrasting with the persistent heat of the day. The skies remained a deep pale blue, but a change was coming. The plane tree leaves began to yellow and the breeze lost its summer playfulness, growing daily stronger and more earnest. Heavy clouds gathered over the mountains, a portent of the autumn rains. The sea, too, was changing. The swell rose and the water, a steel-blue, heaved to a deeper, darker rhythm — a hint of the winter storms to come.

The days fell into a pattern: wander down to check the surf and stop by the *panadería*, return to *Casa Ignacia* for breakfast and an hour of Spanish, before heading to the nursing home terrace to sit on my favourite bench and journey with George Steer through the desperate struggles of the Basque resistance.

After lunch, Mundaca was a kaleidoscope siesta, a dream of warfare and romance, of waves and beauty. And I found myself thinking of the doctor and his patients as often as my brother and sister — and Maite.

In the late afternoon, I'd often return to that same spot, to draw or read, watch the veterans, or simply gaze at the sea.

Battle-axe was usually there, sitting watchfully on the perimeter, ready to tuck in a blanket, or whisk the patients inside when lunch was beckoning, or the sky grew threatening. Otherwise, the veterans were free to roam in their tired memories and drift slowly towards their final destination.

The doctor appeared frequently, moving from one veteran to another, taking blood pressures, listening to hearts and chests, chatting quietly while he went, holding a hand, squeezing an arm, patting a back, endless reassuring. He loved his patients, and they loved him.

My heart moved. Was that my calling too?

No waves appeared. In the evenings I searched the bars, but Maite wasn't to be found. Not even on the weekend. So back I went, day after day, following my feet to that same seat, drawn to the nursing home.

A week after my first visit, I was about to enter the gate when I saw, through the scrolls and the climbing roses, a young woman, her back towards me, locked in conversation with the doctor and the old man with the steel gaze I'd seen that day with Greg. Maite? I watched, but she soon departed through the main building, carrying a parcel they'd given her. She left and I never saw her face. Was it her, or was I just wishing it were?

§

Every Thursday I read the newspaper in *Bar El Puerto* and talked with Manolo in Spanish. There'd been two more *ETA* killings of *Guardia Civil*, one in San Sebastian and another not far from Mundaca.

Manolo seemed restless. He slung his tea towel over his shoulder and leant on the bar. The blue of his eyes stood out against the dark tan of his face and tiny beads of sweat sparkled in the creases of his forehead. 'How's the book going? Tell me what you've learnt.' His face grew mischievous. He reached for a bottle of beer, poured it and passed the glass. 'It may not be the truth.'

'Not the truth? George was there, he saw it with his own eyes.'

'One set of eyes isn't the truth,' Manolo said with a teasing edge to his voice.

I felt the heat rise to my face. 'George always tried to be objective. Franco had him kicked out of rebel-held territory, you know, before he reported from the Basque country.' I picked up my beer. 'His heart was on your side. He could barely fault the Basques,' I put down my beer again, 'only their stubbornness, which sometimes made them uncooperative. And their lack of cunning in waging war.'

Manolo raised his hands in mock surrender. 'It's true, we are not naturally cunning.' His gaze narrowed. 'Although, there are always one or two rogues.' He rubbed his chin. 'I can think of a couple.' He leant towards me. 'What else does your George say?'

'I'm up to the defence by the *Frente Popular* of Guipúzcoa against the Navarrese assault led by General Mola.'

Manolo's face hardened. 'The Navarrese were traitors! Not real Basques.'

'That's what George said, that Navarra was Basque in name but little else, and had no real ambitions to be independent.'

Manolo folded his arms.

'When the Basques were granted semi-independence,' I said, 'the Navarrese military sided with Franco and attacked

Guipúzcoa. The *Frente Popular* tried hard but they were a coalition of militias — communist, anarchist and Basque Nationalist.'

He shook his head sadly. 'Not a proper army.' He polished a glass and studied me. 'You're impressed by George, aren't you?'

'He's passionate about his work.'

'Yes, but he's watching from afar. He's not in amongst it, dodging bullets.'

I bristled. 'He is at times. You can't doubt his bravery.'

Manolo grunted, unconvinced.

'George thinks the Basques were courageous, but amateurish. Poorly commanded and poisoned by factional differences,' I said.

'Unfortunately, it was like that, *muchacho*.' Manolo frowned. 'Too many factions.'

'It's hard to believe that before Irun finally fell and the reprisals began, the anarchists torched the whole town.'

Manolo's face reddened. 'Anarchist bastards! Always ready to torch and run.'

'Then San Sebastian surrendered without a fight and the *Frente Popular* retreated.'

'Defeat and retreat!' His shoulders sagged. 'Enough of our sad story for today, *muchacho*. Pepe will be here soon.' He moved down the bar, polishing while he went. '*Muchacho*, that girl you were with that night.'

'Maite?'

'I think she's the grand-daughter of one of our great Basque fighters, a senior officer with the Nationalists.'

'Really?'

'I'll see what I can find out,' he said in English when Pepe bustled in. 'But if so,' he raised an admonishing finger, 'she's not for you, my friend.'

§

'Am I disturbing you?'

I jumped out of George's book and put a hand to my heart. Maite had crept up on me reading on the nursing-home terrace beneath the plane tree in the golden late-morning light. A vision, she appeared like an autumn leaf that had drifted from above, and come to settle on the seat beside me. 'God! You gave me a fright!'

She laughed and took my hand. 'Sorry! I couldn't help it. I was visiting a friend and saw you. You seemed so peaceful reading, but I'm going to drag you away.'

'You can disturb me anytime you like. George doesn't mind.'

'You're on first-name terms! You *are* making progress.' She laughed again. 'Well, you'll have to put George away for today.' She took the book from my hands, picked up a wine-red leaf to mark my place and handed it back closed. 'We're going painting.'

'We are? Where to?'

'It's a secret. You'll have to trust me.'

'Is there any reason not to?'

She laughed. 'Ah! You have a cheeky side.'

'Just like you.'

'I'm a Basque, a serious one … and an artist too, sensitive. Too many sides?'

'I doubt it.'

She pulled on my sleeve and led me across the patio, through the gate, to her car. The back seat was full of art equipment.

I smiled. 'You aren't as shy as I first thought.'

She laughed. 'You aren't either.'

We drove into the hills beyond Guernica along a road I didn't know. Across the valley, a lone stand of eucalypts caught my eye. Strong and pliable, they leaned and settled, shifting with the restless autumn breeze. They reminded me of home and, in a way, of what I'd have liked to be — at home in a foreign land.

I pointed. 'Eucalypts.'

She glanced at me. 'You miss home?'

'Sometimes.'

'They must miss you.' She dodged a pothole. The scent of wild sage and hay drifted through the windows.

'I suppose.'

'My family missed me when I was away in Dublin.'

'Why Dublin?'

'To study art. I told you. I went with my brother.' The last sentence tumbled out before she could catch it. She bit her lip.

'Did he study too?'

Her mouth tightened and she clutched the wheel. 'No. Inigo was there on … business.'

'What sort of business?'

She squirmed in her seat. 'Commercial,' she said, gaze fixed on the road.

Out the window, wisps of smoke drifted from the chimney of a nearby farmhouse and up through the pale sky. A roving hawk wheeled and dived at something in its adjacent meadow. A chained Alsatian ran barking at the hawk and came to an abrupt, choking halt.

I didn't say anything but wondered, *Why Ireland?*

The road dipped and curved and we reached a fork. A chapel with an ancient Basque cross and weathered bell sat snugly between the two roads. She headed right, deeper into the hills. Her grip on the wheel was loose, her voice relaxed again. 'I'm taking you somewhere important to the Basques.'

'Where's that?'

'Where are you up to in the book?'

'Back near the beginning. Background stuff. I decided to read it cover to cover instead of dipping in here and there. George reckons the Basque character is honest, moderate, moral and law-abiding and says you're all sports-loving Catholics.'

She nodded. 'Do you agree?'

'Mostly.' I hesitated. 'I mean, you couldn't describe *ETA* as law-abiding, could you?'

She glared at me. 'Someone has to fight Franco.'

'At any cost?'

'What would you do? Roll over and be trampled on?'

'I'm not sure. I've never had to face that.'

'Exactly!' Her hands clenched on the wheel. 'Believe me, you're forced to make radical choices.'

'Is that what happened to your brother?'

She was silent for a moment. 'I told you Inigo didn't do anything bad.' Her voice was tight. 'It was all a mistake.'

I tried a different tack. 'Isn't there a peaceful way?'

'Which is that?'

I didn't really have an answer. 'Maybe things will change when Franco dies.'

'Why? Franco's people are entrenched. Fascist rule will continue.'

'Are you sure?'

'Do you think Franco would let his regime fall apart?' Her mouth tightened. 'Don't worry, he's got rat cunning. He's planned ahead.'

We drove for a minute without speaking. She took a big breath, the heat in her face subsiding. The road narrowed through the forest.

'George says Columbus's great sea captain, Juan de la Cosa, was Vizcayan. Elcano too — he navigated Magellan's ships around the world.' I shook my head. 'Incredible!'

'People don't appreciate that. They only talk about Columbus and Magellan.'

'Bilbao was rich, though.'

'And that's why the Spanish wanted to control us, to take our money and resources.'

'They needed them, didn't they?'

'The Basques worked hard to build their wealth. Why should those lazy Spanish take it from us?'

Outside, the day was warming, the breeze firming, the deciduous trees wrestling against it, clinging to their leaves. Maite pulled the car off the road on to a grassy knoll with a view across a plain to a town in the distance.

She reached for my hand. 'Let's get out here.'

We stood, the hills at our backs and stretched our limbs. 'Eibar.' She pointed to the town. 'Where a big battle was fought. We'll paint this scene.'

'Alright.'

'Sketches first, of course.'

She got out sketch pads and pencils from the back seat and we sat on a blanket. I followed the method Greg had shown me. She sat close, legs touching, leaning into me periodically to examine my drawing, gauge my progress. Her perfume mingled with the scent of mountain herbs and juniper.

I spied her sketch. Gentle lines that grew bolder as the form took shape, the whole becoming one, centre and periphery all in balance. Like surfing, all the elements of the artist's repertoire flowing seamlessly, rendering the complex simple. So deceptive.

Catching me looking, she smiled, then grew serious, gently bending to me. We kissed, a delicate brush of lips, soft and swaying like the mountain grass. We kissed again, and she touched my cheek. Tender fingers, barely touching, trailed down to my neck. Sketch pads slipped and pencils slid as we rolled into the grass.

§

She shook me awake. 'I'm hungry.' Her eyes danced with mischief. She grabbed my curls and gently pulled me to my feet. We hugged for a while before she straightened her skirt and I slipped on my shirt.

'*Vámanos.*'

'Where to?'

'There's a tavern not far from here. Friends of the family.'

We collected the sketches, folded the blanket and put them in the back seat. She drove steadily onward towards the town.

'We didn't even begin the paintings.'

She laughed. 'You distracted me.' She squeezed my thigh.

At the bottom of the hills we came to a hamlet with a tavern. 'The food here is good,' she said.

The owners greeted her warmly but regarded me with suspicion. I shifted slightly as their eyes sharpened. There was subtle murmuring in Basque, but Maite seemed to reassure them. They sat us at a table near the window where we could see the outline of the town in the far distance, a church tower rising from it. Maite ate like it was her first-ever meal. The owner's wife, a thick-set woman with weathered features and hands like spades, brought soup with crusty bread. *Vino blanco* accompanied the fish. '*Buen provecho,*' she said. Good appetite was an understatement.

I enjoyed watching Maite as much as the food itself and the food was delicious. 'You *are* hungry,' I said.

'Your fault,' she said, while soaking up the fish juices with a torn piece of bread.

I laughed. 'My fault …? You kissed me first.'

She wagged a finger and smiled mischievously. 'Still your fault.' Next she attacked the flan.

Before we left, the owner's son gave me the once-over. 'It's okay,' Maite said. He handed her a shoebox sealed with tape, which she stowed under the blanket in the back seat.

'What's that?' I asked.

'A few things that need sending abroad,' she replied nonchalantly.

I left it at that.

We returned to the same grassy knoll. Maite set up an easel and painted with oil. I sat on the grass and completed my sketch with watercolour.

'Not bad,' she said, when I had finished.

Hers was alive with beautiful detail, mine dull and flat in comparison. I grunted. 'Not my calling, it seems.'

She put her arms around me. 'Don't be so negative, you've barely begun.'

'I see a mess!'

She laughed. 'The sketch is fair. The colour needs finessing. I'll show you how next time.'

Next time.

No amount of muddy watercolour, mystery shoeboxes or lingering questions about Ireland could compare with the euphoria of kissing Maite. I hummed a tune all the way back to Mundaca.

'When will I see you next?'

'At the weekend.' She drew me to her and kissed me. Swimming in lucid green pools.

I went to get out. 'Can you do me a favour?' she said. 'If I give you the address, can you post this shoebox?'

§

The following day was glorious. The sun washed over the early autumn and with it came a gentle swell. I surfed alone with no human distractions, free to appreciate the ocean. The tide was turning when I paddled across the shallows of the sandbank. The sea, bottle green in the early afternoon light, scalloped by a freshening cross-shore breeze. The waves were fast and tricky and I battled hard to find a good ride. 'It doesn't matter,' I whispered to myself. The cool water, the breath of the wind and the reassuring rhythm of the undulating sea — on days like these, even a few rides were satisfying.

Between sets, when the sea was quiet, Izaro with its ruined chapel was visible. It was said that a monk lived there a long time ago and swam into Mundaca under cover of darkness to meet his lover, swimming the three kilometres back before dawn. 'If it's true,' I whispered to no-one, 'he must have been bloody brave to swim these waters and cross these rocky shores. And desperate too! Could I do the same for Maite, if need be? How far would I swim? What lengths would I go to help her?

Risk arrest, imprisonment, even death?'

I thought about posting the shoebox. Love can make you do crazy things you'd never imagined. I hoped I was never truly tested. Was the shoebox a test?

The sea had initially restored me, but now I found myself clutching at the board.

I returned to land and made my way to Ignacia's house. The village women watched bewildered when I passed by in my wetsuit, board underarm, dripping.

The surf had made me hungry and I ate ravenously to the strains of the Greek pop singer. 'My friend, the wind,' he sang in high-pitched exotic English.

Interesting words. On those beautiful offshore days, the wind certainly is a friend. But on the onshore days, the wind feels more like an enemy. No doubt, far away in the Arctic north where the large ocean swells are born, the wind is whipping up the seas — so there too, I suppose, the wind is a surfer's friend. And I do like those warm winds from the south that carry the searing heat of the Iberian plains, with perhaps a touch of the *sirocco* of North Africa.

But the thought of the task ahead, the favour for Maite, intruded and sent a shiver down my back, like a sudden chilly breeze that came from nowhere.

§

The tiny post office was only open in the mornings. The

postmistress, prim and curt, her dark hair pulled back tight in its habitual bun above severe eyebrows, stood behind her desk sorting mail. Behind her, General Franco glared down at me from the wall.

I placed the shoebox, now wrapped in brown paper, on the counter.

The postmistress frowned, turned the parcel to see the address and read it aloud, 'Mr PJ O'Brien, PO Box 357, GPO Dublin, Ireland.' Her eyes narrowed. 'What's in it?'

I hesitated. 'Gifts for a relative.'

She examined me for a long moment, grunted, weighed the parcel, stamped it and put it aside with some others. '*Dos cientos ochenta pesetas.*'

I gave her 300 and she slid the change across the counter. When I looked up from my wallet, she and Franco were both glaring at me. A chill ran through me. Was she one of his spies?

§

I went to hunt out Manolo who was behind the bar, alone, reading a book. '*Ah! Muchacho!* We meet again.' He took off his glasses and set the book aside.

'I talked with Maite.' I couldn't help smiling. 'We went for a drive in the country — painting.'

He looked at me and frowned. 'Painting?'

'Yes, I told you, she's an artist.'

'Ah, yes! You did.' He began to steam the milk for my coffee.

'She studied in Dublin for a while. Went there with her brother. She's teaching me to paint.' My attention wandered to the wine bottles standing behind the bar, their elaborate labels. Manolo, head down, poured the frothy milk into the coffee. 'Maite's taken over where Greg left off.'

'Dublin?' He stared. 'Is her brother an artist too?'

'No. He was on business of some sort.'

Manolo set the steaming cup in front of me. 'Business?'

I hesitated for a moment but decided to spill the beans. 'He's in prison,' I said. 'For helping *ETA*.'

'Prison!' I watched him chewing it over. Something clicked, his eyes widened. 'The IRA.'

My mouth went dry.

'Yes.' He tapped his chin. 'If he *really* was with *ETA*, he went to Ireland to meet the IRA. They share common goals, both fighting oppressive regimes.' He lowered his voice. 'The IRA helps them get weapons.'

I sat forward on my seat. 'Really?'

'I'm not saying that's what he was doing there, but what other business would a Basque have in Ireland?'

'I don't know. I'm confused.' The shoebox flashed across my mind. I tried to collect my thoughts. 'There are other strange things too, Manolo.'

He leaned forward.

'Well, there was that photo of an *ETA* group being arrested in San Sebastian.'

'Yes.' He nodded pensively. 'I remember it.'

'The girl in it, she seemed out of place, frightened. But her face, so much like Maite … I think it might be her sister.'

'Did you ask?'

'No. I couldn't.' I stirred sugar into my coffee. 'I'd already questioned her about her brother and she didn't like that.'

Manolo straightened and put his hands on his hips. 'Brother in prison, sister arrested. Both with *ETA*.' He shook his head gravely. 'It doesn't look good, *amigo*.'

I told him about Eibar and the shoebox, but not that I'd posted it. 'I'm worried.'

He jabbed the air with a finger. 'You ought to be. Eibar has a weapons factory. Small arms. Pistols, revolvers, that sort of thing.'

'Really?'

He pursed his lips and shrugged. 'Guns in a shoebox. A thought worth considering. Think about it.'

I searched for words. 'Doubt it was guns … she carried it lightly.'

'Money then, or documents, maps. Who knows?' He shook his finger at me. 'That girl looks like trouble. You should stay clear of her.'

I met his eyes. 'It's not that simple.'

§

The following morning, I was in my reading corner at the

nursing home, with George, when she appeared again. 'I always know where to find you!' She laughed.

I smiled. 'Something attracts you. Is it me or the book?'

She adopted a coy expression, eyed the book, then me. 'Don't be silly. Of course it's you.'

'You seem very fond of George's book,' I teased.

'So do you!' she said cagily.

'He's my new hero,' I declared.

She looked hard at me, serious now. 'That's good.' Then she smiled. 'We'll be on the same page.'

I grinned. 'Same page. Very funny. Is that Basque humour?'

She blushed and glanced away. 'Don't make fun of me.'

'Couldn't resist.' I searched out her eyes. 'Hard to resist,' I said slowly.

She smiled warmly. 'How did you get on with the shoebox? Post it?'

'I did.' Franco's glaring face flashed across my mind.

'You look worried.'

'The postmistress was very curious.'

'Was she? She didn't open it, did she?'

'No.'

'Don't worry about her.' She was silent for a moment. 'Coming for a drive?'

'Love to.' I surveyed the river. 'No surf in Mundaca.'

'Bring your surfboard. We'll go to Baquio.'

'Really?' I felt a surge of energy. 'We'll have to stop by the house.'

§

With surfboard atop and all my questions flown out the open windows, we detoured to the lighthouse at Cabo Machichaco. Maite sketched, first in pencil, then ink. The detail was uncanny, the end result almost a photograph.

My sketch showed the signs of distraction and restlessness. I set it aside. 'What is this place?' I asked.

'There was a big sea battle right off the coast here.' She pointed with her pen. 'You'll read about it.' She turned, frowning slightly. 'Where are you up to?'

'Bilbao's knuckling down, preparing. The Basques are fighting to hold at Eibar.'

Her face lit up. 'I told you Eibar was important.'

'You were right.' I paused, thinking of the shoebox. 'Eibar turns out to be quite significant.'

'What do you mean?'

I fumbled for words. 'Well, it's … near where you and I got to know each other better.'

She laughed. 'Oh! I see!' Her face flushed and she reached for my hand. 'Eibar was *very* significant.' She gazed into my eyes. 'A beautiful day, one I'll never forget.' She kissed me and squeezed my hand. 'Come on. Let's keep going.'

We packed up and drove on to San Juan de Gaztelugatxe where we climbed, hand in hand, the steep rough-hewn steps to the chapel above. We circled the tiny hermitage, admiring the dramatic view and found a spot where we could sit and look back towards Cape Machichaco.

'The sea battle took place out there.' The sun caught her earring, a flash of gold in her hair, the perspiration on her face and neck a soft autumnal sheen. She lay back against me, her head on my shoulder, her hair spilling across my chest. 'It was March, 1937.'

'March, 1937,' I repeated, running my hand through her hair.

'A sea battle fought at night in coastal fog. A Basque dispatch trawler, the *Galdames*, and its four armed escort boats, intercepted by the Spanish naval blockade. The *Galdames* was carrying about 200 people, including an important Catalan politician and, unknown to most, secret correspondence and a cipher, and the new nickel currency for Bilbao.'

My hand reached her neck.

'That feels nice,' she murmured. 'Where was I?'

'In a fog.'

She laughed. 'Dry sense of humour you've got, Owen … But can you imagine, fighting at sea, at night, in the fog? Fifty-one died, a cabin boy too. So sad.'

'Poor kid.'

She sat up. 'We lost an important convoy and a little boy died.' She pointed out to sea. 'Out there.'

I sat up too. 'Hard to imagine. It looks so peaceful.'

'Let's sketch it.' She pulled pads from her knapsack. 'You sketch it as you see it, I'll sketch with that night in mind.'

'That won't be easy.'

'Has to be done.' She flushed slightly and bit her lip.

'What do you mean?'

She hesitated. 'Why not use one's imagination?'

'Yes, why not?' I said.

§

At Baquio we strolled arm in arm to the westerly end of the bay where I spied a little crescent sandbank, suitably shallow. A set came through, unfurling perfectly in spitfire succession for about thirty metres, the waves waist-high and hollow.

'Look at that!' I exclaimed. 'Unreal!'

She squeezed my arm. 'Aren't you going to surf?'

§

The sea was a slick, inky blue. The swells oozed in, almost unsighted, and hit the piled-up sand. The waves formed, not by an upward reach of the swell's crest, but rather by the sudden downward plunge of the base. I picked up a few slinking swells. Two strokes and a rapid jump to my feet when the board angled down. Weight over the inside rail, I strained to keep the nose of the board free of the water. Then the rail caught and the board swung into the hollowing wall. With gathering speed, I raced along the fast arching wall, the wave's lip breaking close behind or against me. It was all speed and acceleration — brief but intoxicating. I couldn't get enough.

I rode the short, fast waves for an hour. At the end of each, in the spray, where the wave collapsed, the afternoon light created a fleeting rainbow. Paddling back out, cresting a wave, another appeared.

Back on the shore, I told Maite about them. 'So many rainbows out there! Amazing!'

'I couldn't see any.' She laughed. 'Maybe you're going crazy!' She hugged me.

I kissed her on the forehead. 'Maybe.'

While I dried off, an army truck pulled up near our car and a dozen or so *Guardia Civil* filed out.

'Look!' said Maite, pointing.

I lowered the towel. 'What's happening? What are they doing?'

'I'm not sure. Wait and see.'

The commanding officer marched the men, rifles over shoulders, to the east end of the beach. They halted and made two lines facing the sandy cliff. One *Guardia* set targets. The rest drew their rifles. The front line went down on one knee, the rear remained standing. On the officer's command, they aimed and fired.

'Shooting practice,' I said dismissively.

'More like a firing squad!' she whispered fiercely.

We watched from a distance, neither of us wanting to go back to the car until they'd gone. After nearly an hour, the squadron shouldered arms, regrouped, marched back up the beach, climbed into the rear of the truck and drove off.

By the time we left, the sky had closed in, suffocating the

late afternoon light. It grew dark as we traversed the pine forest to reach the summit at Cabo Machichaco. When we broke from the forest, we ran straight into the bright lights of a truck, *Guardia Civil* flashing us with their torchlights, a metal-spiked device snaked across the road.

Maite became resolute, sullen. 'Don't say anything. Let me do the talking.' She wound down her window to the *Guardia*. Another appeared at my window. Both had their weapons ready, fingers on the trigger.

'Where are you going?' he asked her in Spanish.

'Mundaca.'

He shone the torch into the car, into my face. 'Who's he?'

'A friend.'

'Out! Both of you out of the car.'

We did as he said, the *Guardia* motioning us to the side of the road. '*Papeles! Pasaportes!* Papers!'

Maite produced her ID, but I couldn't. I had nothing with me.

'His passport's in Mundaca,' she said emphatically. The commanding *Guardia* grunted. He carefully examined her identification card. 'Your family name … from Guernica …' He tapped the card on the palm of his other hand. 'Search the car,' he ordered his subordinates.

A sweat broke out on my neck at the thought of what they might find. I stole a glance at Maite. She stood unmoving, arms folded, gazing into the forest, seemingly impervious.

They searched the boot, interior and underneath.

'There's nothing much, *Capitán*, only a wetsuit and towel, a blanket and these drawings.'

'Show me.'

The subordinate handed Maite's sketch pad to the Captain, who thumbed through the drawings.

'Who did these?'

Maite broke from her trance. 'He did,' she said.

The Captain studied her, then me. 'Did you?'

Maite didn't flinch.

'Yes,' I said.

'*Extranjeros. Turistas!*' He grunted and tossed the pad into the back seat. A car approached from Bermeo out of the mist to be stopped by a *Guardia* at gunpoint. 'Stay out of trouble, *extranjero*.' The Captain dismissed us, almost throwing Maite's card at her. 'And beware the company you keep.' The subordinate retracted the metal-spiked device, enough for us to pass, and waved us on with his flashlight.

I felt like I'd escaped a shark. 'Why did you do that?'

'Sorry, but many *Guardia* know my family name. They'd suspect me, accuse me of something. Any excuse to harass me. I knew they wouldn't suspect you, a foreigner.'

'But they're only sketches. We haven't done anything wrong. There's nothing to suspect, is there?'

'No.' She hesitated. 'Like Inigo, we've done nothing wrong.' She reached to find my hand and squeezed it. 'Please, no more questions.'

Her brother was in prison, he must have done something.

178

We hadn't done anything, but I felt like I'd committed a crime. We drove to Mundaca in silence. Maite seemed lost in thought. She kept hold of my hand, only letting go to negotiate the tight corners.

'You are an angel, my saviour,' she said when we reached Plaza Santa Catalina. She hugged me. 'You don't know what you've done for me.'

'I don't think I've done anything.'

She kissed me. 'Believe me, you have.'

'Today was one surfing trip I'll never forget.' I kissed her.

'At least you found waves.' She laughed. 'And rainbows.'

'Better than interrogation and the firing squad.'

She stopped laughing. 'Don't joke about those things.'

'I'm sorry ... it's my Australian humour.'

She snorted softly. 'Worse than my Basque humour.'

I unloaded my surfboard and gear. 'When will I see you again?'

'Not for a week, I'm afraid.'

I leant down close to her face, framed by the car window. 'A week? So long?'

She reached a hand to my face. 'Be patient with me. There are things you don't understand.' She pulled me closer. I was lost now, captive to her eyes, her scent. She kissed me. A pleading kiss.

'Can you do me another favour?' she asked.

'What is it?'

She took an envelope from her jacket. 'Post this for me.'

I took the envelope, turned it over. The same address in Dublin was on the front.

'I'll come on the Friday night.'

My fate seemed sealed.

§

'Ah, *muchacho!* That week flashed past!' Manolo's eyes were the colour of lapis and danced with mischief. 'I have news for you. But, first, sit down. *Cerveza o café?*'

'Beer, please.' I pulled up a stool at the far end of the bar. 'What news?'

He cracked open a bottle and poured. 'Be patient, *muchacho.*' He set the glass down and rubbed his hands together. 'First, your book.'

I felt the cold swirl of bubbles on my tongue. 'Ever heard of Wilhelm Wakonigg?' I asked.

'I've read about him, of course. Businessman, lived for many years in Vizcaya, daughter married to the new chief of the Basque police.' He shook his head, face grim. 'A bad end for him.' He raised a finger. 'But just!'

'Guilty of espionage, passing information to the Germans and Franco. Executed by firing squad.'

'A loyal German to the end.' Manolo sighed. 'So much for assimilation.'

'What is it with firing squads around here?'

'What are you talking about?'

I filled him in on our beach adventure and Maite lying about the sketches.

Manolo didn't understand it, either. 'That's strange,' he said.

For a moment I felt a long way from home. 'Do you know by the time George got back to England, his pregnant wife had taken ill and died?'

'Poor soul!'

'He returned to Bilbao with a death wish, I reckon. He took incredible risks.'

Manolo ran a hand through his hair. 'A broken heart can drive a man to the edge.'

'It got so much worse when German gunners and the reconnaissance wireless arrived.'

'Nazis! They tipped the balance. And the Italians. It was all downhill after March '37.'

'Franco thought Vizcaya was easy pickings. Even easier with German help.'

'The Germans knew it too. They stationed submarines near San Sebastian to protect their interests. Once the Basques were defeated, they expected payment from Franco — iron ore, for the German war machine.'

'Tragic times.' He tapped a finger repeatedly on the bar top. 'It's guerrilla warfare these days. *ETA* has become ruthless too.'

I drained my beer.

'*Muchacho*, it's what I suspected.' Manolo raised a finger. 'Her grandfather *was* an officer in the war. BNP battalion leader, a famous soldier.'

I sat forward, hands restless on the bar. 'That might explain why her brother and sister would be with *ETA*. Why she might be too.'

'The grandfather was in the Mundaca nursing home. He died a few years ago.'

'I know the nursing home.'

'Plenty of veterans there, *muchacho*,' Manolo mused. 'They would have known him.'

'I bet! The doctor too. Can you find out more, Manolo?'

'I'll try, *muchacho* … in the meantime you take care.' The corner of his mouth twitched. 'You may be in danger.'

The shoebox, the envelope, the postmistress's suspicious eyes on each and Franco's glaring portrait flashed across my mind. 'Perhaps.' I stretched my neck. 'Like George, she's fighting the good fight, isn't she?'

Manolo grunted. 'It's a good fight. But not like that. Not those methods.'

'Like she asked me, what are the alternatives?'

Manolo shook his head. 'Enough, *muchacho*.'

'She's right, isn't she, Manolo?'

He waved me away sharply. '*Basta!*'

CHAPTER 8

The casino bar began to fill with a mixture of locals and weekenders. A group of men began passionately debating football and the merits of the club Athletic Bilbao, but when they switched to Basque, I was lost.

I was ready to move on, habitually scanning for Maite, when a foreigner appeared, his shoulder-length blond hair and steel-rimmed glasses familiar. His mate, a short, finely-built man with sandy hair and red-tinged stubble, I didn't recognise.

'Owen!' Jock cried, shaking my hand. 'Are you still around? I can't believe it!'

'Sure am!' I replied, rising from my bar stool. 'How are you, Jock?'

'Fine, *amigo*! Just fine!' he said, with a slightly crooked grin. 'Meet my Aussie buddy, Rob, from Sydney.'

I caught the mischievous glint in Rob's eye while I shook his freckled hand. He had the look of an Irish fox on the trot, tongue out.

Jock took off his glasses to clean them. 'By the way, Owen, any word from Jean?'

'No. He's still in Morocco, I think.'

Jock reset his glasses on the end of his nose and pushed

them back gently with his middle finger. 'Cal headed back to the States a while ago. I don't know where Jean was heading.'

'I don't know either. I didn't have the money to chase after him.' I shrugged and re-focused. 'Are you guys staying long?'

'Well,' said Jock, 'I've got at least another month. I brought Rob down here to try the famous Mundaca waves.'

'You can stay with me,' I said. 'There's plenty of room.'

'Great! It's such a squeeze in that van.' Jock rubbed his long-fingered hands together. 'I'm glad you're still here, Owen. You know, man, I had a strange feeling we might run into you!'

The van was parked alongside Adolfo's upturned navy blue fishing boat, the *Betisalada*, which was lying half-painted on the cobbles beside the port wall. I led the way to Plaza Santa Catalina and gave them a brief tour of the house. 'You're right,' said Jock, running an eye over the walls and ceiling. 'She is an antique.'

'You're not complaining, are you?' asked Rob teasingly.

Jock snorted. 'Anything's better than sleeping next to you, *amigo*.'

'She's a relic, all right,' I said. 'But could you get a better position? And cheap as chips.'

'Love the undulations in the floorboards, mate,' said Rob, arms gracefully outstretched, knees bent, pretending to keep his balance. 'You don't even have to leave the house to go surfing!'

I snorted. 'Wait till you see the river mouth break,' I said. 'You'll be glad for the practice in here.'

Jock laughed, a low chugging rumble.

'Coming back to the bars?'

'Are you kidding, my man? Of course.'

'You've been hanging out with Australians for too long, Jock,' I said. 'You're starting to sound like one.'

'Yeah, I'm turning into a bloody Aussie!' he said, exaggerating the twang.

'Come on, you guys. Hurry up. *Vámanos*,' I said. 'I'm supposed to be meeting a girl.'

'A local girl?' asked Jock, a smile forming.

I couldn't help grinning. 'Well, local, but from Guernica.'

Jock wagged a finger at me. 'I thought there was something to that twinkle in your baby-blues! You sly dog! You found a *señorita*!' Jock's eyebrows were two high arches above his glasses. 'You *have* settled into the place.'

'I love it here, mate.'

'I can see why,' he said, grinning. 'Has she got any friends?'

'She has. She might bring one tonight.'

'Do they speak English?'

'A little,' I said.

'So, how do you talk to them?' asked Rob.

'In Spanish. It's amazing how fast you learn when you're alone and forced to speak. I'm even starting to dream in Spanish.'

'Man,' said Jock, shaking his head, 'my Spanish is woeful!'

Rob rubbed his chin. 'I can't speak a word.'

'It doesn't matter,' I said. 'The girls enjoy trying English.'

'Well, I might comb my hair.' Jock darted into the bathroom.

'It won't make any difference,' Rob called out. 'You'll still be ugly!'

'Not as ugly as you, *amigo*! I'll be a fine-looking *americano*! The girls are going to love me!' He reappeared with a shiny-toothed grin, his hair carefully spruced. '*On y va?*' he asked. 'Maybe they speak French!'

We set off on a *vuelta*, me ever-watchful for Maite and her friends. Carmen wasn't at her usual post. I hoped she wasn't sick. Rosa, her dark-eyed, strong-boned daughter reassured me otherwise. 'She's fine, *muchacho*.' She smoothed her jet-black ponytail with a large hand. 'She's at home, babysitting. It's my baby, Arantza, who's been sick. The doctor came again yesterday.'

'I'm sorry to hear that … I know how it can be.'

Rosa studied me for a moment. 'My mother's mentioned you. Says you're going to be a doctor, too, one day.'

I grunted. 'Then she knows better than I do.'

Rosa laughed. 'Perhaps she does.'

I smiled, nodding slowly, digesting the words. 'Glad you have a caring one.'

Rosa took the tops off three bottles of San Miguel. 'These are on the house.'

'So, Maite gave you a book written in English?' Jock said.

'Yeah.'

'In English?'

'Yes, mate!'

'A bit odd.'

I paused, scratched my head. 'There are a few odd things about her.'

Jock frowned. 'How do you mean?'

Conflicting images flooded my mind. I took a big breath and blew out the air. 'Tell me about *your* adventures,' I said.

§

Around ten, we found ourselves back at *Bar El Puerto*. It was crowded, the bar abuzz with revellers and Spanish music, and too hard to talk. We watched the crowd — the swirl of colour, the scent of perfume and tobacco, the loud voices and wild gesticulations, the laughter, and behind it all the sensual driving rhythms of the Latin beat.

At each bar, while we swapped tales and joked, I kept an eye on the door — ready for her to appear, willing her to do so. And as the night unfolded, my spirits began to ebb.

Jock soon twigged. 'Where are the girls?'

'Let's try *Bodegon*,' I said. 'Maybe they're late.'

We manoeuvred outside into the cool, salty night air. The swell was slack and on the mid-tide, barely breaking. The fishing boats in the little harbour rocked quietly on their moorings, lulled to sleep by the sea's soothing rhythms.

Bodegon occupied the ground floor of the casino building and resembled a small fortress. It was entered by large wooden doors from the side street that ran gently uphill from the terrace that fronted the two bars, *El Puerto* and *Los Chopos*.

Large windows overlooking the harbour softened the effect of the solid stone walls.

We were greeted by the familiar smell of red wine, tortilla, *chorizo*, garlic mushrooms, perfume, smoke and human sweat. With a string of *'permisos'*, we pushed our way to the bar and I shouted the order. The bartender ripped the caps off three bottles, poured them into glasses and, without looking, threw the bottles behind him into a bin. Nothing broke. He took my *pesetas* and rifled back the change. I passed Jock and Rob their beers and ran my eye over the bar.

Maite! For an instant, everything seemed to stop — her beauty and movement transfixed for the smallest fraction of time, like a perfect photograph.

I reached her, breathless, my heart racing.

'I was wondering where you were,' she said. A gentle blush suffused her cheeks.

'We've been doing the rounds, looking for you.'

'We?'

'A friend arrived in town, with a mate.' I beckoned them over.

Maite proffered a delicate hand. *'Mucho gusto,'* she said, smiling shyly.

'Nice to meet the artist,' said Jock.

'We've heard you're talented,' said Rob.

Maite nodded politely, the blush deepened.

Ines appeared carrying two *mostos* and complaining about the crowds. *'Dios mío! Tanta gente!'*

'Oh! Hola, Owen!' she exclaimed. *'Qué tal?'*

'*Bien, bien!*' I motioned with my hand. 'Ines, meet my friends.'

'*Quiénes son?* Australians?' She smiled, holding out her hand.

'American,' Jock said, kissing her hand. 'And Rob here's Australian, from Sydney.'

'*Mucho gusto, muchachos.* Welcome to the Basque country! First time? When did you arrive? How long you staying?' She went at them in heavily accented English with irrepressible energy.

Maite led me away to a quieter corner and came close so we could talk.

'Owen, how are you?'

'A bit tired. But so much better for seeing you.'

She pulled me close. 'I've missed you.'

I could smell the perfume on her neck. I pressed against her. 'God, I've missed you too.'

She laughed and pushed me away slightly. 'You've been busy surfing, I bet.'

'No, not true!' I pulled her closer again. 'Well, a bit of surfing. But mostly reading and thinking of you.'

She nuzzled into my chest. 'I can guess what you were reading. But what were you thinking?'

'Pleasant thoughts,' I said teasingly.

'That's all?'

I pulled her tighter against me. 'Passionate thoughts, too.'

'Sounds more interesting.'

My hug loosened. 'And thoughts about your mysterious side.'

She laughed. 'That's called feminine mystique.'

I laughed too. 'Oh, is that what it is? Nothing else?'

'Mystique, mystery. It's good, isn't it?' She pulled away slightly, smiled coyly. 'Keeps you interested.'

'That's true. Up to a point.'

'Would you rather be with someone you know everything about?'

I mused for a moment. 'Probably not.'

'Then you'll have to have faith, trust.'

'Can I trust you?'

'What does your heart say?'

I drew her close again. 'Maite, you know what it says.'

'Tell me.'

We stole a quick, fierce but tender kiss. She hugged me with a quiet intensity. 'You *must* trust me.'

'Alright,' I said. I took a breath, pushed it out slowly, the tension in my body releasing with it. 'I'm in your hands.'

She squeezed me tight. 'You won't regret it.'

Christ! I hoped she was right.

Maite turned to see the others. 'Look,' she said, when their conversation erupted into laughter.

'She's on a roll,' I said.

'That's an understatement.' Maite grabbed my hand. '*Vámanos!*'

We rounded up the others and stepped into the fresh cool air of the cloudless night. Jock and Rob linked on each arm, Ines led us to the quiet bar in the back streets. Maite and I lagged behind. In the dark of the narrow cobblestone street, I drew her to me, the swell of her breast against my chest, her hip moving against mine when we walked. That strange electric feeling coursed through me. She must have felt it too, because she nestled tighter. At the corner of a cul-de-sac, in the shadow of an overhanging balcony, I stopped and kissed her. She returned my kiss, but the sound of advancing footsteps startled her, and we drew apart. The others had stopped outside the bar. '*Venga, venga!*' implored Ines, herself a little merry.

There was barely space for five to stand on the sawdust floor, and the faded lime-green walls had large patches where the paint had flaked. The owner served us and slumped again. No-one came or went.

Maite and I stood close but not touching. The jaundiced light from the cobwebbed bulb left no dark corners for refuge, but Maite's proximity was enough. She'd put my doubts to rest without giving anything away. And the secret of our liaison heightened our awareness of each other. Even the smallest gestures took on meaning.

The barman finally stirred and shuttered the only window. We finished our drinks and moved outside. In the alleyway, Ines kissed Jock and Rob on the cheek, promising a rendezvous in the near future. I pulled Maite to me. '*Guapa*, lovely *señorita*, when will I see you?'

'Tomorrow evening,' she said warmly. 'I'll pick you up in the main street, next to the bank, about eight o'clock. We'll go to Lequetio. Okay?'

We kissed and Ines called, laughing, '*Maite! Vámonos!*'

'*Agur, Agur!*' called Maite when Ines led her around the corner, leaving us in the silent back streets of the village.

'Ines is cool,' said Jock when we turned for home. 'But feisty.'

'You got her flustered!' said Rob. 'She couldn't understand your accent. She's beautiful! Such fire in her eyes! It's a good thing she finds me attractive. Did you see the way she looked at me?'

'You're joking!' exclaimed Jock. 'She might like your weird laugh, Rob, but she can't resist my charm! Did you see how we talked, her body language? No, my friend, she is mine for the taking!'

'I don't think so, Jock. Ines has got the hots for me! Maybe I don't have that American swagger, but she gave me a look that said ... "Yes!"'

'Forget it, Rob. You're spoken for!'

'Maybe, Jock,' Rob said teasingly. 'Maybe.'

Jock kicked at a stone on the cobbles. 'Anyway, she's quite a lady.' We crossed the deserted plaza. 'You and Maite seemed pretty intense,' he prodded gently.

'Yeah,' I said, exhaling slowly. 'Pretty intense.'

The boys laughed. 'Anyway, it's damn obvious,' Jock slapped me on the back, '*Amigo*, you got hit by Cupid's little arrow ... straight in the heart!'

I sighed. If only that was all there was to it.

§

The sun was well up when we surfaced the next morning. A clean swell was running down the sandbar, the wind offshore and meek. We suited up, ambled to the port and paddled out through the harbour walls. It was a gentle, lazy day, and so good to have mates to surf with. The cool autumn sea soon washed away our hangovers.

We surfed quietly across the morning: long fast rides and the hypnotic paddle back out across the silky, blue-green water. The Pyrenees sat brooding against the naked blue sky and Laga's cliffs shone gold with autumn. I didn't want to think too far ahead. Tonight I'd be with Maite, drift in those luminous eyes, breathe her perfume, and feel the warmth of her love.

It was a perfect day. We returned to land, spent. Not the all-consuming fatigue of frenetic activity, but the pleasant ache of steady, measured paddling — one that brings peace and satisfaction, but leaves the mind alert.

'Who's hungry?' I asked.

'I'm starving,' said Rob. 'A feed, a hot drink and a siesta is what I need.'

Back at the house, lunch behind us, Jock was doing the honours. 'Cup of tea, *amigo*?' he called from the kitchen.

Rob was languishing in a lounge chair, his tousled sandy hair a mess, gaze dulled. The fox had lost his trot.

I nudged him as I took up a chair. 'Tired, mate?'

'Too many beers last night,' he replied. 'But it was worth it ... Gotta love the *vuelta*.' He gave a low groan while he stretched. 'Ines is a character, isn't she?'

'Man, I love these *señoritas*,' said Jock bringing in the tea, eyes bright and blue like the pattern on the cups. He lifted his gaze fleetingly when he poured. 'Imagine hooking up with one of them!'

Suddenly, I saw myself hooked, literally, dangling on the end of Maite's line.

Jock handed out the cups. 'When are they coming back?'

'I'm not sure about Ines,' I replied, 'but I'm meeting Maite tonight.'

Jock raised an eyebrow mischievously, cup to his mouth. 'You lucky devil!'

'She's lovely,' Rob chipped in. 'And you can see she really likes you.'

I set down my cup, the tea almost spilling. 'Really?'

'It's bloody obvious!' said Rob. 'Even if she seems a bit nervous.'

'Well,' I picked up my cup again, 'girls here have to be careful, especially around foreigners. Reputation is everything.' I took a sip. 'This is foul, Jock! Where did you learn to make tea?'

'Give me a break, *amigo*, I'm an *Americano*. A coffee man! … Go on.'

'Imagine the gossip if word gets out, or if her family finds out?'

'I guess,' said Rob, sitting fully upright and stretching. 'They certainly seemed more relaxed when there were no other locals about.'

'Exactly.' I lounged back in the late afternoon light that

angled through the balcony doors. 'So, which of you two is going to steal Ines's heart?'

Rob's brown eyes gleamed with a mix of anxiety and delight. 'I'll have to watch the beer, otherwise I'm done for. Rebecca can read me like a book, even through my letters.' He peered into his cup. 'I'm a hopeless liar — she'd pick up on it straight away if I played up.'

Jock sensed victory. 'So you can leave Ines to me?'

Rob shrugged. 'I'm not sure she really liked you, Jock.'

'What do you mean?' asked Jock, the grin disappearing.

'Well, let's face it … you're an American with no money and limited prospects.' The corners of his mouth began to quiver. 'And a real tight-arse with no sense of humour!' he added with a burst of laughter.

'So funny!' said Jock. 'Lucky you have a girlfriend back home, Rob, because no girl here would go for you, *amigo*, you look like a derelict! You don't even bother to shave. You might be at uni, but you're not that smart.'

'Alright, Jock, settle down. I'm only joking, mate,' said Rob playfully. 'Go for it, my friend. I want to see your sophisticated Yankee charm!'

'Alright,' said Jock, retreating. 'You watch.'

'That's settled,' I said. 'No pressure, though!'

Jock sank back in his chair, looking more defeated than victorious.

'Yeah, Jock.' Rob flopped back and drained his cup. 'No pressure.'

I settled back in my lounge chair with the verandah doors open and continued with my Spanish study. After an hour, I put the book aside and picked up one of Jock's surfing magazines — page after page of beautiful waves. 'Look at these shots of Pipeline, mate! Gerry Lopez dropping into some huge ones!'

Rob peeked over my shoulder. 'Almost as good as Mundaca,' he said, laughing. 'Hey, don't torture yourself reading the mags, Owen.'

'I'm amping myself for the next swell,' I said. 'I wish it would hurry up and come!'

'Owen, you're amped enough!'

I threw the magazine down and picked up *The Tree of Gernika*. I thumbed through the book to find my place. Suddenly, there was a familiar noise, a drum roll and a loud voice in the street below. Jock and Rob raced to the balcony and I ambled over.

The thin elderly man with the kettle drum stood at a nearby corner giving a speech. When he'd finished, he walked to the next corner, stopped, performed another short drum roll and repeated the speech.

'What's he selling?' asked Jock.

'Nothing! That was my first impression too.'

'What's his trip, then?'

'He's telling the news, but it's impossible to understand. It's like he's talking in code.'

'A town crier!' Jock said. Our eyes followed the old man as he turned the corner.

'Yeah, like in movies!'

We stood listening and chuckling until the drum roll and speech was lost in the alleyways. We heard the crier every afternoon when we weren't out surfing. We loved it, and just the sound of the approaching drum made us chuckle. 'Here he comes!'

CHAPTER 9

With the warmer weather, the windows open and a refreshing breeze, the shortcomings of Ignacia's house could be ignored. But it was getting cold and the windows had to be closed. After our morning cup of tea, the boys circled in.

'Owen,' said Jock, 'I don't want to seem picky.' He groped for the right words. 'But this place needs … sprucing up.'

'I've been putting it off.'

Rob fell back against his seat and laughed. 'That's an understatement!'

'Jeez, fellas, give me a break. I haven't spent much time here,' I said, squirming in my chair. 'Occasionally sitting and eating out on that balcony and sleeping, really. What have you got in mind?'

Jock rubbed his hands vigorously. 'A complete overhaul.'

Our first task was to clean. We washed and scrubbed and mopped. We cleaned the walls as high as we could reach. The kitchen ceiling bore the smoky grime of decades of wood fires. We weren't going near it.

We worked hard, but it was impossible to get rid of all the dust. It clung resolutely to the ceilings and the upper reaches of the old walls.

If we could have heated the house to any appreciable degree, we might have got on top of the damp, but there was no heating — a detail I'd overlooked on that first, beautiful autumn day tour with Ignacia.

In the warmer weather it wasn't so noticeable, but when autumn advanced, there was no escaping the damp, drifting in unseen from the now dull grey-green waters of the port. Salty, tinged with boat engine oil, it arrived on the back of the autumn winds and came to rest on every surface. It spread its tentacles through the house, on clothes and bedding, clinging firm, immoveable, like an octopus clamped to a rock.

The lukewarm shower had become intolerable. The gas-fired water heater was good for about sixty seconds and first shower was a privilege. But when winter approached, it was no-one's privilege. We resorted to heating large pots of water on the stove and 'showering' in the kitchen sink.

On the days of long, cold surfing, being caught second or third in line for a 'shower' — standing in the draughty stairwell, numb and blue with only a cold damp towel — was protracted torture.

Winter took hold and the house became unbearably cold. Layers of clothing and a blanket made it cumbersome to sit and awkward to eat. We huddled in the kitchen with the gas stove on, or got back into bed. Mittens or gloves helped with the chill but not the dexterity. Even reading became difficult.

We took refuge in the bars, but there was a trade-off

between spending money there and buying gas for the stove. The balance of finances became trickier as the winter deepened.

The dust we more or less came to terms with. The damp was a losing battle that we gave up fighting. The cold was expected and we coped. But the rodents became a battle of wits and courage.

Early one morning, Jock had an encounter.

I'd seen big rats before, near the markets in Bermeo. Massive creatures with long pink tails, they emerged from the drains to forage on scraps but scuttled nervously away at the sound of footsteps. The thought of facing off with one of those vermin, its back up and teeth bared, was unnerving.

Jock had got up to use the toilet, switched on the hall light and come face-to-whiskers with '*La Rata*'. It had escaped through its hole under the attic door and could be heard ascending the stairs. Jock, stopped cold in his tracks, managed to control his bladder. He retreated to his room, put on shoes, and warily tried again.

We heard about it the following morning.

'Big as a fucken cat,' he snarled, eyes wide.

'Something's got to be done,' said Rob.

'We'll have to catch it.'

'Not me,' I said, raising my hands in protest and retreating a step. 'Can't we just block the hole in the bottom of the door?'

'Maybe,' said Rob thoughtfully.

We went to inspect the door in the hallway.

'Who's going in?' I asked, absolutely certain it wasn't me.

No-one volunteered readily. Jock, cursing, was coerced. He switched on the light and carefully opened the door. A very dusty staircase led into the attic, a roof space where ancient beams sagged under the weight of faded red clay tiles. Cobwebs hung in giant plumes and light invaded in thick fingers where the tiles were broken or missing. Jock proceeded hesitantly to the top of the stairs and peered into the patchily-lit space. All was quiet.

'I'm not going any further,' he said firmly. 'The timber's all rotten. It's too dangerous.' He beat a retreat and rejoined us at the bottom of the stairs. 'Besides,' he added, 'it's full of giant cobwebs.'

We closed the door and locked it. I'm not sure why. That wasn't going to keep the rat out, but somehow it made us feel a little more secure.

We decided to block the hole. Rob found an old magazine and wedged it in tight. 'That should do it,' he said, convinced that no rat could pass.

For a few days all was quiet, save for the scratching of our smaller friends.

Jock announced the bad news several days later, on rising to check the surf. 'The magazine's gone!' he yelled.

Rob and I rallied from our rooms to join him in the hallway.

'Jesus!' said Rob, examining the residual scraps of magazine around the hole. 'The bugger chewed right through it!'

Next we tried an old sandshoe Rob had found in his bedroom cupboard. He rammed it into the hole. 'That will do it!'

Jock and I exchanged looks. We weren't so sure.

The following morning we examined the sandshoe. Eaten through.

'Jeez, man! That thing must have big choppers,' said Jock, eyes bulging with restrained horror.

'We need something metal,' declared Rob gravely. Setting his mind to the problem with renewed determination, he found a cylindrical metal container about the right size, refashioned the hole in the door and wedged the container in.

'Surely, that will do it,' Rob said boldly. But he hadn't convinced anyone, not even himself.

The metal container did work to a degree. It prevented the rat from getting out of the attic, but didn't stop it from trying. In the middle of the night you could hear *La Rata* trying its hardest to break through the fortifications. I didn't like that sound, not my kind of lullaby. I preferred the subtle scratching of the mice.

Eventually, I told Ignacia about our little problem. She arrived the next day with a small bag of green pellets. She studied our defensive arrangements at the bottom of the door and shook her head, bemused, and then scattered the pellets in the attic stairway with her tremulous gnarled hand.

'*No se preocupe!* Don't worry!' she said confidently on leaving. '*Adiós, muchachos! Adiós, rata!*'

And she was right. The tiny scratching sounds disappeared for a while, later to return, but *La Rata* had gone.

§

A large pot, its lid awry, bubbled merrily on the stove, a loaf of crusty bread sat on the bench nearby. The smell of *alubias* and onions filled the house. 'Smells damn good,' I said. '*Vino*, anyone?' I revealed two bottles of *Rioja* from behind my back.

'You bet!' Rob dropped his magazine. '*Vino* goes well with Pipeline!'

We settled around the table in sleeping bags like giant caterpillars. 'To Mundaca!' I said, raising my glass. 'And the next big swell!'

'To Mundaca!'

We drained our glasses.

Halfway through the second bottle, we'd shared our virgin surfing stories and Rob was getting maudlin about Rebecca.

'Maite's brother's in prison,' I blurted. 'Seven years. Something to do with *ETA*.'

'Wow, man, a terrorist!' Jock grabbed at the bottle to pour us all more wine. 'What did he do? Kill someone?'

'She won't tell me. Only that he didn't do what they accused him of.'

Rob swept breadcrumbs into a pile on the tablecloth. 'You'd get more than seven years if you killed someone.'

'Franco's regime is ruthless,' I said. 'They execute people with bloody firing squads, so it can't have been that.' I sat back against the hard wood of the chair. 'They went to Dublin together — she was studying art, but he was doing business of some kind.'

'I've been to Dublin,' said Jock. 'A fun city! Hardly known

as the art school capital, though. Don't recall any galleries.' He laughed. 'Mind you, too busy drinking Guinness in the pubs.'

'That'd be right,' said Rob, picking at the breadcrumbs, his eyes on Jock. 'No sense of culture.'

'Guinness is a big part of Irish culture,' Jock retorted. 'Ask any Irishman!'

Rob waved him away. 'So, Owen, you don't know what business?'

I shook my head. 'She was vague about it. Manolo thinks if he really was with *ETA*, he could have been linking up with the IRA.'

Jock lurched backwards. 'Holy moly! That's heavy, man. I mean, you wouldn't want to mess with them.'

Rob scowled. '*ETA*'s no different, Jock.'

'He's right,' I said. 'Manolo says the IRA helps *ETA* get weapons.'

Rob sat back too. 'Far out.'

I took a gulp of wine. 'And there's more.'

'Jesus!' Rob flicked at the pile of breadcrumbs and they scattered over the table.

'Manolo found out that Maite's grandfather was a famous soldier in the Spanish Civil War. An officer in charge of a Basque battalion.'

'No wonder they're with *ETA*!' exclaimed Rob. 'It all adds up.'

'What about Maite, Owen?' asked Jock. 'Is she involved?'

'She says not, but a few strange things have happened.' I ran a finger around the rim of my glass. 'I'm not sure.'

'What strange things?'

I told them about our trip to Eibar and the shoebox, and being stopped by the *Guardia*, and how she'd said I'd done the sketches.

'She's up to something,' said Jock. 'You better watch out, man!'

'I should ...' I thought about the parcels I'd posted and whether to tell them. I sighed and sat back. 'But she's so lovely. Irresistible.'

'Irresistible!' Jock gripped the table. 'This is serious stuff, *amigo*!'

'Oath!' said Rob, a hand busy at his stubble — a tic developing. '*ETA*? Don't get involved.'

I swallowed. 'I already *am* involved.'

'Maybe you should press her,' said Rob. 'Find out more.'

'She asked me to trust her.'

'Do you?'

'I do.' I toyed with the glass and surveyed the breadcrumbs. 'But there's things I'd like to know — for my own peace of mind.'

'You should keep your distance.' Jock put on his glasses and stared at me. 'What are you here for anyway, man? The surf, right?'

'Yeah,' said Rob. 'Jock's right, Owen. You should focus on the waves. Isn't that why you stayed in Mundaca?'

I sighed. 'Of course, but …'

'No buts, Owen,' said Jock.

I looked at Rob.

He shook his head.

'Alright. I'll try to focus.' I set my glass down and cracked my fingers. 'I *have* been waiting for a good swell.'

'It's going to get big and that'll be something,' said Jock.

'True,' I said. 'Imagine flying down those huge walls. Can't wait!'

'I can,' said Rob. 'Imagine the wipeouts. Don't want to think about it … Bars tonight?'

'Sure,' said Jock. 'Owen?'

'Not me,' I said. '*I've* got a rendezvous.'

They looked at each other, then pounded me with cushions. The cries of 'idiot' rang in my ears.

CHAPTER 10

On the main street was a triangular nook, bordered on one side by the stone wall of the Banco de Vizcaya and on the other by a roughly rendered retaining wall. Dimly lit, I could wait there unseen. A car approached from Guernica, slowed and stopped. Maite!

'*Qué tal?*' she asked, smiling, when I got in. She leaned over and kissed me on the lips. I could smell her perfume, subtle jasmine.

'I started to think you weren't coming.'

She laughed. 'Don't be silly!' She kissed me again. 'Shall we go to Lequetio?'

'Why not? I've never been there.'

'It's beautiful! You'll like it. And I can relax there. No prying eyes!'

'Even better!'

We headed out of Mundaca, across the bridge and up to the lookout. The river, dark and silent, rested in its nocturnal bed, and on the other side of the estuary the lights of Laida hung like lanterns, disappeared into the trees when the car curved down to Pedernales.

'How was your day?' I asked, one eye on Maite, one on the road.

'Tiring. I went to my uncle's farm and then the nursing home … I didn't see you there.'

'I haven't been going since Jock and Rob arrived.'

'Dr Arriaza has noticed. He's disappointed. Some of the patients too. They liked seeing you in that corner seat.'

'Is that right …? I'll go soon — promise.'

Maite yawned.

'Didn't you sleep well last night?'

'No.' She turned briefly. 'I was thinking about you.'

'Really?' I put my hand on her thigh. 'Nice thoughts, I hope!'

'Beautiful thoughts,' she said softly, releasing one hand from the wheel to place it on mine.

'I don't want to get you into trouble with your family for looking sleepy,' I said, laughing.

'You won't. My sister says I seem more alive than usual.'

I swivelled momentarily to look at her. 'Is that right?'

'Yes.'

'How many sisters have you got?'

'Two.' She hesitated. By the dim glow of the dashboard lights, I saw her bite her lip. 'One's away.'

'Where?'

'Away.' She released her hand from mine. 'On a trip.'

Another brick wall. I reached for her hand. 'I know that alive feeling too. Since I met you, I've felt alive like never before!'

'I'm glad.' She squeezed my hand tightly. 'My sister was nosing around today.'

'What did you tell her?'

'That I'd met someone … *alguien guapo y simpático*, someone handsome, nice. I didn't tell her you were Australian.'

'Why not?'

She shook her head. 'If she knew I'd met an *extranjero*, she'd be upset. She'd tell my brothers.'

I pushed out a breath. 'Jesus, is it *so* important I'm not Basque?'

'Of course,' she said with an edge to her voice. 'Around here it's extremely important. Not many people are broad-minded when it comes to family. So I have to be discreet.' She stole a glance. 'You understand?'

'Yeah,' I said reluctantly. 'But it seems ridiculous. What would the rest of your family do if they found out?'

She was silent for a minute, weighing up the possibilities. 'Better they don't know.' She grimaced. 'Much better.'

'Why?'

'My brothers and the other sister are passionate Basques. We all are, but they more than most … They'd do anything.'

I turned to look at her. 'Anything?'

She was quiet for a moment, a silhouette in the thin moonlight. 'Almost.'

'What about your dad?'

'He's a pacifist.' She hesitated. 'He reacted badly to what happened to his own father during the Civil War. Never got over it.'

'What happened to your granddad?'

'He was a brave soldier. He commanded a battalion, saw

terrible things. Many of his men died.' Her sadness was etched by the pallid light. 'He felt responsible and carried that guilt all his life. And he never got over the Basque defeat.'

'Jeez, that must have been hell.' I shifted in my seat. 'I'm sorry.'

'My dad watched him suffer, saw his torment.' Her voice tightened. 'It made him totally opposed to war.' She was quiet a moment, concentrating on rounding a tight curve. 'My father has encouraged us to look for an alternative to violence.'

'An alternative?'

'A more effective way to promote the Basque cause.'

I said nothing. What did 'more effective' mean?

'My brothers and sisters and I don't always agree on how to go about that.'

'How so?'

She was silent for a moment. 'Let's say there are different ways to fight and some more radical than others.'

I could feel my muscles tighten. 'Do you believe in radical options?'

'It depends.'

'On what?'

She searched for words. 'On how desperate you are.'

I swallowed. 'Are you desperate?'

'Everyone gets desperate sometimes.' She seemed deliberately vague.

'Like your brother?' I asked.

She flashed an angry look. 'I told you he didn't do anything!

He's innocent. Don't you listen?'

'I do. You said your brothers and sisters didn't all agree on things. I thought, maybe, he'd gone out on a limb.'

'What does that mean?'

'That he'd taken a more radical course of action.'

'Ah! I thought you understood! You don't listen. He didn't do anything radical. You don't understand anything at all!'

I bit my lip to save myself from saying something I'd regret. Her mouth was clamped like a purse with the strings drawn tight, and she gripped the wheel as if clinging to a lifeboat.

'Jeez, I'm sorry,' I said. I put my hand on her arm. 'It seems *I've* gone out on a limb, overstepped the mark.'

Her grip on the wheel loosened. 'You have.' She shrugged and her face relaxed. 'There are things you may never understand.'

I bristled slightly. 'It can't be *that* complicated.'

She glanced at me. 'It is and it isn't.'

'Hell. What does that mean?'

'We have a sense of duty. To our family. To our fellow Basques.'

'I can understand that.'

'Can you?'

'Of course.'

'Then why aren't you with your family?'

It was a question I hadn't expected. 'They ... don't need me at the moment.'

'Don't they?'

'No.'

'Are you sure?'

'They cope without me.'

'And your brother?'

'I told you, he's travelling.'

'Your family's dispersed. That wouldn't work here.'

'Well, you went to Dublin. And your sister's away. What's the difference?'

Her voice tightened. 'The difference is those things happened for a purpose, for something we believe in! What's your purpose? What do you believe in?'

I didn't know what to say. 'I'm trying to work that out. That's why I'm travelling … to discover my purpose.'

She was quiet for a moment. 'What *do* you believe in?'

'Believe in?' I chewed on my lip, thinking. 'Freedom. Peace … I'm against war.'

She stiffened. 'You wouldn't fight for anything? Your country? Your home? Your family?'

'I mean,' I said, squirming, 'I wouldn't be a soldier, invade another country. Like Vietnam, it makes no sense for Australians to fight there. We were dragged in by the Americans.' I clutched at the seat. 'My next-door neighbour was killed there, but what for?' I reached for her. 'Of course, I'd defend my family, my home — if I had to. But I've never had to really think about it.' I took a breath. 'It's not an issue for us, for me. It's not a reality.'

Her face hardened. 'It is for us, for me. It's a daily reality.'

'It's different for you,' I pleaded. 'Your cause is obvious. You were born into it.'

'That's true.'

'I absolutely love it here, I really do.' I squeezed her thigh. 'And I feel for you. I've read nearly half George's book and I can see how the Basques suffered, people in this area, and how you're still suppressed.' I hesitated. 'I'd fight for it too.'

She frowned. 'Would you?'

'Why not? In my own way. Like George did.'

'I knew you'd understand.' She dropped a hand from the wheel and clutched at mine. 'So you're on our side?'

'I'm on your side.'

'And you trust me.'

'Of course.'

'So, best we keep things to ourselves, okay? It's much simpler that way. Otherwise there might be consequences.'

'Alright. If that's the way it has to be … I want to be able to see you, but I don't want to get you into any trouble.'

I didn't know exactly what the consequences might be, but I was willing to take the risk. Jeez, I could only imagine what her brothers might do. For her, restrictions and a curfew, no doubt. For me — hunted down, beaten up, or worse. I didn't want to think about it.

§

Lequetio appeared subdued. On the footpath, I put my arms

around Maite and she snuggled against me. We kissed for some time, content to be alone in the shadows.

'*Vámanos,*' she said eventually, gently breaking free.

Maite seemed completely relaxed while we walked hand-in-hand and began our *vuelta*. The beautiful old port was lined with restaurants and rustic bars. At each bar she chose the *pinchos*, delicious morsels of seafood, and we sipped our *tintos*.

'How does it feel in the sea and riding waves?' she asked.

My hands lovingly traced the form of the swells and the fast-flowing path of the surfer, while I tried to portray the powerful emotions.

She laughed. 'Surfing, I'm not sure I understand it. It's so dangerous! But I can see you love it. It's your passion!'

'The surf and the beach are a big part of Australian culture.' For that moment, I wanted nothing more than to take Maite home.

'The surfing is important to you.' She crinkled her brow. 'But you're in the Basque country. You must learn about *our* culture.'

'Will you teach me some more Basque?'

She laughed playfully when I tried to roll my r's. Basque has a lot of them.

Between bars we walked beside the port. In the middle of the bay was a large island. Maite said at low tide you could almost walk there. We stood for a while, silently gazing across the water, content in each other's company. I was overjoyed to be with a beautiful girl who was fast becoming the centre of my world.

She took me to a famous old bar that specialised in *jamón*. Cured Spanish ham, sliced thinly, melts in your mouth. Dangling from the cobwebbed ceiling, not far above head height, were dozens of various size and age, swaying ever so slightly in eerie noiseless patterns. Maite ordered drinks. The *pinchos*, all *jamón*, were delicate, rich and lightly smoked.

I reached to touch a nearby ham. '*Cuánto cuesta?*' I asked the bartender, an older, jolly, rotund man.

'Fifteen thousand pesetas,' he said. 'Or thereabouts.'

'*Ooh la la!*' I said. 'There's a lot of money hanging from this ceiling.'

He laughed merrily, his bushy eyebrows arching upward, and shook his right hand in the air in the customary way. '*Mucho. Mucho.*' He retrieved a plate from further down the bar. 'Try this,' he said. It was older, more expensive, better, but I was no expert. 'That one's on me.'

We left him amongst the myriad hams and walked to the port. Two *Guardia Civil* appeared. Not again! My pulse and breathing quickened with a surge of adrenaline, like when a big wave approached. Maite's hand tightened in mine and she slowed, trying to delay the inevitable.

They halted in our path. '*Papeles.*'

Maite handed over her ID card. The *Guardia* examined it carefully with his torchlight and gave it back.

'*Usted,*' he said, looking up at me.

'*Es extranjero,*' said Maite. '*Australiano.*'

The *Guardia* regarded me suspiciously. '*Pasaporte.*'

'*Está en Mundaca,*' I said. '*Tengo esto.*' I took out my wallet and gave him the extract of my birth certificate.

'*No vale,*' he said impatiently. '*Hay que tener el pasaporte.*'

He interrogated Maite with the charm of a Doberman. '*Qué hace usted aquí?*'

'*Una vuelta.*'

'*Por qué está usted con extranjero?*'

'*Es un amigo de Mundaca.*'

'*Mundaca? Qué hace en Mundaca?*'

'*Hace surf. Es surfista.*'

'*Es hippy?*'

'*No.*'

'*Fuma marijuana, toma droga?*'

'*No.*'

'*Vamos a cachearle.*'

I knew where this was going. I stood with my legs apart, arms out, already feeling violated. The subordinate *Guardia* searched me and found nothing. He started again with Maite, convinced she was meeting someone clandestinely. '*Y usted? Se encuentra con alguien?*'

'*No.*'

'*Por qué está en Lequetio?*'

Maite didn't give an inch, repeating what she'd said earlier. '*Le dije antes. Hacemos una vuelta.*'

At this point, a group of men came out of a nearby bar. The

Guardia's attention was drawn to them. '*Papeles,*' he said. A second *Guardia*, finger on the trigger of his submachine gun, waved us away and proceeded to question the others. We moved off swiftly, the voice of the *Guardia* smothered by the slap of our shoes on the hard cement path.

'Bastards!' Maite fumed, once well out of earshot. 'They hate us.'

It was difficult not to share her contempt. My own experience of the *Guardia* had been minimal and relatively harmless. Officious, unfriendly, unpleasant — yes. But abusive — no. At least not to me, yet I could sense the hatred, the menace, and it made me shiver.

Nowadays the plight of the Basques appeared such a straightforward proposition. Why should they be persecuted? 'It's thirty years since the German and Italian fascists were defeated,' I said, when we reached the car. 'Manolo's right. Franco's Spain exists in a vacuum. It's got almost no political allies in the Western world. Franco will die, Maite, and when he does you might get the reform you've waited for so long.'

She studied my half-shadowed face for a moment and kissed my cheek. 'I'm really sorry,' she said, a little mournful, 'but I'm tired and I don't want to talk about it anymore. Let's drive back and I'll drop you off.'

'Will I see you tomorrow?'

'Yes.' She eked out a half-smile. 'Tomorrow night. Same spot.'

When we arrived in Mundaca, she reached into the back seat

and brought out a rectangular parcel from under the blanket.
'Would you mind?'

It felt much heavier than the others. 'What's in –'

She interrupted me, a finger to her lips. 'Trust, remember?'

§

The boys and I stood on the headland beneath unhappy clouds, surveying the sea. Across the river the autumn light broke through, highlighting the pine-covered headland, the Laga cliff and the white sands of Laida, soon snuffed out by the mass of heavy clouds that pushed in from the sea. A cooler onshore wind rose up out of the north-west and cut across the grey-blue sea, arriving in disorganised scurries that tormented the moderate swell.

On the sandbar, the swells transformed into disparate dark peaks that lurched skyward and crashed, discharging their pent-up energy in a series of dull dis-synchronous explosions. The spume was whipped sideways and disfigured peaks rolled across the sandbank, pushing their force horizontally, creating a seething sandy mass of froth. The channel was a battleground of the out-surging river torrent and the churning, chopped-up swell, with no consistent victor.

The wind stiffened and ripped across the estuary. The chaotic sea issued a steady growling roar — a warning to all would-be seafarers. Jackets fastened, hands buried deep in pockets, we stood watching. The salty wind carried an uninvited chill from the deeper outlying Atlantic, catching our faces and ears, buffeting our jackets and well-worn jeans.

'Man, what a mess!' said Jock. 'I told you it wasn't worth looking!'

I chuckled. 'Surfers ritual, Jock. You gotta check it, no matter what.'

'Stuff this,' said Rob.

We headed back to the house to bunker down. I went back to bed, plunging back into the depths of a disquieting dream of being in Lequetio with Maite. After interrogating us, the *Guardia Civil* made us face a stone wall near the port with our hands up, waiting for the order to shoot. It came and the sound of machine-gun fire rang out around us. But the shots eventually gave way to the mocking laughter of the guards. Then they told us to get lost.

I awoke in a state of agitation. I'd never seen anyone die. Never been to a funeral, not even my sister's. Two great-aunts had died at home, in a bedroom upstairs, a bedroom I'd occupied, and would occupy again when I went home to study. I never saw the bodies. I was shielded, protected. I remembered the smell, though — the scent of death mingled with old age. You don't forget that. But they were old, death was expected. To die young, that was different.

No-one warned us Louise would die. It came as a shock, even to my parents. Her days were always numbered, we didn't know it, and she didn't know it either. She lived one itchy, scratching day to the next. And then, one day it happened.

She was gone. Dad came and told me at school. I had to sit in the classroom at lunchtime. It's the only time I remember him crying, but, for me, it wasn't real. It was as if she'd disappeared, gone on a long holiday, drifted away to another life. It wasn't that she'd *died*.

To die, I couldn't fathom.

My uncle fell off the back of his fishing boat once, engine still running, halfway between Rottnest Island and Perth. Drowning, he said, was preferable to a shark. His life flashed before him, like they say it does. I heard him recount the story to my father after a few whiskeys in our lounge room. It stayed with me, but it was only a story.

Death was a theory. Violent death, that was even more far-fetched. I hated violence. I'd been punched a few times, not really beaten, but hit hard enough to make it memorable.

And, anyway, to die like that, shot against a wall in a fishing village, was that really my destiny? Would I die for the Basque cause like George had been prepared to do? But hadn't George been half-dead from grief, from losing his wife and unborn child? He didn't seem to care whether he was dead or alive. That wasn't me.

George admired the Basques, grew to love them, threw himself in with them, wholeheartedly. That I could understand. But he wasn't fighting only for them. He was fighting for justice — justice here and justice at large. He was committed to discovering and communicating the truth to the world at large, uncovering the lies and deception, documenting all the sadness, horrors and tragic truths of war. When it came down to it, he was a war correspondent — a war correspondent who'd happened on the Basque country. That was *his* destiny.

Would I fight for Maite? Yes. Die for her? That was a different matter.

I reached for my book. George was back in Bilbao and the terrifying daily air raids had begun. Like everyone else, he spent much of his time scampering to and from shelters. Only bad weather, when the planes didn't fly for fear of smashing into the mountains, offered any respite. On the battlefront too, the aerial bombardments were pinning down the Basque troops and creating paralysing fear.

George described the *mystique* of the air — the sheer physical dominance of the German air force and its devastating effect on morale. It was the noise, smoke and fire, as much as the bombs that created the terror — a terror that affected the troops on the battlefield, not unlike the civilians in the city. This, he thought, was the first war where air power had had such a major impact on the course and outcome of a war.

I laid the book in my lap and tried to imagine Melbourne skies filled with aircraft, the sound of their engines, of bombs falling, whining, the explosions, buildings destroyed, smoke, people rushing for cover, confusion, the relief at finding shelter, the silence underground, the smell of fear, the tears and whimpers, the terrified children, the consoling grandmothers, the moans of the wounded, the last gasps of the dying. And after, the air raid over, surfacing nervously, surveying the wreckage, smoke and flames, searching for loved ones, neighbours, friends, always glancing skyward. No, not in Melbourne. Impossible.

I looked up at the ceiling where a patch of mould was thriving. Poor Bilbao! About to be starved out by Britain's refusal to come into port and France following suit, like a castle under siege. What must they have thought of the British, their supposed friends?

In Britain, amid a rising tide of public opinion, the matter was debated in parliament for weeks. Through his newspaper articles and by passing information to influential British politicians, George's exposés helped reverse British policy, though they wouldn't guarantee safe passage across the three-mile coastal limit into Bilbao itself. George claimed it was his duty to not only report the truth but also to counter misinformation.

The peeling, faded wallpaper was stirred by a current of wind sneaking though the gaping crack between the door and the architrave. George wasn't afraid to go out on a limb. No fear. He used his craft, his influence, to aid the cause to his utmost. And he succeeded. Is that how it was done? Was the pen mightier than the sword?

The wallpaper flapped. I pulled up the blanket and the book. The troops are rattled and Memaya is lost, Elgueta and Elorrio next to fall, but somehow Beldarrain and his troops escape. I wiggled my toes and stretched my restless legs. Good old Beldarrain! He seemed to have a sixth sense. But where are these places: Elorrio, Memaya, Elgueta? Maite would know them.

My leg was going numb. I shifted position and turned the page. George meets Jaureghuy at his hotel, an undercover French military advisor to the Basques, fronting as a Salvation Army journalist. Salvation Army! We had them at home, fighting for Christ. A different battle, different weapons. How strange to have their own foreign correspondent. Was that believable? The French must have thought so. I had to chuckle.

Outside, a few dark clouds had gathered above the village. To think those German planes had gathered here too, above the river mouth where we surfed, to turn and make their run down the inlet to Guernica, to practise their *blitzkrieg* — a thought that made surfing here seem completely surreal.

But it all happened out there, out beyond where we surfed, out amongst the swells in an ocean we doted on for little else but waves. Hard to imagine with everything so calm and peaceful these days. Merely fishing boats on their daily forays and the play of the wind across the sea. Surfing, after all, was about finding enjoyment and peace. Envisaging the river mouth as a fulcrum for destruction was unimaginable. The war had reached our doorstep! Guernica, Mundaca and Bermeo. It was all too close.

I got out of bed. The wind had backed off a little and the clouds seemed less threatening. I decided to walk up the hill behind the village by way of the post office. George had given me courage to send the parcel and maybe there would be a letter from home.

The few locals who ventured out were wrapped in coats,

berets pulled tight, their manner brisk and purposeful. Umbrellas, useless in this wind, were furled and tethered and used as canes or not at all. We scanned the skies, sensing a heavy autumn downpour.

The postmistress gave me the usual once-over. 'Another parcel for Ireland?' She raised an eyebrow.

'Yes,' I said sheepishly.

She lifted it and grimaced slightly. '*Pesa bastante.*' She weighed and stamped it, and placed it aside.

'*Cuatro cientos veinte cinco pesetas.*'

I paid the money. '*Señora, hay correo para mí?*'

She huffed and turned to peruse the pigeonholes behind her. She thumbed through a bundle from *Correos Listos* and, reading out the names in thick, measured Spanish, halted at one. '*Sí, hay uno,*' she said stiffly, and handed it to me.

'*Gracias.*'

'*Adiós,*' she murmured. Both she and Franco were watching me when I left. I pulled the door hard against the wind and made for the hill.

The long grass furled and unfurled in swirling patterns where the wind funnelled through. A few stray seagulls careened overhead, bouncing off the sudden gusts. There were no farmers or their wives about today. They stayed close to their *caseríos*, stone farmhouses in the lee of the hills, protected there from the wilder weather. I was alone, save for the letter in my pocket, and Franco's eyes still boring into my back.

Near the crest of the hill, between two fields, there was a

stone terrace wall where blackberries had taken hold. Here, out of the wind, I sat and gazed out over the village to the estuary and beyond, to Izaro, besieged by the wind-lashed, blue-black, Cantabrican Sea.

Mum had a lot to say. They were all missing me, especially Rosie. She wanted me to come home. I swallowed back tears. I missed her too and felt guilty being away so long. There was no recent news of John. Why didn't he write? She presumed that wherever he was the post was hopeless. We didn't hear from him for five months when he was trapped on that island in the South Pacific. She was resigned to a long wait, but you could tell she was hurting.

Dad wrote mostly about the government. The Whitlam dream was falling apart. A swag of new policies had been introduced too rapidly, he said. The neighbours' curtains were still closed. They rarely saw them and, when they did, they looked grey and drawn and spoke only briefly. Vietnam had been so cruel to them.

Whitlam had made important social changes, but the economy was falling apart. Scandal and other political mischief, with the government trying to gain control of the senate. Malcolm Fraser, the leader of the opposition, was gaining ground. He wondered where it would all end.

They'd been out to the crematorium at Springvale to visit Louise's grave, on her birthday. They'd taken flowers.

Tears dropped on the page. I'd forgotten about the lingering anguish, the dark cloud sitting over the house. I felt overwhelmed with sadness. 'Poor Louise,' I whispered to the wind. 'It all comes back to you. Too much suffering.'

Louise had fought a battle of attrition, for survival, a slow, unwinnable war. I could draw from her strength to fight against the negative forces that held me back. 'Is that what you're experiencing, John, an internal battle?' I whispered. 'A battle to make sense of it all? Is that why you left and never come back?'

Is that what George had done when he lost his wife and child? His grief was raw. Ours, mine, was different — distilled over time, the essence concentrated, a residue to carry inside forever.

'Too many thoughts,' I whispered. 'Where are they taking me?'

The wind was wreaking havoc, distorting the land and seascapes, disfiguring their composition. In places it uncovered their stark underlying fabric, revealing terrain I'd not yet seen. The sea's form endlessly changing as the wind cut and thrust across its surface, the swirling patterns in the pines on the headland across the river mouth where the trees, tightly grouped and deeply rooted, strained and bent, but held fast.

The sky, too, put on a show, rapidly transforming under the hammer of the wind. Clouds scuttled past, herded down the valley towards the higher Pyrenees. Rain whipped up in a stinging spray. I pulled up the hood of my jacket, but the wind caught it and flung it backwards.

Fearing the worst, I headed back to the house. The path was

slippery. At least the wind, now at my back, forcibly kept my hood in position. It rained heavily and the path was treacherous. I moved hesitantly but slipped and slid on my backside. 'La hostia!' Muddied and cursing in Spanish, I got to my feet, my hands caked in mud. I could have laughed.

The others certainly did when I flung open the door. 'Sewer rat!' said Jock.

'What happened?' asked Rob, who had a fair idea what had happened. 'Are you mad, Owen? It's wild out there. You dirty, filthy boy!'

'Mate, I had to stretch my legs!' I peeled off the damp layers at the door and retreated gingerly to the bathroom for a torturous shower. The hot water ran out well before the mud was off. My dignity restored by fresh clothes, I joined the others in the kitchen.

Jock was still shaking his head and chuckling. 'Coffee?'

'Sure,' I replied.

'Milk?' enquired Jock. 'Or do you want it ... mud black?'

'Bloody comedian, you are, Jock! Well, you guys missed quite a show up there on the hill.'

Rob shook his head in mock concern. 'Life's one slippery slope for you, Owen.'

§

The wind scaled back across the afternoon and by early evening all that remained was a stiff breeze. Heavy clouds had given way to thick, white cumulus forms that sailed past at altitude. Pale lemon shafts of light broke through from the west. My thoughts and mood moved with the weather. The anguish and guilt wrought by the letter had given way to gentler, calmer feelings. Home seemed so far away.

Unsettled by Maite, the doctor and that intense man, a puzzle I couldn't yet solve, my mind turned to the ocean. I needed to focus on the here and now, on my own battleground. Where was the giant swell I'd been waiting for? Why couldn't the real battle begin, the one I was really here for?

I rounded up the others. There was little point checking the waves, but we did anyway. The sea, simpering, messy and defeated, snatched at every citron ray of light, extracting energy to repair itself. Hunched in jackets, we murmured to each other, shrugged and adjourned to *Bar El Puerto*. Having been cooped up for the better part of the day, we were in a mood to cut loose.

Carmen, arms folded, was holding fort behind the bar. She half-smiled, half-grunted when we entered, as if her wayward children were late coming home, but she was still pleased to see them. She leant against the bar and tried to put on a grave face. '*Muchachos! Cerveza o café?*'

'No more coffee thanks, Carmen,' I said. 'We're thirsty. *Cerveza.*'

'*Cerveza.*' She raised her eyebrows in resignation, and reached below the bar.

'How's the grand-daughter?' I asked.

'Been coughing for a month. Cough, cough, cough, vomit.'

'Can't the doctor fix her?'

'Whooping cough. Says it will last three months. She's losing weight.'

'I hope she's okay.'

'We all do. I'm going to see her as soon as Manolo gets here.' She scowled. 'Late as usual.' She levered off the bottle caps, poured each glass half-full and slid them towards us ruefully. '*Tres cervezas.*'

'Your shout, Rob,' said Jock sheepishly. 'I left my wallet back at the house.'

'Typical bloody Scottish!' exclaimed Rob.

'Scottish *Americano*,' Jock retorted. 'Or, to be exact, an *Americano* with a hint of Scottish.'

'A hint?' Rob laughed. 'More like a whiff!'

Carmen shook her head. '*Salud pilluelos*. Ragamuffins.'

I raised my glass. '*Salud, Carmen! Salud muchachos!*'

The boys raised theirs. '*Salud!*'

Jock took a sip and spied the newspaper lying on the bar, a photo of a Spanish correspondent taken hostage in Lebanon on the front cover.

'Crazy bugger!'

'Gutsy bastards, those war journos,' said Rob wistfully. 'It'd be an interesting job, though.'

'Depends,' said Jock. Off came the glasses, out came the handkerchief. 'You need huge *cajones* for that.'

Rob laughed. 'No problem there.'

Jock grunted, cleaning his specs. 'I can't see Rebecca sitting at home while you dodge bullets around the globe.'

Rob chuckled nervously. 'I'm not really the war-zone type.' He motioned towards the sea. 'The only bullet I want to dodge is a ten-foot wave.'

'I'm with you there!' said Jock, specs and crooked grin back in place.

'Boys, there'll be plenty of bullets flying down the river mouth when the big swells come,' I said.

'Don't keep reminding us, man.'

'Don't you want to fly down the line, Jock? Feel all that energy and speed?'

'I do, I do. But I don't want to get killed in the process.'

'You won't get killed!' I said loudly.

Carmen frowned and reached for a broom.

'How do you know, man?'

'You know how to surf, how to survive,' I said in a softer voice. 'Have a little faith.'

'Faith?'

'Yeah, faith. Your survival instinct will kick in. You'll be okay.'

'A bit hard to have faith with a broken neck.'

'We'll all be out there,' I said. 'We'll keep an eye on each other.'

'In the end, you're on your own,' said Jock. He grimaced. 'You know that.'

'Jock's right,' said Rob. 'Even if you're brave, or mad, like your mate George, you still have to survive on your own wits.'

'Of course. But survival's inbuilt, isn't it?'

Anxious eyes regarded me.

'Fellas, a few more days of smaller waves and you'll be ready to taste the bigger ones.'

Jock finished his beer. 'Owen, I think that book is playing with your mind.'

Rob fidgeted with his empty glass and set it on the bar. 'I know what I'm ready to taste. Another beer. *Otro bar?*' He laid down the *pesetas*.

'*Sí, otro bar, amigo.*' Jock stretched his shoulders like he was going for a surf. 'Enough talk of bullets and war.'

Carmen stopped her sweeping, bemused. 'Your Spanish is improving, *muchachos*. *Agur!* And if you want to learn about survival skills, go and watch Mohammad Ali — over at the casino.'

The great man himself was not at the Mundaca casino, but his fight with Joe Frazier was going to be telecast live in the upstairs bar.

Like most surfers, we were underdressed and out of place in this dignified establishment. This evening, however, a smattering of locals had gathered to watch the brash Ali face off against the ageing Joe Frazier in a re-match dubbed 'The Thriller in Manila', and so we didn't stand out too badly.

We swayed and grimaced while we watched. From the groans, the locals were feeling every punch. In the final rounds, a few were on their feet, ready to swing. As his opponent wilted, Ali delivered a series of devastating blows. A staggering Frazier barely made it to his corner before his trainer threw in the towel. At least the opponents were well-matched and the rules abided by. My mind flashed to the Basques fighting the fascists, on the ropes, getting pummelled.

The celebrations began with a rush to the bar.

As night descended on the village, we adjourned for the post-mortem to a quieter watering hole in the main street, the one opposite the triangular nook.

'About time we saw the girls — Ines,' said Jock, after we'd dispatched with the boxing gloves and I got up to leave.

'Jock's got to ply his charm, remember, Owen?' said Rob.

'Yes. How could I forget?' I *had* neglected Jock's romantic yearnings, but that was the last thing on my mind right now. 'I'll see what I can do.'

I hadn't forgotten my appointment. Before that, I wanted to see Manolo.

I headed along the lanes that twisted and turned through the heart of the village, my mind a sea of unrest, thought waves crashing into each other from every direction. My shoes scraped the cobbles, the echoes ricocheting along the narrow passageways between the tenements. The sulphurous glow of street lamps, like distant lighthouses in a sea mist, drew me forward — a spotlight of raw yellow revealing me briefly when I passed beneath. The light at my back a sallow wash that turned my form to shadow — a shadow that stretched and led me back into darkness. And there, half-blind, alone with the smell of mould and brine, I felt my way along the sweaty walls of old buildings, over cobbles slippery like fish, to the main street.

Manolo leant on the bar, powerful arms, like posts, holding him erect, his head cemented on a thick, strong neck that grew out of a formidable torso, a torso once steeled by muscle but now cushioned by age. A blurry portrait through the steamed-up window.

He was holding court, arguing with three local fishermen, *boinas* clamped tight against the wind. From outside I'd seen their hands flying, but when I entered, the conversation stopped.

'*Hepa*,' they said, almost in unison.

I nodded and grunted in customary fashion.

'*Muchacho! Qué tal?* Where have you been hiding?' He reached out a paw. 'A drink, *muchacho? Cerveza?*'

'Please.' I took a stool at the far end of the bar, out of earshot.

Manolo brought the beer. 'You look worried, *muchacho*. What's up?'

'Too much.' I ran my hands through my hair. 'Too much happening.'

'*Muchacho*, I can't talk for long.' He glanced down the bar to the fishermen. 'Customers. There'll soon be more, but I wanted to let you know what I found out.'

'Yes?'

He leant forward, almost whispering, 'A soldier who fought alongside Maite's grandfather during the war and disappeared for a long time afterward is in the nursing home. He's old, unwell. The doctor was with them too in the war, a medic. Seems they were all extremely close, life-long friends since that time. They're loyal Basques,' he said. 'But *ETA*? I couldn't say.'

The door was flung open and a group of men blew in with the wind. '*Manolo, hombre, cinco tintos!*'

'*Vengo, Señores!*' Manolo collected himself. 'I've got to go, *muchacho*. Come back when it's quieter. We'll talk, okay?'

§

Maite arrived at our meeting place soon after I did. She didn't want to go to the bars, so we drove up to the lookout and parked. I told her about the letter from home and about Louise. She listened quietly, not asking too many questions, looking out across the river into the darkness.

'Death so young is too tragic,' she said. 'Illness or war, the result is the same.' She gripped my hand. 'I fear to die young.'

'Me too.' I pulled her close. 'This is a bit gloomy,' I said. 'Do you want to come to my place?'

§

I led her up the stairs into *Casa Ignacia*. All was quiet, save for the usual sighs of the roof and the creaking groans of the floorboards.

'Is it haunted?' she asked.

'Of course,' I replied. 'The walls whisper at night and tell me stories of the previous inhabitants, the long dead.'

'*Mentiras!* Lies!' She clutched me tight, as if she believed every word.

A mouse scurried across the floor into its hole when I turned on the kitchen light.

I laughed. 'One of our little pets.'

She scowled. 'I'm not sure I want to be here.'

'Don't worry. I'll protect you. Come this way.' I led her down the corridor, pausing at the bathroom where I flicked on the light. The tap in the sink was dripping and a fold of mouldy wallpaper rustled with an eddy of breeze. 'The spa room. No sauna, unfortunately.'

She screwed up her face. 'It's ancient.'

'Antique,' I said. 'Priceless.'

'I feel like I'm walking uphill.'

'You are,' I said. 'But come, it's downhill from here to the balcony.'

'That's good,' she said. 'Up hill, down dale. You'll stay fit living here.'

'You'll see.' I opened the balcony doors. 'The view is perfect.'

'Is it safe?'

I reached for her hand, coaxing her into the dark. 'It's old, but strong.'

She stepped out gingerly — like I had done on that first tour with Ignacia — clinging to my arm. I pulled her close. She nestled in, advancing cautiously with me to the rail. The half moon slid shyly behind a dark cloud. The port lights — pale, thin, yellow — cast an eerie, damp light over the tiny harbour.

'How romantic,' she said, gazing out. 'Like a painting of Venice in winter. Cold but humid.'

'Look, you can see the waves in the river mouth.'

'A surfer's dream home.'

I laughed. 'Almost.'

'Did you take it for the view?'

I grinned. 'In a way. The price was attractive too.'

'Hmm. I can imagine.'

'But I've grown to love the place.'

She laughed. 'That, I *can't* imagine! And besides, love is a strong word.'

'The place grows on you! You have to remember I came here at the end of summer, when it was still warm. With the doors and windows wide open, the sound of the sea and the wind, it was beautiful sitting here on the balcony, reading, looking out, breathing it all in.'

She turned to me. 'You are a romantic at heart, aren't you?'

'I suppose. Anything wrong with that?'

'*I* don't think so.' She smiled. 'But many people don't see things that way.'

'A different perspective?'

'A different sensibility.'

'Sensibility, that's a good word.' I looked up at the night sky. 'A different sensibility. That explains it perfectly … another world someone can't experience or appreciate.'

'Like art. Everyone has their own artistic sensibility. And when you find someone with the same sensibility, it's like meeting a kindred spirit on a bridge crossing a wild river.'

'That's poetic.'

'Well, I think it's quite rare. Don't you?'

'I'm not sure. Shared passions attract, I suppose. They lead you down the same path. Maybe it's destiny.'

'Destiny.' She shrugged. 'Destiny suggests we don't really have a say in things, that we can't make anything happen, that it all simply unfolds.'

'True. But maybe it's a guiding force.'

'So, how do you proceed in life?'

'Easy. Follow your instincts.'

She laughed. 'That could cause trouble! Imagine everyone following their instincts. There'd be chaos!'

'I don't mean following your base, animal instincts. I mean, if you're not sure which way to turn, trust your instincts.'

'Well, there's truth in that.' She sought out my eyes. 'So, what are your instincts about me?'

'Hmm.' I kept a straight face. 'Let me think.'

She pushed me away. 'If you have to think, it's not instinct!'

I laughed, pulled her close again. 'My instinct is to kiss you.'

'Then, don't be afraid.'

'I'm not afraid.' I brushed her lips with mine. 'Shall we go to my room?'

She grabbed my hand and pulled me in that direction. 'I should trust *my* instinct too, right?'

I laughed. 'You bet!'

Maite pushed George's book off my bed to the floor. 'I've lived with that history every day of my life,' she said.

§

Around midnight, Maite dressed at speed and set off down the corridor, spiriting herself forward by the paltry lamplight from Plaza Santa Catalina. After a few steps, there was a half-muffled scream.

She'd accidentally kicked a rat the size of a cat with her boot. The rat, equally surprised, hissed, took off down the corridor and bolted through a new hole at the bottom of the attic door. Not again! Was it the son of *La Rata*?

§

I met Maite again the following night at the usual spot. True to her word, she brought Ines, but Bego was now living in Bilbao and couldn't come.

Jock was all smiles. We made a *vuelta*, and he and Ines seemed to naturally hit it off. Over the ensuing days, the ribbing from Rob and I fell away and Ines became a regular weekend member of our little group.

Maite brought a guitar along to the house, determined to teach me a Basque protest song. I battled with the chords and unique style of strumming. She left it so I could practise, but

Jock, his fingers twitching as I wrestled the instrument, circled in. 'How about a turn, Owen?'

'Can you play?' I asked.

'Are you kidding, my man?'

Thereafter, the old guitar rarely left Jock's arms. He entertained us day in, day out, playing all the popular songs, the original version and hilarious variations. We laughed ourselves stupid. The guitar transformed the house. Suddenly, we had music — music *à la Jock*, but music no less.

During the week, Maite and I joined Jock and Rob in the bars for a while, before heading back to the house. This was to become our routine. The only thing that varied was whether we joined the others at all, and, if so, what time we left them.

Often Maite would fall asleep in my arms, wake with a start after midnight, dress, then scurry off into the darkness. I'd listen, half-asleep, to the faltering purr of her little SEAT car break the stillness in Plaza Santa Catalina and trail off into the night. And after, I'd fall into a deep, contented sleep, overjoyed by my inexplicable good fortune.

§

Maite came for me a few days later, at the house. I'd stopped reading at the nursing home. The terrace was too cold and the wind cut through me. Dr Arriaza had offered a room inside with a wonderful view, but Battle-axe clearly didn't approve.

'Is the rat gone?' Maite asked.

'Ignacia's pellets did the trick. Not a squeak, or a hiss.'

'Just as well … I've brought a picnic lunch,' she said. 'Bring a jacket.'

I took my jacket from the back of a kitchen chair and we started down the stairs. 'Where's Truende exactly?'

'Between Bermeo and Bilbao.'

'I suppose the road is winding?'

'And steep.'

We reached her little car and got in.

'Did you read any more of the book?'

'Is it so important?'

'If you understand the book, our history, you might help our cause.'

I wasn't sure what she meant. How could I help?

She reached for my hand. 'You would help me again if I asked, wouldn't you?'

'Of course,' I said. 'I'd help.' Jesus, what the hell was I saying? While we drove through the hills, I wondered what she might ask next. What had I put myself in for? What would Jock and Rob say if they found out? Mum and Dad would be horrified. And I could imagine what John would say: 'You bloody idiot, Owen!' He'd be right, of course.

'The fascist, Mola, thought he could break through to Bilbao.'

'Mola?'

Her eyes flicked from the road to me and back again. 'Are you listening?'

'Yeah … sure.'

'He attacked the Basque defence along a broad front, but the front was *too* broad, German air support stretched too thin. The attack failed and Bermeo became encircled. The Italians were cut off.' She negotiated the bends to the foot of Mount Truende. 'A Basque battalion counter-attacked from Mount Truende, near the pass.'

'Up there?' I asked, pointing to the summit.

'Yes. They drove the Italian column back, captured arms, supplies and several Italian soldiers. Hundreds were killed.'

'A good win for the Basques,' I said.

'Yes, and not only here. Another Basque battalion forced the Italians back from Mount Sollube to Pedernales. And on the southern side of Sollube, the Basques repelled rebel advances from Rigoitia and at Urrimendi.'

'The boys and I walked through the hills from Mundaca to Bermeo the other day and ate *paella* at a bar called Sollube, close to the *paseo* beside the port.'

'Sollube is close to the Basque heart.' She rounded a tight curve and I clutched at the arm rest, fighting nausea. 'That night, in the dark, Basque fighters snuck down to the coastal road and dynamited the bridge at Mundaca.'

'Jeez, they blew up the bridge?'

'Yes, to cut Bermeo off from Guernica.'

'Hard to imagine.' I shook my head. 'I've walked across that bridge many times, on my way to the lookout.' Car sick, I wound down the window halfway.

'George risked his life and went with a supply vehicle from Bilbao to Truende, dodging bombs and machine-gun bullets.'

'I told you he was crazy,' I said.

She scowled. 'He wasn't crazy. He was brave.'

'He could've got killed.'

'Any of them could have. Any day. Everyone took risks.'

'But he was a journalist, not a soldier.'

'He was on our side.'

'True.' I wound the window fully down, took a deep breath, the wind licking at my face. 'What happened at Mundaca?'

'We were bombed off the road.'

I swivelled to her. 'God! I don't believe it! Beautiful Mundaca bombed.'

She grunted softly. 'Many beautiful places were bombed.'

I glanced back at the twisting road. 'I haven't noticed any scars around the village.'

'You could ask the old folk.' We had almost reached the summit. Maite pulled the car to the side of the road. 'There's a spot over there. See, between those two big rocks. We can eat and I'll tell you the rest of the story.'

I took the blanket, Maite the picnic basket, and we made our way across to the sheltered grassy patch. Maite unpacked *bocadillos* of *jamón*, tomato and cheese, a flask of *vino blanco* and two glasses.

'Cheers,' I said, touching her glass with mine. 'That's what we say in Australia.'

She clinked me back. 'Cheese.'

'Not cheese!' I laughed. 'Cheers, meaning good cheer.'

She laughed too and moved close against me. 'I know it's cheers, but at first, in Dublin, I thought people were saying cheese.'

'Oh, I get it!'

'Shall I tell you what happened next?'

'Will I get indigestion?'

She frowned at me. 'Don't make jokes. It's serious.'

'Alright.' I raised my hands in surrender. 'No more jokes. Carry on.'

'You know where we were stopped by the *Guardia* on our way back from Baquio that day?'

'Jesus! How could I forget?'

She smiled sweetly and kissed me on the cheek. 'You were so loyal that day. We –' She hesitated, the smile dissolving. 'I … will never forget that.'

I gazed down the mountain. What did she mean by 'we'?

She reached for my hand, squeezed it, and leaned in to me, searching out my eyes. 'Shall I continue?'

'Yes, go on.'

'The Italians were forced back and gave up for the day.' She reached for her drink. 'But here at Truende, the Germans fire-bombed for an hour before an Italian column advanced towards the pass.' She pointed down the road. 'There.' I followed her finger. The road snaked up the mountain. 'There were eighteen Italian tanks in pairs, supported by ground troops in the cornfields on either side. But our Basque fighters had blocked the road near the crest with three logs, which the tanks couldn't cross.'

'What did the Italians do?'

'Because of the steep banks, the tanks couldn't turn or move off the road. They got stuck. Sitting ducks. And the foot soldiers hid in the corn, afraid of our snipers. Our men,' she pointed to the summit, 'were waiting for anti-tank explosives from Bilbao. They could only roll grenades down from their trenches until one brave fighter snuck down and exploded a grenade right under a leading tank. Kaboom!'

'What a gutsy effort!'

'That did it! The Italians gave up, retreated.'

'Victory!' I grabbed a roll, raised it to the sky, then bit into it.

'Yes! A good day for the Basques. George rode here with the supply vehicle carrying the anti-tank grenades, terrified he'd be blown up. When they finally arrived, the Basques were already celebrating with a victory dance.'

'Could they hold the mountain?'

'At dawn the next morning, twenty rebel soldiers, Moors, waltzed in and took Sollube while our men, Asturian replacements, were having coffee in their shelter behind the ridge. The Asturians fled, the Italians arrived, and up went the Monarchist flag on Sollube's peak.'

'What a bloody disaster!'

'Basque morale was crushed.' A tear ran down Maite's cheek before she could catch it. 'The men panicked, there was total chaos. Troops at Truende and Cape Machichaco, fearing they'd be cut off and receiving no orders, retreated to the coast. And, to the south of Sollube, the Asturian battalions fell away.'

'Far out! Those Asturians were useless.'

'Aguirre was furious at the loss of Sollube. The Basque Council of War sat to try the deserters.'

'The verdict?'

'All guilty.'

'The punishment?'

'A few were shot.'

'Shot?'

The muscles around Maite's mouth tightened. 'Desertion in the time of war is a serious offence, you know … it can be infectious.'

I shivered. 'I can imagine it would be.'

'Aguirre sacked his Chief of Staff and temporarily took command himself. He ordered an immediate counter-attack on Sollube.'

'Any luck?'

'No. And there was other bad news. The Asturians lost Rigoitia and deserted a key mountain position close to the *cinturón* at Vizkargi.'

'Perhaps their heart wasn't in it?'

'True.' She shook her head. 'They wanted out. The Basques had to go it alone. They counter-attacked for four days at Sollube and for seven at Vizkargi. They fought hard, but ultimately failed.'

'The beginning of the end?'

'In a way.' She pushed a wind-blown lock from her face, leant on one hand and gazed down on me, framed by sunlit hair. 'Had enough?'

I reached up to brush aside the hair obscuring her eye. 'Uh huh.'

§

'Let's paint,' she said. 'I'll get the sketchbooks from the car.'

I raised myself onto my elbows to watch her pick her way across the slope to the car. She came back with pads, pencils and paints and sat beside me.

'Here.' She handed me a pad. 'Draw — imagining those Italian tanks coming up the road towards the logs.' She took a tiny camera out of her pocket, held it to her eye and fired off a couple of shots across the panorama.

'Wow! That's the smallest camera I've ever seen! Almost like a spy camera.'

She flushed. 'I like to take a photo sometimes, to refer to, if I don't finish the drawing.' She put the camera away and opened her sketchbook.

'Makes sense,' I said, but such a tiny camera didn't make sense.

In an instant she was gone, buried in the drawing.

When she was finished, she nestled in against me and said, 'If a parcel arrived from that address in Ireland bearing your name, could you collect it from the post office and give it to me?'

I pushed out a breath. 'I said I'd help.' Jesus, this was getting way out of hand.

§

The surf was steadily building. Each day the sea grew stronger. I could feel the energy change with the season. The playful days seemed to disappear, replaced by heavier waves that drew from the deeper waters of the Atlantic. We surfed everything we could and while the surf progressively grew, Jock and Rob's confidence grew with it.

With the stronger swells, came a few seasoned surfers. An American called Gary had been living in Hawaii for a few years and had surfed the famous Pipeline break on Oahu's north shore. He brought with him a prized hand-crafted surfboard, sleek and yellow with a red lightning bolt on the bottom.

We watched in awe when he casually paddled into the critical part of a peaking swell, dropped vertically down the drawing face, shifted his weight over the board's inner rail at the bottom of the wave, gliding effortlessly into the wave's interior while the lip passed overhead. At times he might bow his head or dip his shoulder to dodge the powerful descending lip, but once secure inside the wave, he set a perfect trim that matched the speed of his board with that of the pitching wave, using only his left hand against the wave's face to temper his speed and delay his exit from the wave's interior.

Gary's surfing was a small miracle. Precise and simple, no

acrobatics, no tricks, perfect technique and timing, he nonchalantly made the difficult look easy.

We watched, mesmerised, sometimes to our detriment.
Several times I got hit by waves when I paddled back out and
stopped to watch him gliding effortlessly towards me. It was
worth the drubbing.

Gary wasn't a professional, there weren't many, and he
didn't surf in competitions even though he could have. We
were somewhat in awe of him, but he was happy to show us
how to ride the 'tube' inside the wave.

We sat in Ignacia's lounge, recovering from a session and a
long lunch. Jock had Maite's guitar in his lap, and was strumming away. We'd heard all his songs many times over. Rob was
fed up. 'Give it a bloody rest, Jock! Tell us about Pipeline, Gary.'

Gary watched Jock set the guitar aside, musing, like he was
chewing on a piece of straw. 'Pipeline?' He spoke in a quiet,
measured manner, like a farmer talking about the weather. We
listened, respectful, like disciples. He sat back, creases forming at the corners of his mouth. 'Pipeline's unique, mythical, a
beautiful beast, the ultimate challenge — powerful, shallow,
the coral *so* sharp, the rip *so* strong.'

'Yes, and the wave itself?' asked Rob, urging him on.

'Not for the faint-hearted, man. When it's big, you can die.
You need finely-tuned skills, a lot of courage, a cool nerve. You
have to know the place, know its fickle nature.'

'I bet,' said Rob, like a fox with his tongue out. 'What's it
like to ride?'

'Like this,' Gary said, a light shining from within, sitting forward to shape the descriptions with his hands. 'The swell approaches, the adrenaline starts to flow, you paddle across. Is this one rideable? Am I in a good position? The swell hits the reef, it stands up, tall, double what it seemed. You're ready to pounce, you paddle furiously, rapid strokes, totally committed.'

Rob's mouth fell open. Jock rolled his eyes, but we were all hooked.

'Then it happens, lightning quick, a beautiful blur, speed and fear, board's snatched up, wave lurches higher, sheer drop, you leap to your feet, plunge, straight down, a glimpse of coral.' He rose gracefully to his feet. 'You're airborne now, feet cling tenuously to the board, spray in the face, blinded, thunder behind, mind on fire.'

We were all taking the drop with Gary.

'Falling fast, leaning in, rail catches, board's nose clear. You're at the bottom now, wave's arching, you press hard with feet, intense pressure in ankles, sudden acceleration, board's flying, a blue cavern surrounding you, swirling deep and dark. A moment of stillness, all is quiet, fingers caressing the wall. Board's singing, blue dissolves, you're bursting free, flying to light, blue turns to green, singing slows, heart slows, gliding to calm.'

'Jesus!' said Rob. 'Sounds bloody awesome!'

'Awesome all right, but brief,' Gary said, sitting again. 'Over in a flash. Not like Mundaca.'

'Too bloody dangerous for me.'

I shivered. 'Gee, that sounds intense, mate.'

'You need to know the place, man, how it ticks.' Gary picked up the guitar, set it firmly in his lap and ran his left hand gently up the neck. He let the back of his fingers fall across the strings and a sweet chord sounded. 'Make the wrong choice on a big day and it could prove fatal.'

'That reef sounds ridiculous,' said Jock. 'Give me Mundaca's sandbar any day, even if it is shallow.'

'Mundaca is better in many ways,' said Gary. 'So much longer. And safer. Pipeline's a blink. A heart-stopping blink.' He settled back in his chair and began to play. He had a relaxed style and didn't sing. We listened, glad for the change, happy with the silky, smooth rhythms that made us drift. You could close your eyes and see the palm trees, Pipeline in the distance.

§

When I walked in late that afternoon, bearing the parcel I'd collected from the post office, Manolo was alone at the bar restocking the fridge. 'Where have you been, *muchacho?*'

'Surfing.' I pulled out a bar stool. 'The swell jumped.'

'Too busy to pay me a visit?' he asked rhetorically, wiping down the bar.

I made a face. 'Of course not.'

He stopped wiping and gave me a penetrating look. 'Your girl's sister, the one in the newspaper? It's true. She's with *ETA*. That car bombing two years ago. She's under arrest.'

250

'You're kidding!'

'No joke, *muchacho!*'

I looked at the parcel, the name 'PJ O'Brien' on the back. I couldn't wait to give it to Maite that night, get it off my hands.

Manolo eyed it too. '*Cuídate, muchacho,*' he said. 'Be very careful.'

§

I hadn't visited Dr Arriaza for a while, so the following afternoon, feeling a little guilty, I went to the nursing home. Out the front was a car I knew only too well. My pace slowed.

At the gate, through the branches of the climbing rose, I spied Maite on the patio. She was talking to the doctor and an elderly man, wheelchair-bound and swaddled in blankets, the same intense character who had helped decide which of Greg's paintings to buy. Maite handed him the parcel, the one from O'Brien that I'd given her the night before. The conversation flashed through my mind.

'So what's in it?' I had asked her.

She hesitated.

'Can't you trust me with the truth?' I implored.

'I can, but it's better I don't.' Her brow crinkled like it always did when she was anxious. 'It's safer that way.'

'Safer? Safe from what?'

She put the parcel aside and took my hands. 'I can't tell you. I'm sworn to secrecy. You have to understand.'

'I don't.' I pushed her hands away. 'How can I?'

'I'll tell you one day. Then you'll understand. Please be patient.' She drew me to her and hugged me.

I didn't respond at first. 'Patience,' I whispered in her ear, 'I'm running out of that.' I pulled her tight against me, kissed her neck and she moaned softly.

Soon our frustrations were swamped by passion. We fell asleep in the sweat that followed and I stirred only briefly when she left sometime across the night.

Now, as I watched, she kissed the stern man affectionately on both cheeks, farewelling him as if he were her own father. She and the doctor started towards the gate, towards me. I had to walk on.

When I looked back from the shadows near the bridge, she was getting into her car, the doctor seeing her off. She also kissed him on both cheeks, like she would a close uncle. She drove off and the doctor went inside.

I followed him a few minutes later.

He was standing alone on the patio beside my favourite seat, as if he'd been waiting for me, smoking, seemingly lost in thought. '*Muchacho! Qué pasa?* Where have you been?'

'Surfing. Some friends came to town and we've been hitting the waves.'

'Lost interest in drawing?'

'No, not all. But, I have to confess, surfing takes priority.'

'I knew something had distracted you.' A mischievous look crossed his face. 'I assumed it was a girl.'

I felt the heat rise to my face and smiled. 'Speaking of girls, I saw you out the front saying goodbye to one.'

'Ah yes!' He studied me carefully then drew on his cigarette. 'The grand-daughter of an old friend. A great man, committed to the end. He's dead now.' He pointed to an empty reclining chair. 'Died right there.' Smoke drifted from his nostrils, ushered away by a faint breeze. 'She's a lot like him. Same spirit. Same passion. Same commitment and dedication.' His eyes lit up momentarily. 'Beautiful too.'

'An irresistible combination.'

He eyed me carefully. 'Few could resist … Only a fool would.'

It was my turn to study him. 'Sounds like a girl you could really trust.'

He held my gaze. 'Absolutely.' He drew hard on his cigarette. 'Anyone who'd spent time with her would know that. No questions asked.'

'No questions?'

A faint smile played across his face. 'No questions, *muchacho*.'

'Unquestioning trust. That's a big risk for anyone, Doc.'

'Life is full of risks. In difficult times you have to trust others.' He motioned to his stomach. 'The feelings here tell you who.'

'Gut feelings alone?'

He blew out a steady stream of smoke. 'If you can't trust your gut feelings, what *can* you trust?'

§

Manolo stood outside the post office on the other side of the street, talking to the postmistress. He nodded sheepishly when I passed on my way back to the house. The postmistress, as unflinching as the portrait on her wall, stared as I nodded cautiously in return.

At *Casa Ignacia* the boys were in a stew. They'd been to the shops and returned to find the house upside down, our belongings strewn everywhere.

'Someone's ransacked the place!' said Jock.

'You're kidding!' I said. 'Who?'

'Who do you reckon, mate?' said Rob.

'No idea!'

'Well, Rob and I have a fair idea,' said Jock.

'*Guardia Civil*,' said Rob.

'*Guardia Civil*!' I said. 'But why?'

'We've got a theory,' said Jock. He looked at Rob.

'A theory?' I said. 'What do you mean?'

Rob gave me the once-over. His eyes sharpened. 'Who's PJ O'Brien?'

'Oh, shit!'

'Rob saw that parcel you had,' said Jock. He folded his arms across his chest. 'We think they were looking for that.'

'What was in it, Owen?' said Rob.

'I don't know.'

'Come on, Owen, spill the beans!'

'I swear to God, I've got no idea! I gave it to Maite unopened, like she asked.'

'Are you crazy?' said Jock. 'No wonder the *Guardia* have been here!'

'And worst of all, you didn't let *us* in on it,' said Rob. 'Your mates!'

'She made me promise I wouldn't.'

'Blinded by love!' yelled Jock 'That's what you are!'

'Jeez, I'm sorry, guys. I wanted to tell you.'

'Bit late for that, Owen,' sighed Rob.

§

It took a few days for the boys to forgive me, and only after I'd told them all that I could. Of course, there wasn't a lot to tell that they didn't already know. They understood that a promise was a promise; they just weren't happy about it. A few days of being slapped around the head seemed to fix the problem, much like a bad wipeout tends to set you straight.

CHAPTER 11

Jock called from the balcony, a note of concern in his voice, 'There's a little red MG in the car park with roof racks and a board on top. I think it might be another Pom!'

I was rugged up in bed, reading. It was mid-afternoon, a dreary day in early November. 'God help us!' I yelled, and winced at the lingering memory of the Englishman, Graham, whom we'd adopted briefly but had to kick out of the house for not pitching in or paying his way.

'*Amigo*, let's go for a look-see,' said Jock, his face a mixture of curiosity and suspicion.

I marked my place, set George on the bedside table and climbed out of bed.

We rounded the edge of the port through a light misty rain, the sky grey and sullen. I pulled up the hood of my jacket. The port was silent, no fishermen in sight. We climbed the steps on the casino side to the headland. The river mouth was subdued. Signs of a swell but nothing breached the sandbar at this high tide. The slate-grey sea lay heavy like a metal plate. Where a sea mist had formed, sky and sea merged on the horizon. There was no wind.

We inspected the MG at close quarters. The surfboard

bore a large number of scars, but the car was impressive. You couldn't live in this little roadster, but it would be fun to drive.

We found him in *Bar El Puerto*. The newcomer was standing, coffee in hand, wearing a midnight blue plastic rain jacket over a heavy black seaman's sweater and dark blue corduroy trousers. He had his back to us and seemed to be studying the rows of bottles behind the bar.

'Nice car,' said Jock when we drew near. The guy half-turned towards the voice and a spark lit his brown eyes.

'Jock!' he said, reaching to shake his hand, a grin on his half-shaven face. He took my hand, his grip strong and measured, and followed it with a bear hug. 'Little brother! You look so different, all grown up.' He stood back, examined me. 'You look fit. Really fit. Lots of waves, hey?'

Jock's glasses had steamed up. '*Jean!* I don't believe it, man! Is that really you? You look like a Nordic fisherman.'

'John!' I exclaimed. 'This is amazing! Where have you been?'

'I was in Morocco.' A broad grin overtook his face. 'But then I met this girl –'

Jock laughed and looked up at the ceiling. 'Must run in the family.'

'How do you mean?'

Jock tipped his head in my direction and winked. 'Owen too.'

'Owen … a girl.' John frowned, stared at me. 'You *have* grown up.' He shook his head.

'What happened next, man?' said Jock.

257

John was still focused on me. 'Mum's letter arrived saying Owen was here with you, so I borrowed a car for a few weeks.'

I smiled meekly. Had he come to see me or Jock?

'Rob, remember me telling you about *Jean*,' said Jock. 'The Aussie from last summer.'

'How could I forget?' They shook hands. 'Jeez, you've gotta helluva grip, mate,' Rob said, jiggling his hand.

John laughed. 'Sorry! Working the boats, hauling ropes and buckets — and God knows what else — gives you hands of steel.' He examined them. 'Look at the bloody cuts! Still healing. But it's been a trip.'

And he was off and running. John knew how to tell a story. He had a way about him, a feverish look in his eye when he spoke, as if he were there and you couldn't help but go there with him. He held court like a tireless raconteur. Where he got it from was a mystery. Not our parents. His enthusiasm was infectious, his appetite for life, boundless.

I was proud to be his brother. He reminded me a little of George — same adventurous spirit, same tireless passion, same descriptive powers — George with his pen, John with his tongue. John had always inspired me. He'd pushed the boundaries, defied the odds. No wonder I'd followed in his footsteps.

But I'd stepped out of his shadow now, followed my own path, hadn't I? And, if part of him had rubbed off on me, was there anything wrong with that? I wanted him to be proud of me.

'The landscape!' he said. 'Especially dusk and dawn. By day, an unforgiving desert, muted, washed out by sun. But dusk, at Anchor, out on the rocks, where burning desert meets the cold Atlantic, a fiery sun melting into a restless, purple sea. It's incredible! So beautiful! And the stars! Solitary at dusk, but when night closes in, the sky comes alive — a celestial sea.'

'How about the surf?' Rob asked.

'The surf! Agadir! Incredible! Anchor point was even better, camped there for months. What a crew of crazy guys! Surfers from all over — Americans, Brits, South Africans, Aussies, Kiwis.'

'And the waves?' Rob licked his lips. 'What about the waves?'

'Anchor was crowded but we managed, surfed in shifts of sorts. The shoulder's fat, but it's a nice long ride. Water's chilly though — it's that crazy, cold current, like in Portugal. You really need that wetsuit.'

'Sounds incredible!' said Rob, hand working at his stubble.

'It was, it was. But it seems an age ago. Denmark snuffed it out.' John ran his fingers through his hair, combing it back. 'I'm itchy for waves, real quality. What about the surf here?'

'Tide's too full. There'll be a decent wave at Baquio,' said Rob.

'No problem. We'll take the MG.' John rubbed his hands together.

'Will you get us all into that little thing?' asked Jock.

'Oh, yeah,' said John with unwavering confidence. 'I'll get you in.'

We headed back to the car and I tried to explain the directions to Plaza Santa Catalina.

'Get in and direct me,' he said.

§

'Our humble domain,' I announced, when we climbed *Casa Ignacia*'s dusty old stairs.

'Humble's the word,' said John, hesitant to handle the rail.

We showed him through and reached the lounge balcony. 'She's old and creaky, but look at that view!' I said.

John whistled. 'It's beautiful all right.'

'You should see it when the surf's firing!' Rob clutched at the rail. 'It's unreal, isn't it, Jock?'

'It is, my man! It is.' Jock scanned the view. 'But not today, *amigos. On y va?*'

We tied the boards to the MG's roof with some pieces of old cord that John had in the boot, then Jock insisted we toss a coin for the front seat.

'Bugger!' I clambered into the back with Rob.

John inched out onto the main road. While he accelerated up the winding road towards Bermeo, he flicked a switch in the wood-grain dash and the cabin filled with a haunting melody. A strong female voice backed by piano — Carole King. It had a potent, melancholic feel, and I felt decidedly homesick. Away for eleven months, on this still grey day in Spain, my thoughts drifted to my own country — summer on the way, the comforts of a warm family home and my closest friends. John's presence only seemed to make it worse.

We drove through Bermeo and out past the cemetery where the narrow road snakes into the patchwork of fields, to the long series of gentle uphill switchbacks. John couldn't resist and we raced towards the summit, to the pine forest where the scent of juniper begins.

'Pull over,' I pleaded. 'I need air or I'll throw up.'

'Poor bugger! What a curse,' said John, turning into a clearing.

Jock jumped out, lurched the bucket seat forward and I stumbled out. I took a few long, deep breaths, hands on knees. What a horrible feeling! It took me back to the Great Ocean Road in Victoria — hunched over at the roadside, wave upon wave of vertigo traversing my head, trying not to vomit. When I was a child, I always vomited.

'How are you feeling, mate?' John asked, patting me gently on the back.

'Not so good,' I replied, focusing on the long, slow, deep breaths, my trusted panacea.

'Your colour's coming good,' said Rob.

I stood up. The vertigo and nausea had retreated, but I continued breathing deeply until I'd regained my equilibrium. 'Getting there,' I replied. 'Give me a few more minutes.'

'Reminds me of all those surf trips with Dad,' said John. 'God you suffered.'

'I don't want to think about it.'

The others strolled to the edge of the clearing. In the foreground, the fields to Bermeo and its port, and beyond, the sea,

Izaro and the rugged Pyrenees. A thick sea mist hung over the distant seascape.

'Still spectacular! Can't wait to see it with a swell running. Jock, you'd better get in the back unless you want Owen throwing up all over the back of your head — remember when you did that to Dad?'

They all laughed and so did I. Poor Dad!

§

The base of the island at San Juan de Gaztelugatxe was shrouded in mist, giving the peak and chapel a mysterious, fortress-like appearance. Baquio was eerily quiet, the beach deserted. A solid swell slunk in from the Atlantic and rolled across the sandbanks. Six-foot waves, oily smooth.

We paddled out — Jock, Rob and John to the sandbank in front. I wandered the shoreline about 150 metres away, dodging plastic bottles and tar balls as I went. The waves were fast, clean, increasingly bigger and I rode one after another, a hypnotic session punctuated by bursts of activity. Between the waves, I absorbed the grey mood. No rainbows today, no Maite on the beach — no *Guardia*, no guns, no shooting — only the ghosts.

It was mid-tide when I made my first mistake. A rogue set appeared out of nowhere. Paddling deep inside on the first wave, I dropped late, made it to the bottom, but looking down the line, realised I wouldn't make it onto the wall, not even with the best bottom turn. An enormous thud caught me from behind. The lip had actually missed me and the back of my board, but the force of the exploding wave catapulted me forward.

Airborne, I tried to go deep when I hit the water, but I was out of control, helpless. I somersaulted along, pushed by the surging whitewater. Relaxing was the key to minimising oxygen consumption and surviving. I was shoved deep under the rolling mass, and still tumbling, completely lost my bearings. A sudden jerk on my leg rope, when the wave pushed the board forward, halted the tumbling, but now I was being dragged underwater. I couldn't pull hard on my leg rope to escape in case it snapped, so I relaxed, waiting until the power of the whitewater diminished. My breath began to run out when the pressure on the leg rope eased. I carefully flexed my leg, a counter-pressure, until the resistance dissipated completely and I was released. I scrambled to the surface, careful to protect my face.

A single gasping breath was all I could take before the next wave was on me. I duck-dived deep, but I couldn't escape the dragging. I resurfaced, snatched a breath, and headed under the next wave. Eventually, I was washed to the edge of the sandbank. I hauled myself onto the board, grateful that the leg rope had held, and lay catching my breath.

After a minute, I'd regained my composure. That was close. A slap in the face, a reminder not to disregard the forces of nature. 'Push the limits at your peril, you fool,' I whispered. Had my instincts deserted me?

I felt battered and weary but not enough to kill the desire

for another ride. I paddled out and across to the others. 'Are you all right?' Rob asked, his brow knotted.

'I thought you were going to drown!' said Jock.

'I'm all right.' I stretched, rubbing my neck. 'Wouldn't want to go through that again in a hurry. What a thrashing!'

'Stay wide and rest up for a bit, *amigo*.'

John looked at me, grinned, and shook his head. 'That's a hell of a way to get fit!'

§

After the surf, we went to the same bar I'd gone to with Jock that first time. The others started quizzing me about my little sandbank in 'the corner'.

'Short, fast and hollow,' I said. 'But only enough waves for one surfer at a time!'

'One surfer at a time, hey?' said Jock, an eyebrow raised.

'I came here once before, with Maite, and a firing squad turned up for practice at the end of the beach.'

'Bizarre!' said John. 'I bet surfing under the spectre of Franco wasn't what you had in mind.'

'Not at all,' I said. 'It was surreal.'

He strummed his fingers on the table. 'Perhaps,' he mused, 'if you were more aware of political developments, you might have anticipated an increase in military activity. According to the Danish newspapers, Franco's ailing, hanging on by a thread, and speculation's rife.'

'I thought I *was* aware.'

Rob jumped in. 'Owen, there's probably more accurate news in the foreign press than you'd get here.'

John put down his tortilla. 'He's right. It'd be controlled, censored, here.'

'But I hear things from Maite, too,' I said defensively.

John grunted softly. 'She'd have her own slant.'

'And the foreign press wouldn't?'

John frowned.

'She's a proud Basque,' I said, 'but no zealot.'

Jock and Rob exchanged a look. 'From what you've told us,' said Rob, choosing his words carefully, 'she seems fully *committed* to the cause.'

I leant forward, gripping the edge of the table. 'Yes, she's passionate. She gets emotional about it. Why wouldn't she? She's involved on a personal level.'

'And now,' added Jock coolly, 'so are *you*.'

They stared at me. Would they mention the parcels or the raid on the house? I hoped not. I sat back. 'Perhaps, but she doesn't tell me everything. I'm sure she's seen and heard many things and hasn't told me.'

Jock leaned towards me. 'It's what she's *not* telling you that worries us.' He wagged a finger. 'We warned you to be careful.' He turned to John and raised his eyebrows. 'Your little brother's blinded by love.'

'He's got himself a girlfriend who's in *ETA*,' said Rob.

'Oh, Jesus! Is that right?' asked John.

'No,' I said. 'We don't know that.'

He hunched forward. 'What have you got yourself tangled up in, Owen?'

'Tangled up in?' I frowned out the window at the sea. 'She's wonderful, beautiful,' I said. 'Wait until you meet her.'

'She *is* lovely,' said Rob. His eyes skipped from John to me. 'But can you trust her?'

'Of course,' I said defensively.

'Completely?' asked Jock. 'Her family's obviously involved in politics, *ETA*.'

I pursed my lips, thinking. They were all watching me. 'It's true, she can be elusive. But she's asked me to trust her.'

'Do you?' John tapped the table with an index finger. '*ETA* is serious business, Owen.'

'I *do* trust her.'

'Why?' John asked. 'You don't seem to know what she's really up to.'

'Instinct.'

'Instinct?' John raised his eyebrows. 'Is instinct enough?'

I thought of Dr Arriaza. 'It's all I've got when I don't know.'

John sat back, folded his arms across his chest and grinned. 'Where was your instinct when you got hammered in the waves today?'

I glared at him. 'What do *you* think I should do?'

'I'm not sure. I just arrived.' He tilted his head towards Jock and Rob. 'They'd know better. Based on what I know from earlier in the year and what I've read, all I'd say is be extremely careful.'

'*Jean*'s right.' Jock stabbed the air with a finger. 'Be *really* careful, Owen … remember why you came here, man. To surf. Right?'

Jock wasn't wrong. Our days were dictated by the rhythms of the ocean. Our pursuit was apolitical. But that was before I understood anything. The Frenchmen had sparked my interest. George with his book had lit a slow burning fire, and Maite — with her smouldering determination — had allowed me to feel its heat.

'I'm not saying ignore it,' said John. 'But be aware of what you're doing, what you're getting involved in.'

I glared at Jock. 'We can't simply surf and ignore where we are and what's going on around us!'

'Of course we can!' said Jock. 'It's none of our business!' His gaze narrowed. 'You're under her spell. And as for that book and George Steer, they've got you hostage.'

I gritted my teeth. 'Isn't dictatorship and repression everybody's business?'

Rob groaned loudly. 'Come on, settle down, fellas.'

I eased back in my seat. 'Jock, read George's book when I'm finished. You'll feel differently.'

Jock's shoulders dropped. 'I'm sympathetic,' he said, 'but we're only foreigners passing through. There's nothing we can do.'

'That's true, Owen,' said Rob. 'What can you do?'

I bit my lip. 'I'm not sure. Something, perhaps.'

John snorted. 'You?'

If he only knew, I thought. I stared at him and said nothing.

'Strange.' He sat back, his hands behind his head. 'I've read a bit about the Civil War, but I've never heard of George Steer.'

'He's an amazing man!' I said leaning forward again. 'Intelligent, brave, big-hearted, loves the Basques. A real hero!'

'You talk like he's still alive.'

'I told you,' said Jock, shaking his head, 'Owen's obsessed. Maite's got him hooked on the Basque cause. Her brother's in prison, sister's in custody.'

John glared at me. 'You're on the edge, Owen. *ETA* may be closer than you think.'

I held his glare for a while before looking out the window, chewing on my lip. A set wandered in. The breeze grasped at it, contorting the wave faces, holding each back, stalling them until they broke free, rolled over and continued on their path to shore.

'Let's go,' said Jock. 'It's getting gloomy.'

Rob stood up and stretched. 'Those curves won't be fun in the dark. Owen, you better sit up front again. I don't want you throwing up on me.'

John sighed. 'No throwing up full stop, little brother.'

'I only get sick in the back.' I eased out of the chair and stood up. 'Come on, guys, chip in, I'll fix up the bill.'

Jock shrugged sheepishly. 'I left my wallet at the house.'

'Jesus, Jock!' Rob grappled him into a mock headlock. 'Same every bloody time!'

John laughed. 'Nothing's changed!'

'I forgot, man.' Jock wriggled free, adjusting his glasses. 'An oversight.'

'You can tie the boards on,' said Rob. 'Punishment.'

§

We were stopped by a *Guardia* roadblock at the edge of the pine forest, the same place Maite and I had encountered one.

'How often does that happen?' asked John, a strain in his voice.

'Second time for me,' I said. 'In a car at least. Maite and I were stopped walking in Lequetio.'

'Not particularly friendly, are they?'

'I suppose they're looking for weapons,' Jock mused.

'Or fugitives,' Rob added.

'Maybe it's a manhunt!' said Jock. 'Those *Guardia* were certainly looking for something ... or someone. I hope it's got nothing to do with your girlfriend, Owen.'

'Come off it,' I said defensively. 'But something's happened.'

'It should be in the news,' Rob said.

We had nothing to hide, but the torch-lit faces of the *Guardia*, the guns, and that spiked metal device were unnerving.

'They seemed jumpy,' Jock added.

John snorted. 'This is the kind of trouble you just don't need, Owen. They must know something we don't.'

'Something's definitely up,' I said. 'You can feel it.'

John stole a sideward glance at me while he ran the MG down through the fields towards Bermeo. 'Instinct, hey?'

'You could say that.'

He laughed and put his foot down. It didn't take long to get back to Mundaca.

§

John settled into the spare room while Jock and I prepared a meal of anchovy fillets. We ate in the kitchen and talked. Surf was first, like always. 'And Mundaca?' John asked. 'Have you had it any good?' He lit up when I described the last big swell, the rides and the wipeouts. 'Bloody hell! I wish I'd been here for that!' His brow crinkled. 'We'll get decent waves soon, won't we?'

'Hard to say.' I snapped a piece off the crusty breadstick. 'It's getting stormier every day, the swells are steadily building.'

'It'll be unreal!' He rubbed his hands together. 'I just need to get surf fit.'

We had a long catch-up in the kitchen. John did most of the talking, but we all had our turn. 'George has made a big impression on you,' he said. 'Perhaps I should read this book of yours.'

'George is a legend!' I wiped crumbs from the corner of my mouth. 'In certain ways, you remind me of him — same adventurous spirit, same love of a good story.'

'Me ... like George? I doubt it.' John sat back, scratched his head and mused. 'Adventurous spirit, maybe. Stories, yes. War zones? No. In love with the Basques ...' He pointed a finger. 'That sounds more like you.'

I smiled wryly.

He wagged his finger. 'Make sure that love doesn't get you into trouble.'

I folded my arms. 'Don't worry, I'm not joining *ETA*.'

John sat back in his chair. 'When Franco's dead, maybe *ETA* won't be needed.'

'George never really foresaw *ETA*,' I said circumspectly. 'But he said the Basques would never be suppressed for long.'

'The Basques have been suppressed *far* too long.' John leaned back, hands behind his head. 'But, Owen, let's face it, it's not really your business, is it?'

'It's a cause worth fighting for, isn't it?' I swallowed, thinking of Maite's passionate devotion. 'What would you fight for?'

John shook his head and groaned softly. 'Little brother, where are you going with all this?' He leaned forward, picked up my sketchbook from the table and began leafing through it.

'Wait till you read the book.'

'I'm looking forward to it.' He raised an eyebrow. 'Your drawings?'

'Yep.'

'Not bad. Too realistic though, Owen. No interpretation. You haven't captured the spirit, mate.' He tossed the sketchbook aside, smiled at me. 'You'll make a better doctor than artist.'

I sighed. 'You're right. I tried to tell them I had no artistic talent.'

'I wouldn't say *no* talent. You gave it a shot. That's important.'

'I enjoy it, but you can see I don't have the feel. Greg taught me the basics ... a lot of other things, besides. Mate, what a surfer! He taught me how to really ride a wave. The artful approach!'

'A soul surfer, hey? Sounds like a brother as much as a friend.'

'You could say that.' I was silent for a moment, glad to have my real brother at hand. 'And Maite taught me a lot too.'

'More than drawing it seems?'

I smiled. 'A lot more.'

§

In the casino, we chatted, waiting for the weather report. Jock stopped us, pointing at the television. 'Look at this!' A grim reporter related how three agents of the *Guardia Civil* were killed by a car bomb in the neighbouring province of Guipúzcoa.

'What did I tell you?' said Jock, eyes bulging. 'It was a manhunt!'

A shiver ran through me. 'No wonder they seemed so tense.'

My brother gripped my shoulder.

'Don't worry,' I said, releasing myself.

The weather girl appeared with the latest synoptic chart behind. A low-pressure system near Iceland was visible over her right shoulder, 982 in its centre.

'Is a big storm brewing?'

'Could be.' I checked my watch. 'I'm going to meet the girls. I'll bring them back. You'll see.'

§

Maite, Ines and I found the boys in *Los Chopos*, still talking travel and surf. I peeled John away after introducing them.

'John,' Maite said, 'we have the same name in Basque — *Jon*.'

'Common name.' He winced. 'I prefer the French version. You can call me *Jean*, too, if you want.'

She smiled. 'I prefer the original, it sounds Basque.'

'I don't mind what you call me,' said John, a grin forming, 'providing there isn't a swear word attached.'

Maite laughed. She studied him. 'So *you* are the long-lost brother Owen's been telling me about.'

'I wasn't lost, simply out of reach. The Moroccan postal service is not the speediest, at least not from Anchor Point.'

A mischievous light played in her eyes. 'Do they use camels?'

John laughed. 'Not quite, but the result's the same. It took four months for one letter to get home.'

'Your poor parents. They must have been worried.'

'Naturally,' said John. 'But there have been longer gaps. Mum worries regardless.'

'Mothers always worry,' she said. 'Brothers and sisters too.' She appeared momentarily distracted, no doubt thinking of her own family, before touching my arm. 'Owen was worried about you.'

'Was he?' John sized her up. 'Brothers can be a worry, can't they?'

'They can.' She bit her lip.

In the moment of awkward silence, John stole a glance my way. 'Owen and I narrowly missed each other back in early summer.'

'So I heard,' she said. 'A near miss.'

'It wasn't meant to be,' he said. 'Anyway, he obviously didn't need me to hold his hand.' He gave me the once-over. 'He's transformed into a fully-fledged man since I last saw him.' He smiled. 'Besides, he might never have met you, if we'd hooked up.'

She felt for my hand. 'True. Destiny took its course, brought me a true friend.' Her fingers slipped between mine and grasped tightly.

I squeezed back.

John raised his eyebrows, shook his head at the two of us. 'I can't believe my brother has a girlfriend. Who would have thought?'

Maite frowned. 'You took off a long time ago, didn't you? He's not the boy you remember.'

John stared at her but said nothing.

'Well, he's a man now.'

'So it seems.' John shrugged, changed tack. 'Owen tells me you're an artist and that you've taken him sketching.'

She scowled slightly, as if I'd betrayed her confidence. 'We've been on a few picnics.'

'Baquio too, I hear.'

'Yes. Why?'

'We got stopped there today by the *Guardia*.'

'Same place we were stopped,' I added.

She looked at me questioningly.

I shook my head discreetly to indicate I hadn't told John what she'd said to the *Guardia* about the sketches.

She relaxed slightly and turned to John. 'Have you seen the news?'

His eyebrows went up. 'About the *ETA* killings?'

'Yes. There are *Guardia* roadblocks all over the place.'

'I wonder why they're looking around here, when the killings were in Guipúzcoa?'

She flushed and moved closer to me, until we were touching. 'They look everywhere. Everyone's a suspect under Franco. Even you.'

John laughed. 'I don't think they'd be too worried about foreigners.'

'You might be surprised. Foreigners have helped us in the past.'

'Like George Steer?' John raised an eyebrow. 'Owen's been telling me about the book.'

'George,' she said. 'And others. There was an International Brigade during the Civil War. Men of conscience, from far and wide.'

'I know about the International Brigade. Hemingway fought

with them.' John brushed a crumb off his sleeve. 'But that was a long time ago.'

'Their spirit lives on,' she retorted, her voice rising, her face red. 'Not everyone's given up on us.'

'I wouldn't know,' said John.

'That's right,' she said passionately. 'You don't know. You have no idea.'

John said nothing, brooding, as if turning the possibilities over in his mind. Maite, her face still burning, clutched me with one hand and reached for her drink with the other. She took a long, slow mouthful, calming herself. I watched the colour settle, felt the tension in her body ease slightly. She put down the glass, tried to smile, squeezed my hand and excused herself. We watched her walk to the rest room, dragging Ines from Jock as she went.

John toyed with his glass. 'She's quite something.' He pursed his lips, searching for the right words. 'A tender beauty ... with real fire in the belly.'

'She's wonderful,' I said. '*Now* you understand a little more about what I'm feeling.'

'I do.' He frowned, like Mum did. 'But, Owen, you still need to watch your back. Passion can be misleading.'

'You think I'm being led astray?'

'I don't know.' He hesitated, ran a hand through his hair. 'That's for you to find out.'

We rejoined Jock and Rob and the conversation was back to travel and surf by the time the girls reappeared. Maite, her composure restored, searched out my hand, then watched and listened. I thought she enjoyed seeing John and I reunite, but sensed a sadness too, perhaps imagining a reunion with her own brother.

'He's a strong character,' she said, when I walked her to the car. 'A lot like my own brothers.'

'I've always admired him.'

'I can tell.' She was quiet for a moment. 'You're strong too, you know.'

'You think so?'

'Yes, I do. John might be a wanderer, an adventurer, and that's fine, but you can stick things out — commit, persevere. Those traits will help you to become a good doctor.'

'I suppose.'

'Look how you've stuck it out here in Mundaca, waiting patiently.'

'I love it here,' I said, when we reached the car.

'It's more than that.' She pulled me to her. 'It's about who you are.'

§

It was good to see John, but I didn't feel quite the way I'd imagined I would. John had changed but not that much. He looked older, had roamed the world, was more knowledgeable, and had become very sure of himself. No, it wasn't him who'd really changed. It was me. When we finally had some time alone, we talked about home, about Mum and Dad and Rosie and shared what was in our last letters.

'They went out to the crematorium,' I said hesitantly.

His head sank and he ran his hands through his hair. 'Jesus, I'd rather not talk about that,' he said quietly, and then, looking up at me with a pained expression, 'Do *you* want to talk about it?'

'Not really.' My chest felt hollow and I looked away.

'There's not much to say, is there?'

'I suppose not,' I said, mouth dry.

'Another time, alright?' he said, his face set.

You can't run away forever, John, I thought. One day you'll have to face it.

CHAPTER 12

Friday night came and we went on a *vuelta*, starting in the casino where we could catch the weather report on the television. The weather girl spoke in long, breathless bursts. The synoptic chart appeared. An intense low-pressure system sat to the north and west of Iceland. The isobars were tightly drawn and in the centre the number 946. A king-size swell was in the making in the North Atlantic.

Jock and I stared at each other in disbelief.

'Nine-four-six,' Rob mouthed.

'Oh my God!' I exclaimed. 'It's going to be huge! This is what I've been waiting for!'

'Are you mad?' Jock's eyes were wider than the river mouth. 'This is going to be the mother of all swells!'

John, surf-less in Denmark in recent months, swallowed hard. 'Oh Jesus! First not big enough, *now* too big!'

No-one knew how big a swell the sandbar could hold, but we'd soon find out. It would arrive in about thirty-six hours.

I met Maite at the usual place at the usual time. She could see how excited I was when I jumped into the car and laughed, while I feverishly told her in jumbled Spanish about the coming swell. We drove to Plaza Santa Catalina, parked, and when we walked to the bars, she told me about the alert to all seafarers.

The others were still holding up the bar in the casino.

'Nine-four-six,' Jock kept saying, with a shake of his head.

'Nine-four-six — what's that?' Maite asked, before tiny creases appeared at the corners of her mouth. 'Ah! The big storm, the big swell that's coming!' She laughed.

'I've been waiting ages for this.' I chewed on my lip, trying to imagine the seas.

Rob turned to John. 'What do you think, mate?'

John shivered. 'Not sure I'm up to it!'

Rob's eyes darted mischievously. 'Not as brave as your little brother?'

John didn't take the bait, but pretended to. 'Owen's not little,' he said. 'Look at him, he's fully-grown. There's no competition.' He took me in a headlock.

I played along. 'Let go!' I called out. 'You're hurting!'

The others laughed. He released the pressure and I wriggled free. 'You bastard!' I said, rubbing my neck and trying to keep a straight face. 'Just like the old days!'

'Brotherly love,' said Jock. 'Nothing like it.' More laughter.

'Don't worry, John,' I said. 'You'll manage. We'll keep an eye out for you.'

Rob smirked. 'Don't know about that, mate. *I'll* be busy surviving.'

'Me too,' said Jock.

'Nice friends you are!' said John. 'Every man for himself, hey?'

'Don't worry.' Rob patted him on the back. 'We'll fetch your body if it washes up downstream.' He let loose with a characteristic staccato laugh.

Maite watched us laugh, shaking her head. 'You're all mad. You won't be able to surf, anyway. It will be too wild.' She eyed each disbelieving surfer. 'Trust me.'

Perhaps she was right, time would tell, but her last words hung in the air, the double meaning clear.

Maite sensed something was amiss but misunderstood our reaction. 'Believe me, our beautiful Bay of Biscay will turn into a monster. You wait.'

The others, squirming, waited for me. I had to get back on track. 'We've all surfed big waves,' I said resolutely. 'John might be rusty, but Jock and Rob are ready and I'm itching to go.'

Rob winced. 'I'll give it a crack ... if it's not *too* big.'

'Me too, I guess,' said Jock. 'How big can it get?'

Maite raised her eyebrows.

'Don't worry,' I said. 'Once you get a taste of those big long walls, there'll be no holding you back.'

We talked of the deep-drawn swell speeding towards us from the north and how we would ride it. Maite laughed at us. 'Impossible! Far too dangerous! Don't even think about it.'

We tried to argue with her, but she'd seen it all before. Giant swells that sent fishermen scurrying; boats tied down hard inside the walls of every port; mountainous seas that seethed and smashed; the seafarers, landlocked, grimly watching on until the beast lay still.

But we were surfers. We lived and breathed the ocean swells. We travelled far and wide to search them out, hunt them down, and ride them. And the bigger — the better. We all had our limits, but those were rarely tested.

'You'll see!' said Maite, smiling wryly.

She and I left them to the bars and went home. And there, later, beneath the salty blankets, our energies spent, she cautioned me again. 'The sea will be terrifying, you have no idea. Don't do anything silly!'

'Don't worry, I love surfing but I'm not going to die for it! I'm not that stupid.'

§

The next day we stocked up on food in Bermeo. We weren't sure how long the swell would last. In its old port sat a few of the beautifully shaped, wide-hipped, wooden boats that ran to the Canary Islands off Morocco to fill their hulls with tuna and cod, the catch quickly whisked to the covered market across the road.

At the butcher, alone behind his counter, we bought ham and salami and a whole chicken. At the grocer, the locals, all women, studied us at arm's length as we entered, their tongues momentarily silenced. They watched as we dipped into the sacks of flour and pulses and baskets of vegetables. The gossip began again when we plucked a few garlic bulbs and peppers from the strings that hung from the cobwebbed ceiling, then intensified as we scoured the shelves for tinned fish, tinned tomatoes, fresh bottled olives and a few haberdashery items.

It was the usual gossip — our appearance, our habits, where we lived, what we did, the surfing, why we didn't work, how long we had been around, how long we would stay.

At the counter we waited quietly. The storekeeper chatted endlessly with the womenfolk as he chopped, cut, poured, weighed, wrapped the produce, counted the money and dished out the change. One old lady, garbed in black, like a widow still in mourning, gave us a withering stare. 'Look at these four. Fish out of water.'

The others laughed until gently rebuked by the manly shopkeeper, who eyed us sheepishly.

I smiled. 'Don't worry, *hombre*. We're used to it,' I said in Spanish.

The shopkeeper laughed. The women flushed, their tongues momentarily anchored. As we left, grinning, they whispered tactfully in Basque.

We bought a few luxury items, including a bottle of excellent red. 'Not like that flagon rot-gut you told us about!' Jock said later, with a dreg-filled smile.

'Hey, don't knock the flagon!' I replied, recalling the dreamy moon-filled nights at Baquio, the smell of earth and sea, and the swish and sway of the breeze-swept corn.

§

The fish market reverberated with the catch-cries of the burly fishwives. The fisherwomen, tense, talked of their menfolk racing home across the seas. In the damp of its sluiced cement floors, one fishwife hauled and butchered a thirty-kilogram tuna fish. Glistening with scales, apron besmirched with blood and guts, and reeking of the sea, this rubber-gloved fishmonger was a formidable woman. Her knife flashed across the white-tiled benches as she scaled, chopped and filleted the fish with power and precision. Almost finished, she gave us a long hard stare, mopped her sweating brow with the back of her bloody glove. She wiped her knife on her apron, and looked at John. '*Qué quiere, hombre?*'

'She's cute!' said John, under his breath, a wicked glint in his eye.

She grunted, picked up the fish's guts and tossed them into a bin beside her, leaving the fish head on the bench.

'Not my type,' Rob replied, biting his lip. 'Yours?'

'I don't think so,' said Jock, trying to keep a straight face.

She glared at us. '*Bacalao?*'

We'd tasted *bacalao*, salted cod, in the bar, and it was good. But I knew from Adolfo that the de-salting in fresh water took two days and was beyond our patience and resources.

'Tuna steaks, a few anchovies and some *merluza* fillets,' John said in Spanish, his eyes still glinting.

She weighed and wrapped the fish. We paid and made to leave. '*Muchachos,*' she said, brandishing her giant fish knife, 'Some of us speak a little English, you know.' She brought the knife down hard cleaving the fish head in two. 'You aren't so cute, either!'

At the hardware shop we bought rubber tubing, nylon cord, fishing line, a strong dog collar each and a couple of handkerchiefs. Knowing we were strange foreigners who rode waves, the storekeepers regarded us curiously, as if to say: 'Surely, they wouldn't be mad enough to venture out.'

As we were leaving Bermeo, a steady stream of boats scooted into port, sighing with relief when they rounded the walls to safety.

In *Casa Ignacia*'s dilapidated lounge, we set about making our extra-strong leg ropes. Scorned by purists, the leg rope had become crucial. All committed surfers knew how to make them, like they knew how to work with fibreglass and resin to repair a damaged board.

We threaded the nylon cord through the thin latex tubing and, taking an end each, stretched out the tubing and tied the ends off with fishing line. The leg rope was secured to a special fixture in the ventral side of the tail of the surfboard. The other end we tied to a handkerchief or dog collar, which in turn could be fastened to the ankle.

The leg rope had to be strong but carefully tensioned to withstand a sudden force — a bit of give, a bit of stretch, but not too much of either. Too much stretch and after a wipeout the board might recoil into your head, too little and it would snap. With luck, it might save us from a long and dangerous swim and the board from damage on the rocky shore.

After lunch, we checked the sea. Not a hint of a swell. It was still too early, and we were too anxious.

Back at the house, bored and restless, Jock and I decided to cut each other's hair — long and wild after months of neglect. We laid a plastic raincoat under a chair.

'I'm not having a bar of it,' said Rob. He scuttled to his room to write to Rebecca. John, leaning against the door jamb, watched on suspiciously.

Jock assured me he knew what he was doing, so I agreed to go first. Curls fell steadily to the floor.

'There goes your strength, Samson,' said John. 'At least Jock can cut.'

Using a mirror, Jock guided me through cutting his own hair.

'Jock, are you crazy?' said John. 'You'll look like a robber's dog!'

'Not a robber's dog,' he said, checking in the mirror when all was done. 'Not even a dog.'

'A few snips short of an Afghan, I reckon,' said John.

Jock laughed.

'At least he's not a stray,' I said. It had slipped out before I could catch it.

A dark cloud raced across the room. John bared his teeth and looked ready to take me by the throat.

'Hey, easy, boys!' said Jock. 'No need for that ... Besides, I've got an idea,' he said, inspecting the floor, grinning. He picked up one end of the raincoat. 'Take the other end, Owen, and follow me.'

John put his teeth away. 'You idiots.' He shook his head.

We carried the raincoat full of curls and locks out of the house, down the narrow walled-in path towards Santa Catalina chapel and the port, chuckling as we went.

We mounted the seawall. Jock, fighting off the laughter, conjured a few semi-spiritual words. 'Oh gods of the oceans and seas, send down big waves — big, beautiful waves.' With that we threw our 'offering' into the sea.

There was something strangely sobering about the arc of the fall and the way the curls floated and disappeared — the thought of injury, death and a watery grave — but after a moment of eerie silence, we were laughing so hard that we nearly toppled in, then chuckled our way back to the house.

John was waiting at the top of the stairs, glaring, mostly at me. 'You've both gone mad,' he said, when Jock explained the empty raincoat. 'Surf fever.'

Indeed, a temporary madness had taken hold.

An hour later, nerves on edge, we re-checked the sea. There was a pulse! A small consistent swell had arrived. The tide had dropped, and the swells began to break, but it was still a little full. A fishing boat snuck into port.

'I'm in,' said John, when a wave broke along the full length of the sandbar. He was chewing at the bit to ride the famous waves and, at that first break, he shot off to change into his wetsuit.

'Hmmm. It's tempting,' said Rob, taking his hands from his pockets. 'What about you guys?'

'I'll wait for the tide to drop a bit further,' I said.

Jock hesitated. 'I'm with Owen. It's only going to get better. I'll conserve energy.'

Another set arrived, each wave broke teasingly down the line.

'Don't wait too long,' said Rob. 'The crew from France are bound to descend on us.' He raced off to the house in pursuit of John and, almost immediately, a van pulled into the car park, and then another. Soon a posse of surfers had formed on the headland.

The swell was now about four feet. We spotted John heading down the slippery stone steps on the side of the little port and launching into the water. He paddled out through the harbour walls into the channel, picking up the current, then stroking quickly out past the rocky point with its little chapel, to behind the break.

While the rest of us stood chatting, we spotted a local fishing boat, a traditional Basque one — the old heavy wooden sort — with beautiful lines and about five metres long, coming back to port from the far side of the river mouth. We didn't think too much about it at first, because we were watching John and the waves, but the boat kept motoring steadily towards us. John had paddled across to the take-off area at the far edge of the sandbar and positioned himself, sitting on his board, waiting.

Another set appeared. Even when the waves were only a few hundred metres off the sandbar, the boat kept coming. The two fishermen seemed unaware that the swells would turn into breaking waves.

The chatter stopped as the boat drew near the edge of the

sandbar, our eyes magnetically drawn by its relentless course and speed. 'Check this fishing boat!' an Aussie surfer yelled. 'What the hell are they doing?'

The fishermen were locals. They knew the sandbar. They'd fished here all their lives. They were masters at judging the tide, the swell, and when to run their boats across the sandbar to get in and out of the little port. They never took chances.

'Buggered if I know,' I replied. 'They're going to cop a hiding!'

The boat kept coming. And then I realised … it was Adolfo's boat!

John positioned himself for a wave out the back. He'd let the first one go and it reached the sandbar, reared up and broke with a heavy thud.

It was too late. Hit side-on by a wall of whitewater, the boat rolled over, pitching the two fishermen into the sea.

We were transfixed. Was this really happening?

After a few long moments, flailing limbs appeared in the froth. God, I thought, I hope they can swim! It didn't look that way and the upturned boat was bloody close. If they didn't watch out, they'd get it in the head!

The next wave broke and rolled through, washing the boat and the fishermen further down the sandbar and into the river mouth. Again, the fishermen disappeared under the water only to bob up, arms flailing. They looked to be in big trouble.

There was a loud cry for help from about fifty metres along the railing. Raul had stirred from his hangover to raise the alarm. He shouted and waved his arms towards the port and the bars. Locals appeared from everywhere, running, yelling, one or two barking orders. Almost in an instant, it seemed the whole village had converged on the headland.

Carmen, tea towel in hand, was amongst them. She gripped the nearby railing. *'Dios mío! Qué pasó?'*

John must have seen the boat heading to port and guessed what had happened. And so, with all eyes on him, he had to ride that wave with no mistakes and get to the fishermen — fast. He rose to his feet and raced across the wave's face, speeding down the line of the sandbar, manoeuvring artfully. He covered the distance with amazing speed, every movement of his body and surfboard matched to the fast-breaking wave.

Gliding off the end of the wave, John lay prone on his board and streaked into the midst of the drowning men, then slid off his board to help them grab hold, steadying the board so it didn't turn over.

On the headland, an infectious hysteria had taken hold, women screaming and crying, men shouting, but when John rode that wave it was watched in silence, breath held, eyes fixed on his flight downstream, and when he reached and saved them, you could hear and feel the collective relief.

Rob launched into another feathering wave and streaked down the river mouth to lend support and the fishermen's survival seemed assured. I wasn't aware of any cheering, but there might as well have been — that's how it felt.

From that moment, the surfers could do no wrong, our

uncertain reputation instantly transformed. Now we were heroes. Not just John and Rob. All of us.

The coastguard arrived from Bermeo and whisked Adolfo and his crewman away, but the boat and all its gear — the fishermen's livelihood — were still adrift in the river mouth, so we surfers suited up and headed out *en masse* to recover them.

Many hours later — and with the help of a tugboat from Bermeo to drag the righted fishing boat off the sandbar — all was saved. Well, almost all. Adolfo and his crewman had lost face in the worst possible way. They'd made a catastrophic error of judgment and would never live it down.

After all was done that could be done, it was time to warm up, to eat, drink and celebrate. Naturally, we took to the bars.

Many of us surfers had only just met. Today brought us close like brothers. It would not be forgotten soon, although perhaps Adolfo would wish it otherwise. We had to do a round of the bars, all together, and go over what happened from every angle, from every point of view. The whole village was grateful. Drinks were on the house, or shouted, well into the night.

It started in *Bar El Puerto* with Carmen watching on. John was the centre of attention, Rob by his side. Jock and I stood to the side.

'What you don't realise,' John told the gang, 'is that when I slid off the board to help the fishermen, an octopus — part of the fishermen's catch, I guess — wrapped around my neck and I could feel the tentacles slithering.'

'Was it alive?' asked Dwayne, an American from southern California.

'I'm not sure!' John laughed. 'There wasn't time to find out …! It slid away when I grabbed the two men and dragged them onto the board.'

'Radical, man!' drawled Roger, another American.

'One of the guys was so desperate to clutch onto something, he pushed me under.' John, using his hands, ducked and weaved, re-enacting the moment. 'I thought I was going to drown, too … But that slithering sensation, so cold and slimy.' He put a hand to his neck. 'And the feel of those suckers on my skin — it'll stay with me forever.'

'Jesus, mate. We couldn't see that part from the headland,' said Ian, an Aussie from Sydney. He chuckled. 'You're gonna have some nightmares, alright!'

Jock turned to me and winked. 'John's on a roll, Owen.'

I shrugged. 'Same old … right place, right time … He falls on his feet wherever he goes.'

'In his element now.'

'That's his gift. Holding court.'

'Look at them hanging on every word. They think he's been here forever, not just a few weeks … If anyone's a local, it's you.'

'No foreigner's ever going to be a local, Jock.'

'You know what I mean.'

The door flew open and Raul was carried in on the shoulders of a group of fishermen, his head bobbing in customary turtle fashion. His thick lips parted and he burst into song. They set him down and he staggered to the bar, leering. 'Carmen,' he shouted, bringing a fist down on the bar top, *'Vino para todos!'*

Unable to suppress a smile, Carmen raised an eyebrow, grunted, and filled a long line of glasses with a single pour. A fisherman passed them around.

'A John y todos los Australianos!' Raul yelled, with a slur. *'Salud!'*

'Salud!' came the response, before we downed the shot of rough red.

'Carmen, por favor, más vino,' John called out.

She poured another line.

John raised his glass. *'A Raul!* The lifeguard!'

'A Raul!' came the booming response.

Raul was in heaven. He burst into song. The fishermen shouldered him again and headed for the door. He didn't quite duck in time and there was a dull thud as head met wood. He barely noticed, but the fishermen swayed. One reached up to pull Raul's head down and off they went. The bar erupted in laughter.

I sidled up to Carmen. 'Nobody's shushing the town drunk tonight!' I said.

She was silent for a moment. 'I'm sure Adolfo and Jose might if they were here.'

'Raul helped save their lives.'

She shrugged. 'He did, but their lives will never be the same. Doctor Arriaza came to our *piso* again earlier, to see the baby. The men are in the nursing home. He said their broken bones will mend. Their spirits, he's not so sure about.'

'Poor buggers!'

'Yes, a tragedy, but their families are grateful … As for Raul, he certainly helped, but your brother was the real hero. You must be proud of him.'

It was my turn to be silent. 'And Rob.'

Carmen studied me for a moment. 'Rob too,' she said.

I surveyed the bar. John, once more, was surrounded by the pack of ogling surfers. 'I have to go.'

Carmen smiled. '*Maite?*'

I nodded.

'Where are you off to? You can't go!' the group exclaimed, when I made to leave. John frowned, his story disrupted.

I gave a vague answer about meeting a friend and promised to return.

Rob winked, smiling that knowing smile.

Jock looked enquiringly. 'Ines?'

'I think so.'

'Check the surf, won't you?'

§

Under the stars, accompanied by Maite and Ines, we had a final look. A cool breeze pushed down the valley. The tide was close to low. Huge swells loomed out of the night and pitched onto the sandbar. Unbroken, they were difficult to discern, but once they pitched, their sound and size were unmistakeable. Ten feet, we gauged, and growing fast. The swell was unrelenting.

'Oh, God!' mumbled Jock through the checkered scarf that half-enveloped his face. 'Not sure I can do this.'

Ines snuggled against him reassuringly. 'Then don't,' she said.

John plunged his hands deep into his blue jacket, his face partially masked by its upturned collar. 'I hope it doesn't get much bigger!'

'Jeez, me too,' I said.

Maite ran a hand lovingly through my depleted curls. '*Guapo loco*,' she murmured in my ear.

We shifted nervously in the brisk night, peering into the dark while line after line of purple-black swells exploded onto the sandbar, their plumes of spray bright with starlight. We shuddered with each exploding wave, like soldiers approaching the battlefront, the cannon fire steadily magnifying. Steaming walls of whitewater thundered symmetrically down into the darkness of the river.

'Let's get some sleep,' I said, knowing this would be impossible.

We returned to the cold damp house.

Maite and I lay together for a while, but I was far too restless. We could hear the others rustling in their rooms. Even John, our hero, was unsettled. The giant swell had dented his swagger. I grunted to myself.

'What was that?' asked Maite.

'Nothing … just thinking.'

'You seem pleased about something.'

'Pleased?' I sighed slowly. 'Scared, more like it.'

She hugged me tightly. 'Tomorrow's a real test, isn't it?'

I hugged her back, burying myself in her warmth.

§

Maite left earlier than usual and I accompanied her downstairs to the little plaza. *'Buena suerte!'* she said quietly, after a long embrace. 'You'll need it.' She kissed me on the forehead like a mother would, got in the car and wound the window half-down. 'And take care!'

'Don't worry! I will.'

She inched off into the mist and I was left standing in the empty plaza, listening to the pounding of the surf, its drumbeat ever stronger. I shuddered. Of course I would take care. I loved my surfing, but I was no martyr.

I returned to my room and there in my cold bed, her arms not around me, I lay tired but awake. My body called for restful sleep, but each boom of the breaking swell reverberated through the house, and through me. I could hear, between the explosions, the others moving restlessly in their beds. I wasn't alone in my fruitless search for sleep. I tossed and turned and gave up. I picked up my book. George, too, was mustering courage.

It's June 12 — Bilbao's day of reckoning. Gastelumendi must be held. Steer and his journo friend Corman rise early to an eerily quiet hotel. They hitch a ride to Urrusti at the front. With shells raining down, George moves amongst the sad and bitter troops in the trenches and shelters. Resting, he reads a book of poetry by George Herbert. A massive aerial bombardment begins and he's nearly killed. Tanks and infantry advance with endless shelling. George sees the faces of two young Basque soldiers, standing beside him, blown away.

Gastelumendi is taken.

Bullets singing around them, George retreats with the troops. At the back of the hill, he discovers Corman and the car have gone. He walks to Zamudio, strafed as he goes, arriving with a headache, sore eyes, deaf ears and a dry mouth. Two Basque commanders revive him with wine. When Larrinaga, the Chief Communist Political Commissar, leaves for Bilbao to report the fall of Gastelumendi and Cantoibaso, George grabs a lift.

Back in Bilbao, everything is quiet. At the Presidencia, George reports what he's seen at the front, retires upstairs, quaffs sherry and falls asleep in an armchair. The first shelling wakes him. Twelve-inch armour-piercing shells narrowly miss the Presidencia and blow up nearby houses. From a window, he sees the dead and dying; the police, Red Cross and journalists' cars all rushing about in the dust.

Bilbao is crumbling. Only the steep ridge of Santa Marina stands against the enemy. It falls the following day, and when German planes begin to machine-gun Bilbao, people prepare to flee. At midnight, Aguirre meets with his senior advisors to decide whether to defend the city, or not. Four hours later they commit.

The enemy advances along the ridge from Santa Marina to San Roque. The Basques try to counter-attack but fail. Soldiers return to their homes in Bilbao, carrying fearful stories from the front.

At dusk a massive evacuation of Bilbao begins — to the west and to the sea. Motor lorries packed with people and possessions pour out of the city. Every boat in the Nervión is mobilised to carry refugees to Santander and France.

The road evacuation to Santander rumbles through the night strafed by enemy aircraft. It continues, night after night, until nearly 200,000 — half of Bilbao's inflated population — has fled. Basque troops hold back the enemy advance, but with desertions increasing, large holes appear in the defence line.

George stays to the end, to witness the evacuation and the final defence of the city. When the enemy cuts the water supply, there's mass hysteria. And later, with aircraft constantly overhead, total desperation. Machine-gunning starts in the streets, followed by shelling and shrapnel. The aerial bombardment becomes continuous. The front is close to the Nervión. Bullets singing overhead, George crosses the river to witness, up close, the Basque soldiers fighting tooth and nail to hold the slope. By evening the Nervión side of the city is encircled in flame. Before dark, the Basques make one final effort, sending their last three battalions against the enemy — in vain.

§

The dawn sunlight was a crisp pale glow. It stole around the rotten wooden shutters, across the cold glass pane fogged by my nocturnal breath, filtering through the grimy faded curtains to reach me.

Jock burst into my room. '*Amigo*, you have got to see this!'

I threw on clothes and raced to the balcony. Rob was already there. 'Oh, God!' I said, gripping the rail.

A monstrous set steamed past the top of the seawall and unleashed its force, sending massive spumes of spray into the thin dawn light. John, stirred by our movement, surveyed the view through sleep-encrusted eyes.

The port itself was a whirlpool. Six-foot waves smashed through the entrance into the fishing boats and bounced off the inner port walls. The incoming waves met the rebound in a confusion of refracting waves that lurched high and broke. A vicious rip beyond the entrance was all the while sucking water from the tiny port.

But this was a sideshow compared to what was happening beyond, something disturbingly beautiful. Last night's steady breeze had firmed and a stiff biting wind raced seaward down the valley to meet the mountainous swells. It gripped the top of the enormous peaks, wrenching them higher, sending huge arching sheets of spray backward and skyward. A cloud of settling seaspray engulfed the breadth of the river mouth. And when the sun rose out of the hills behind the village and caught the spray, the air above the river mouth turned to rainbow.

The massive swells marched relentlessly in from the deeper

Atlantic. They approached the coast and wrapped around the island of Izaro, where they split and ran down each side, at times obliterating the island from view. On the leeward side they steamed through, unleashing their fury on the shallow reef, gigantic but seemingly rideable.

Then the swells re-gathered, continuing their coastward march undiminished. They approached the sandbar as whale-blue, bay-wide ocean masses that reared up in the sudden shallows, their tops feathering, to fold over and crash onto the estuary's sandy bank. The waves rebounded off the sandbar, sending a secondary wall of whitewater careening skyward. This too was caught by the wind and the spume whipped seaward.

The scale of the waves was beyond anything any of us had seen.

'Let's check it from the headland,' said Jock, his voice hoarse.

'Good idea.' Rob was pale, almost whispering.

John was speechless.

'Come on, mate,' I said. 'Let's go!'

We scampered nervously down the stairs to Plaza Santa Catalina and a still-sleeping village. All the shutters were closed, the inhabitants locked down in the safety of slumber.

Striding abreast down the cobbled street to the port, we edged gingerly around it at the feet of the houses, away from where the sea spewed over the port wall. We couldn't stand in the usual spot on the headland. The spray made that impossible. It didn't matter. The view from anywhere was spectacular.

Impossibly huge waves, at least fifteen feet high, were breaking perfectly down the river mouth's sandbank before closing
out in one giant mass in the shallows, 300 metres down-river.
The channel was a torrent, running along the shore, carrying
what water it could back out to sea. It tried to squeeze out
through the gap between the rocky point and the sandbar,
but more often than not met the broken waves that closed
out the channel.

Was it possible to ride one? If you could harness the
paddling speed to catch one, it was possible — theoretically
possible. But how could you get out there? You'd be sucked
instantly and uncontrollably into the rip that ran to the narrow
passage. To arrive there at precisely the right moment, when
no waves were breaking, would require extreme luck. If you
were that lucky, you'd have to escape the outbound rip, paddle
behind the breaking swells, somehow locate the right take-off
position, contain your fear of a rogue set, and then launch,
blinded by spray, into one of the massive beasts. If you made
the blind, free-fall take-off, managed to draw a huge, long
bottom turn onto the glassy mountainous wall, and rocket
down the hollowing wave, trying to control the chattering
board, you'd still have to exit early enough to avoid the almost
certain death when the wave closed out in the shallows. If you
lost your board, leg rope broken, you'd be alone, helpless, and
swept back out to sea, probably to drown. If you broke bones
or were knocked unconscious, it was certain death.

Even with perfect luck, it would be impossible to paddle

across the torrential rip and get back to the near shore. At low tide, with supreme luck, you might get washed down-river, recover, paddle from the sandbank to Laida beach on the far side, and wait for someone to drive around and pick you up.

But imagine the feeling of conquering one of those magnificent beasts, the sheer ecstasy of flying along a rolling, glassy mountain and imagine what the others would think. It would never be forgotten.

'I'm going out!' I declared.

John regarded me dismissively, thinking I was joking. Rob, mute, stared out to sea. Jock eyed me gravely through his steel-rimmed glasses moist with spray. 'You *are* joking?'

'I'm not.'

'Don't be crazy! You'll get killed!'

I glared at him. 'No, I won't ... I can do it.'

A few of the other surfers, bleary-eyed, approached from the vans. 'Man, look at that!' cried the American, Roger, as a huge set poured through.

I started to move off.

Rob looked at me. 'You're not going out, are you?'

'Yeah. I am.'

'Are you mad?!' He shook his head. 'What are you trying to prove?'

'Nothing ... I have to try.'

'Owen, don't be an idiot,' John yelled.

That was it. I ran back to the house, suited up, grabbed my

board, rounded the port again and jogged towards the others on the headland.

Against the noise of the sea, John shouted, 'Are you completely insane?'

'I know I can do it,' I yelled back.

'What happened to your instincts? Have you lost touch with reality?'

At that moment a rogue set heaved into the river mouth closing out the entire breadth of the estuary. Wave after wave smashed along the sandbar and obliterated the passage.

'Have you?' John yelled again. He shook his head grimly at the port, which was seething with fury. 'Grow up!'

'Grow up?' I threw my board down on the grass. 'What do you care?' I yelled back. 'I can make my own decisions ... *You* do as you please!'

'What do you mean, *do as I please?*'

'You just pissed off! Left us in the lurch!'

John's mouth fell open. He stared at me, searching for words. 'Jesus, Owen, I had to. I had to escape!'

'What about the rest of us? Mum, Dad, me! We couldn't escape! We had to deal with it!'

John's shoulders sank. 'I know. I shouldn't have left, but I just had to. Something inside told me to.'

'So bloody easy to run, John. We needed you ... I needed you!'

'Owen, I was sixteen ... I would do things differently now.'

'Would you?'

'What do you mean?' His eyes blazed. 'You don't think I've suffered too? I feel like I failed her!'

'We all do. All of us bloody do!'

John's head sank. 'I'm sorry, mate … I really am.'

'We're all sorry,' I said. Tears ran down my cheeks. I felt my shoulders fall. 'No-one's fault.'

John nodded. He took a big breath, pushed it out, and looked at the ocean. 'Owen, go on. Go out, surf if you have to. But don't get killed. There's no point wasting your life … you'll never be a doctor then, never know your destiny.'

'Doctor? Destiny?' I pushed at the board with my foot. 'Who cares?'

'Mum and Dad … me. Louise would have.'

I took a giant breath. 'I guess.' I looked at the heaving sea and picked up my surfboard. 'Louise probably bloody hated doctors.'

Jock and Rob and the other surfers hadn't taken their eyes off us, hadn't moved.

A huge set poured through and we watched for a long time — I, for one, feeling small and vulnerable, witnessing nature's raw power — a breathtakingly beautiful force.

§

The dawn gave way to a clear morning and the village came to life. The fishermen were the first to appear. Anxious and weary, they checked their boats. It was too late to do anything

about it if they weren't still securely tethered. Women —
spinsters, black-garbed widows, girls, and yawning wives
with their bleary-eyed children — appeared in search of the
day's first bread. Then the tradesmen, the pensioners, the bar
owners, the bartenders, the shopkeepers, and the new mothers with their swaddled babes tucked tight in their prams and,
later still, delivery men, local farmers and other passers-by
— all drawn magnetically to the headland, to stand with the
surfers at the railing beneath the denuded plane trees and
marvel at the ocean, all gossip strangled by the sea's pounding and roaring.

§

I met Maite at Plaza Santa Catalina in the evening and we
went to the house. She'd visited a friend in Bermeo where all
the talk was of the fishing boats that hadn't made it back to
port in time. She let me rave about the waves, the upcoming
day and our hope for rideable surf. 'Don't you get stranded at
sea,' she said gravely.

'I won't. I'm not that brave.'

I was drifting into half-sleep when she said quietly, 'Franco
is dying.'

'Yes,' I replied, dreamily, 'so they keep saying.'

'This time it's true. He's going to die any day. I heard it from
a close friend of the family … Patxi, the friend of my grandfather's in the nursing home.'

I raised myself on one elbow. 'You've never talked much about your grandfather's friend.'

'No.' She was silent for a moment. 'He's suffered a long time, from war injuries.'

'Oh.' I pulled her close.

'He was a journalist who knew George,' she whispered.

'He knew George?' I was wide awake now.

'Yes.' She hesitated for a moment. 'They met during the Civil War. He's old, very unwell these days. His contacts say Franco is on his deathbed.' Her nails dug into me. 'If the monarchy is restored, there might be an amnesty for the prisoners.'

'Do you really think they'll release prisoners?'

'There's talk of it! We're hoping!'

'I'm glad,' I said, hugging her close. 'At least there's hope.'

'Yes, finally.' She held me tight, her nails no longer biting.

My thoughts turned to George and the grandfather's friend, Patxi, but then her hands began caressing and distracting me.

We fell asleep in each other's arms, spent and emotionally exhausted. Much later, Maite awoke with a start, slipped out of bed, dressed at speed, kissed me and raced off into the night.

§

I got up with the sun, threw on a sweater and pants and scampered to the balcony. The swell had dropped a little, but the waves were still huge. A brisk offshore wind skated down the river valley, meeting the waves head on. I ran to rouse the others.

306

Rubbing his eyes and yawning, John was first to join me on the balcony. 'Holy hell!' He was soon wide awake.

'Check it out!' I yelled. 'What do you reckon, fellas? Rideable?'

'Far out!' said Rob. 'That's the best bloody surf I've ever seen!'

We raced across the Plaza with boards underarm. The sun broke through the clouds and the sky began to clear. 'A good omen!' said Rob, raising his free hand to the skies.

'I hope you're right!' said Jock. 'This is scary, man! Crazy scary!'

I swallowed hard when we rounded the cannon. The tide had turned and was on the rise. The port was turbulent, but nothing like yesterday. We nimble-footed down the steps, launched into the water and began to paddle. You could feel the sea start to draw, feel it clutching. 'Christ!' Jock muttered when he stroked alongside.

We nosed nervously out. The rip was drawing fast. We paddled carefully into the grip of the rushing current, to be sucked out to the passage between the rocky point and the sandbar. Timing our transit was crucial. There was a pause between sets. I made it through easily, Jock was fine, Rob too, but John barely scraped over the first wave of a large set. 'Be careful, brother,' I whispered as I hauled up the face of the next wave.

Stroking to the take-off area, I felt the inward surge of the ocean. We paddled in tentatively, fearful to get too close. A set loomed and broke with a thunderous boom. I edged in a little closer, keen. Jock stayed wide, watching. Rob lingered in between us. John had been carried way out by the rip and was steadily making his way towards us. I could feel my heart wild in my chest. We didn't have to wait long. A solid set of about twelve feet approached and I felt the water drawing hard off the sandbar. It was difficult to hold position.

'Here we go!' I dug the back of the board in and lunged forward. The wave peaked and for a moment I thought it had passed me by, but the board gathered speed, the wave started pitching and I dropped steeply down the face of a massive watery mountain. It was a long way down, the spray blinding. I angled the board while I dropped and my eyes cleared. At the bottom I drew the longest turn I could muster, unsure of controlling the centrifugal force. The turn held and I began rising on to a giant hollowing wall, rocketing, barely in control. The vast blue came alive around me, like a whale, its mouth open, drawing me inward. For a moment I was deep inside. I reached to touch the silky lining of the beast's innards but was pushed out by a sudden harsh breath. Stung into action, and varying the pressure through my feet, I manoeuvred the board along the wall. So intense was my focus, it all seemed to unfold in ultra-slow motion.

It was long and fast, a ride of exhilaration and terror. Bloody hell! I felt like screaming. I did! A blood-curdling, primordial scream from a primitive place within.

Near the end, bent on surviving, I turned out of the wave early, scared the one behind was bigger and would consume me. I met the crest, was launched upwards and flew for several seconds, toes barely touching the board, before landing on flat water behind the wave. As I sailed through the air I thought I heard a faint cheer. 'Holy hell!' I yelled, mimicking the words of John. 'What a blast!'

A few locals had gathered on the headland to watch, mostly fishermen, but some of the fishwives too. Maria stood, hand to her mouth, Carmen beside her. No Adolfo, but Dr Arriaza was there, scratching his head.

The next wave was smaller and I was able to pause and regroup. But I couldn't linger. Ten minutes of hard paddling against the swell and incoming tide to finally reach Jock and Rob. Jock, sitting wide of the break, was looking anxious, Rob only marginally more comfortable.

'How was that?' Jock asked, wide-eyed.

'Un-bloody-believable!' I said. 'My heart was in my mouth on the take-off, but once on the wall, I was absolutely flying, and then I got swallowed like Jonah and spat out! Incredible!'

'From behind it looked like you were going to get annihilated!' Rob's gaze flicked nervously back and forth to the horizon.

'You've got to get into the wave really early and make the drop. That's the hard bit. The rest takes care of itself. You just gotta go for it!'

John joined us after a laborious paddle. 'Got stuck in the current, buggered already!' he said, sitting up on his board, planting his hands on his thighs and breathing deeply. He stared at me. 'Owen, I saw that monster you caught … Holy

hell! And you made it through — saw you fly off the end ...
Must've been a helluva tube.'

'Like nothing on earth! Gary, that Hawaiian, taught me how
to ride 'em.'

'So it seems.' He snatched a grin between breaths. 'Who's
the hero now?'

'Hero ...? No way. Just surviving.'

After a minute another large set approached.

'Who's going?' I asked.

'I'll try the last one,' Jock said hesitantly.

'I'll take the one before Jock,' said Rob.

'John?' I asked.

'I'll watch for a bit,' he said, his hands still planted on his
thighs, shoulders rising and falling. 'Have to catch my breath!'

'Alright. I'll take the third one,' I said.

The first two waves rolled through and we rose and fell
like flotsam. When the third approached, I felt more relaxed,
more conscious of the elements. Now I could better see the
wave, its magnificent shape, the line of the wind-swept crest,
all the shades of ocean blue; feel the patterned texture of the
wall beneath my fingers, the bite of breeze on my face and
the steady thunder behind me as the wave crashed on to the
sandbar. What a rush!

I focused on timing and control, modulating the speed to
stay marginally in front of the breaking part of the wave, in the
'pocket', where the power is centred and the ride is best. The art
was remaining there, without getting struck by the arching lip.

The wave careened down the sandbar, I with it, locked in a perfect high-speed trim. I didn't really need to do much, except keep on it, vigilant, and let the wave unfold.

Down the line, the water drew upward as the wave face formed and fell in a glorious arc. Blues turned to greens, dark to light, smooth became rippled and scalloped — a world of sensations unfolding at great speed to be later recalled and relived in countless daydreams. This was heaven!

I flew off the wave, airborne and attempted a controlled landing, but came adrift from my board, somersaulted and crashed. I surfaced to see Rob racing towards me, weaving, balletic, in full control. He flashed by, eyes lit, a blur of elegant motion bathed in swirling blue.

On the next wave came Jock, crouching low over his long green board, maximising his speed, barely escaping the wave's unleashing force. He raised his arms in a victory salute and hurtled past before a flying exit. 'Whoo-hooo!' came the cathartic holler of celebration, when he sailed through the air and plunged into the sea behind the wave. There was cheering from the headland when he surfaced.

Jock collected himself and paddled to where Rob and I were waiting, his grin wide like his eyes. 'Never in my life!' he exclaimed. 'Amazing, man. The biggest, best, scariest wave of my life!'

'You should have seen your face, mate!' I said. 'And look at the crowd.' Half the village were now on the headland, some yelling and waving, many shaking their heads in disbelief.

The other surfers stood close by, looking on. A few shot off to change into their wetsuits.

Jock laughed, the haunted look replaced by nervous excitement.

'Hey, we'd better get moving!' said Rob, pointing. 'Look what's coming!'

Jock and I didn't need urging. We paddled in earnest, well wide of the break, back out to sea. Halfway out, another set arrived.

John, who'd drifted inside, scratched over the first few. The third wave was smaller. He caught it, but was a tad slow and, by the time he was upright, the wave was pitching well over him. Somehow he made it to the bottom and slightly off balance, turned tightly, taking him into the hollow depths of the wave. The wave threatened to engulf him, but he clung tightly, deep within it. With his weight forward, he gathered speed and shot forward, catapulted down the line. He let out a cry of exhilaration and in a blink he'd passed us.

'How was that?' Jock asked breathlessly.

'Bloody lucky!' Rob exclaimed. 'He nearly got it on the head!'

'We will too, if we're not careful,' I cautioned. 'Let's move it!'

On my next wave, I passed John paddling back out, a broad grin leaping from his face and a triumphant fist raised.

Three hours passed before we started to flag. Back at the take-off zone, we decided on a last ride each. 'We're stuffed,' Rob said to the others. 'We're heading in.'

Roger nodded. 'Take care, man! You know how it is when you're tired.'

We all made our waves to the end, except Rob who fell on the take-off and was smashed.

'Oh, shit!' yelled Jock, as we sat up on our boards at the edge of the rip and surveyed the sea. He paled, as if he'd lost his own brother. 'Where the hell is he?'

It was impossible to see beyond the next surging mass of whitewater. All the memories of Greg's near-drowning came rushing back. 'Wait!' said John. 'There's his board!' It was being pushed towards us by a dying wave. Jock paddled across, grabbed it by its leg rope and held tight.

'And there's Rob!' yelled John.

Attempting to bodysurf, Rob was washed in, flailing, on the following mass of foamy water. Jock paddled towards him as the wave gradually died on the edge of the rip, and he passed Rob his board.

Exhausted and breathless, Rob hauled himself on and slowly paddled over. 'By Jesus!' he whispered harshly. 'I'm stuffed!'

'God, you gave me a fright,' said Jock, still pale.

'A close call,' said John. 'A brush with death.' He glanced at me. 'Must be careful.'

When Rob was ready, we made the final dash across the rip, all together, back to the calm waters of the little port.

The villagers surrounded us when we mounted the steps to the top of the port wall. There were smiles, slaps on the back, and endless shaking of heads. '*Locos! Bravos y locos!*'

Carmen stood to the side, baby in her arms, Dr Arriaza beside her. I approached them, board under arm, dripping.

'You boys are crazy! Brave, but absolutely crazy!' he said.

'A calculated risk!' I grinned. 'It's worth it!'

Carmen raised an eyebrow, grunted and suppressed a smile. 'Calculated stupidity, more like it.'

I laughed. 'And how's the baby?'

Carmen smiled, 'On the mend.' She tipped her head to Dr Arriaza. 'Thanks to him.'

The doctor reached into his coat pocket, fumbled out a pack of cigarettes and lit one up. 'I didn't do much. Not much I could do.' He drew on the cigarette. 'Whooping cough, you have to ride it out.' Smoke drifted out of his nostrils. 'Hope that nature is kind.' He patted Carmen on the back. 'We got lucky. Nature isn't always kind.' He looked at me, studied me for a moment. 'You don't win every battle.'

I thought of Louise. 'No,' I said.

He stroked the baby's head. 'But you never give up, do you? You keep on fighting, struggling to find a way, even if the path isn't clear.'

§

The swell lasted for five days then petered out. The last day was a sprightly four to six feet, without the intensity of the previous days. The sun was bright and piercing and reflected uncomfortably off the ocean's sleek surface.

We surfed with casual abandon, no longer confined by the discipline of surviving unscathed. Mistakes were made, we fell, the consequences mild and tolerable. No-one was going to get killed. We surfed in a mood of total celebration, like playful children larking — noisy, smiling, quick to laugh.

CHAPTER 13

Snow began to appear on the distant peaks beyond Guernica. The air grew cold and sharp, and the salty damp was everywhere. The days were closing in. The wind whispered under the door. I went early to buy bread. The streets were quiet like always, the villagers going about their usual activities.

'*Franco Ha Muerto*' in massive print filled the front page of *El Correo*. There was to be a period of mourning followed by a state funeral. Franco's enemies had waited long and patiently for this day. And for them, surely, this was a day of celebration. Finally, the tyrant, the dictator, the oppressor was dead! From the street you couldn't hear the champagne corks popping or the clink of glasses. You couldn't see the relief, the quiet joy, the excited whisperings. In the streets of Mundaca there was no marching band, no fanfare, no celebration. Life appeared eerily the same.

Even the town crier on his afternoon round of the village remained strangely subdued. I guess no-one wanted to appear too elated.

And for good reason — the military and the *Guardia Civil* had been placed on high alert.

§

When we met that night, Maite could speak of little else. 'Franco is dead! It's finally happened! Can you believe it? But what next? His men are still there, still in control. And now the military and *Guardia Civil* are everywhere. I think it will get worse.'

'I hope not,' I said. 'It's bound to be tense for a while. Then you'll see. Aren't you being too pessimistic?'

'So many emotions today.' Her shoulders sank, as if it were all too hard. 'I feel exhausted.'

I wanted to ask her about the parcels, what was in them, but it wasn't the right time. I drew her to me, held her tightly. She snuggled in close. There was urgency now to our nightly rendezvous, for these were our final days. The clock was ticking down and it would soon be time for me to leave.

I was deeply in love with Maite. She occupied my waking and my sleeping dreams, taken hold of me. My heart, gladly tentacled, could not contemplate departure from this place and her. But l had to. Time and money had run out.

§

It was two nights later, when we lay, regaining our breath, that I was able to broach the subject of the parcels. Maite had brought me a gift. 'It's very beautiful,' I said, gazing over her shoulder at the candlelit painting propped against the wall.

She turned briefly to look. 'He's an excellent painter ... a friend of my grandfather.'

'Your grandfather seemed to have a lot of friends.' I waited until she faced me again. 'How's the one in the nursing home — Patxi?'

'Getting worse.'

'What's wrong with him?'

She sighed. 'Everything. He's old and broken. He was injured in the war ... most of them were. His body's giving out. And he's exhausted from finishing off a project.'

I turned her words over in my mind. 'Is he getting good care?'

'Of course. The doctor's his best friend. He gets special attention.'

'At the nursing home here in Mundaca?'

She frowned. 'Yes, of course. Why?'

'Is he that frail, old intense character in the wheelchair?'

'Yes, I go there regularly to visit him. I'm sure I told you that.'

'I saw him give you a parcel.'

She was silent for a moment. 'He often gives me a parcel. And then I return it to him at the next visit. Some we send away. The ones I gave you to post.'

'What's in them?'

'Our secret project.'

'You can't tell me what it is?'

'No.' Her eyes narrowed. 'It's best you don't know.'

'Why not?'

'Not yet.'

'When?'

'When you leave.'

I sighed.

'You have to trust me.' She pulled me close, wrapped herself around me, whispered softly in my ear, 'As I might have to trust you.'

What did she mean by that: 'As I might have to trust you'?

§

Jock and Rob were the first to go and we saw them to the station. They'd held out for Christmas but couldn't wait for the New Year.

We hugged in that restrained macho way, slapped each other playfully on the upper arms, made promises of correspondence and a rendezvous, and joked, tight-throated.

The train wheezily erupted into life. A railway official moved along the length of the platform, closing doors. He checked both ways, held up a flag and whistled. The train grunted, rocked, spat and inched forward.

Jock, half out the train window, his glasses fogged, the breeze catching his straggly blond locks, yelled, '*Adiós, Jean!* Look after yourself, Owen! *Ondo ibili!*'

Rob's head pushed into view beside him, eyes darting, searching us out. '*Adiós*, boys!' he cried. '*Agur!*'

The ageing train hissed and pulled away from the short, narrow platform. Its rusty, faded carriages rocked discordantly when it picked up speed.

John waved. '*Adiós, amigos!*'

'*Agur*, fellas!' I called, the words half-catching in my throat. '*Ondo ibili!*'

Jock and Rob hung out the window, their arms outstretched in final salute until they disappeared around the curve of the hill.

§

'I don't think I can leave,' I said.

John, his mouth half-open, turned to look at me. 'Are you kidding, Owen?' The lines in his brow stood out like the tracks beside us. 'You know what I'd do? I'd grab the opportunity. No question! Go back, study medicine.'

I shook my head. 'I want to stay here.'

'Owen, wake up! You can't stay here. The Basque country is fascinating, Mundaca is a wonderful village and Maite's a beautiful girl, but you have to move on. Your future lies ahead. What would you do here? Even with perfect Spanish, what work would you get? Be realistic.'

He regarded me earnestly, his hand on my shoulder. 'Owen, I couldn't study like you. But you can. You should.' He took me by both shoulders. 'Even your mate, George, knew when it was time to leave, didn't he?'

I shrugged half-heartedly. 'He did.'

'There are certain times in life when you just have to cut and run.' He seemed suddenly overtaken by a profound sadness. 'I had to get away after … just had to.'

'I know … I might have done the same at your age.'

§

'I could stay and get a job,' I said to Maite the following night. She'd been distant, distracted, but now I had her full attention.

'What kind of job?' she asked. She touched my face gently. 'I want you to stay too, but you have to be realistic.' She frowned, hesitated. 'Besides, you *have* to leave … the sooner the better.'

My throat tightened. 'Why?'

'I'm being closely watched. We all are.'

'By who?'

'Franco's spies. They're still in place.'

'Me too?'

'Almost certainly.'

She nestled into me. 'I'm scared. I can feel something in my bones. Our project's finished, and it's as if they know.'

'Are you in danger?'

'We all are. You included. You must get away. It's important.'

'Important?'

She held me close. 'Yes, important you get away safely.'

I sighed. Destiny was conspiring against me. 'New Year, then. The day after tomorrow, when John leaves.'

She kissed me warmly, placed a finger on my lips. 'In the meantime, don't tell anyone what I've said, not even your brother. And stay calm, act naturally.'

I nodded ruefully.

'You can always come back,' she said tenderly. 'And, Doctor … there's one final favour to ask.'

§

On New Year's Eve, the sky was low-slung and oppressive and a scything wind knifed down the valley and cut into the ink blue sea and rising groundswell. In the port, a confusion of waves jostled the fishing boats, which pulled at their moorings like disgruntled mares.

In the afternoon, we pushed through slanted rain up the slippery cobbles to the bars to say farewell to the various bartenders and the regular patrons I'd come to know.

'*Hombre! Te vas?* You're going?' they asked.

'Yes,' I said glumly. 'I must.'

'Don't look so sad!' they said. 'You love Mundaca! You'll be back.'

'Of course,' I said. But that day felt a long way off.

New Year was now sniffing at the door. The village was rousing from a pre-emptive siesta, readying for the long unchaperoned night ahead. We rolled into *Bar El Puerto* on a swell of red wine, flushed with emotion and the salty slap of the wind.

Carmen grunted knowingly when we entered the empty bar, and put down her tea towel. 'So! The brothers are leaving!'

'Afraid so,' I said.

'Dragging him by the heels!' said John.

She smiled mischievously, her eyes narrowing. 'Someone has to.'

'You sound just like Manolo,' I said.

She shrugged. 'Apples from the same tree.'

'Haven't seen him for a while,' I said. 'Where is he?'

'At the post office again, haranguing the *señora*. Says she's withholding the books he orders from overseas.'

That got me thinking.

'Censorship?' whispered John.

She raised her eyebrows. 'Well, there are books … and there are books.'

'Is he here tonight?' I asked.

'Bilbao,' she said, 'visiting family. It's Rosa and I *all* night long.'

It seemed strange to not say goodbye to Manolo, like unfinished business, and left me with a premonition.

'I'll see you again. I'm sure,' she said brusquely. She eyed John. 'Watch out for him, won't you?'

He grinned. 'I'll do my best!'

'*Gracias por todo, señora!*' I said. 'You've been so kind, like my own mother.'

Carmen beamed for a moment, then fumbled for her tea towel. When she looked again, her composure was restored, her face firmly set. Only her eyes betrayed her. '*Cuídaos, muchachos! Agur!*'

'*Agur, Señora! Agur!*' we replied and left, through those same weathered doors that Arturo had brought me through on that first sunny day in June.

And from there, we launched headlong into a deep, dark, *tinto*-ed night. Bar after bar, round after round, the village became a swirl of glasses, berets, creased fishermen's faces, lipsticked beauties, stolen glances, sonorous voices, slippery cobbles, sawdusted floors, cigar smoke, lilting Basque, impassioned music, and lurking, in the shadows of the church, the black-booted, black-helmeted *Guardia Civil*.

Maite was due at midnight for a long-awaited, uninterrupted night together. She found me outside *Los Chopos* on the terrace, seated under the leafless plane trees in a sorry state, undone by wave after wave of *tintos*. I'd taken refuge in the sobering, salty wind above the port, where the fishing boats bobbed and jumped to the tune of the wind and the music that drifted down from the bars, as if they too were full of drink.

A sober, fur-coated, now crestfallen Maite nursed me, swaying, back to *Casa Ignacia*, where, beyond repair, I was put to bed, and all the while, between sickly groans, apologising. She stayed for a long time, applying cold compresses to my forehead, soothing me — dutiful, but disappointed. I didn't hear her leave, lost as I was in an untidy, wine-soaked stupor.

§

Something woke me. Was it the pounding in my head, the

ocean or both? I nursed myself out of bed, dressed clumsily and reeled outside to check the surf.

New Year's morning was a miracle of winter light. The unhappy clouds of the previous day had been pushed aside like curtains to reveal a bright, powerless sun that rose sheepishly above the valley mists to wash across the village.

All was silent, the bars locked, barred and curtained. A docile breeze sidled through the streets and down to the little port, where the fishing boats were silent too, asleep on their sandy beds.

A crisp six-foot swell strode into the river mouth, rose up against the Pyrenean breeze and unfurled along the shallow sandbar with a cracking sound, like that of a slowly splitting mast.

I hauled a cursing John out of bed. 'It better be good, Owen. I feel horrible!'

'Get your wettie on, mate. You won't regret it!'

We lumbered down to the port and gingerly paddled out between its cobbled walls.

The first solid set caught us unawares. Still dumbed by *tinto*, we'd drifted too far inside, and the set's first wave washed over and through us, sending us spinning and tumbling downstream. In an instant we were awake, whisked from the clutches of the hangover, slapped back to life, shipwrecked into action.

We regrouped. A deep, dull headache was now all that remained of the New Year's revelry.

No more mistakes. We were alone in the beautiful, milky-green waves of the Mundaca river mouth. We sat with the sea rising and falling when the swells passed beneath; the crisp clear waters of the river; the long curving valley; the distant beach of Laida leading to the pined headland; the sheer, pale cliffs of Laga falling into the ocean; and, far in the background, the snowy peaks of the rugged Vizcayan Pyrenees. The village with its proud church, streets and houses and shops and bars and, tucked into the corner, peeping out between protective walls, the tiny port, with its humble fleet of brightly tinted fishing boats.

This was to be our last surf, and a beautiful one it was. Wave after wave of silky speed, ride after ride of weightless euphoria. John was all smiles, and so was I.

'No regrets, John?' I asked, while we sat catching our breath at the take-off.

'No regrets, Owen.'

Deep into the morning, brimful of confidence, I dropped late into a steepening wave, fell, plunged deep, and resurfaced to find my beloved board broken in two. It was an omen. I floated in on one piece, dragging the other with me.

The mourning had begun.

§

John had stretched his two-week sojourn to six, to breaking point, repeatedly reassuring his girlfriend he would soon be back. He stowed his meagre possessions in the car and lashed his surfboard to the roof.

We said our goodbyes, hugged.

'Say hi to Dad and Rosie,' he said. 'Tell Mum I'll write soon.' He slid into the MG and fired up the engine. Down came the window, a half-grinning face emerging, eyes moist, a familiar glint. 'Don't miss that boat, will you, Owen!'

§

Maite was driving me to Santander in the afternoon, to the ferry bound for Southampton. On the steps of *Casa Ignacia*, I waited, recalling the pledge of letters and a reunion, but it could not dispel a deep aching sadness that had overtaken me in the final week.

The whine of an engine pierced the quiet of the narrow street leading into Plaza Santa Catalina. My ears pricked. The pitch was not quite right. A SEAT car of a different colour sped into the plaza and halted in front of me. The door flew open. A woman got out. It was Ines.

'Quick!' she called. 'Get in. We have to go!'

'Where's Maite?' I yelled.

'She's been arrested!'

'Arrested?'

'Yes.'

I flung my backpack into the rear seat, jumped into the car, slammed the door.

Ines looked a mess. No make-up, hair unkempt, face drained, eyes frightened. 'What time does the boat leave?' she asked.

'Four o'clock.'

'Just as she said.'

'Is she okay?'

She stole a glance as we accelerated into the main street. 'I don't know ... she said to keep calm ... that *I* have to keep calm ... *you* have to keep calm.'

'When did you see her?'

'Last night. She was on edge, sure something was about to happen. She asked me to drive you to the ferry.'

'When was she arrested?'

'Early morning. Her mother called me.'

'Oh, God! This is madness. It can't be true!'

'It is.' She took a big breath, exhaled slowly, forcibly relaxing herself. 'Got to keep calm.'

'What about the others?'

'Who?'

'You know.'

'As Maite said: *I* don't know any others, *you* don't know any others. Better that way ... and better not to talk. You understand?'

'Of course.'

'Besides, I'm exhausted, and I need to concentrate.'

She glanced in the rearview mirror, relaxed her grip on the wheel and turned on the tape deck.

We slipped through the Pyrenees to the sound of that

strange, haunting Greek voice and I drifted in and out of sleep, taunted by flashes, an incoherent mix of images from the last six months, and an imagining of what should have been — our final goodbye drifting into the salty mist of the gangway.

But it wasn't to be. In Santander, as I turned to walk the slippery planks, it was Ines who gripped my arm, stopping me, bending down to wrestle a large parcel from her bag. 'Open it when you get on board. There's a letter inside. Read it carefully. Maite said you've trusted her. Now she must trust you.' She gripped me tightly again and kissed me on both cheeks. 'She said to say, "*Te quiero.*"'

I put the parcel under my arm and headed onto the ship.

§

The coast's outline was lost in the gloom. I went to my empty cabin and cut the strings around the parcel with my pocket-knife. There was a folder, tightly bound, and with it, the letter. I sat on the bed.

Querido Owen,

By now you are on your way to England, gone from our beloved, troubled region. I'll miss you so much.

I have a great favour to ask.

The folder is for a publisher in London, the address enclosed. This is our secret project, a manuscript, El Arbol de Gernika, a Spanish translation of George's book, illustrated by myself with photographs by my brother and the translation by my grandfather's friend, Patxi, assisted by Doctor Arriaza. The layout is by our friend, Mr O'Brien, in Ireland.

Owen, I'm so sorry I couldn't explain this to you before. My brother, Inigo, was taking photographs for the book when arrested by the Guardia Civil. They thought he was plotting a bombing for ETA. He's not with ETA, none of us are, except my cousin. Marta had gone underground several years back but was arrested a few months ago. You may have seen her photograph in the paper.

Owen, it's all about the book.

You see, my grandfather, Patxi, and Dr Arriaza all fought together in the war. They met George Steer and became great friends of his, grew to admire and love him. They had tremendous respect for what he did for the Basques, his passionate commitment to our cause and, of course, the brilliant book he subsequently wrote about our struggle. It was always their intention to honour him, to ensure the book was widely read, not only in English, but in Spanish too. One day we'll do a translation in Basque.

Of course, this project is illegal. Franco would never allow publication of the book in Spain. Inigo met with a publisher in Dublin when we were there together. They declined to publish it, but put him in contact with a London publisher who eventually agreed. Patxi and Doctor Arriaza worked hard on the final version, only recently completing

*it. I've been busy doing the illustrations based on drawings
I did of the main battlefields. There are a few from our
trips together. Several of Inigo's photographs are included,
together with originals. Our friends at Eibar gave me a
box-full taken during the war.*

*I wish I could have told you all this before. I wanted to.
But Patxi, the mastermind, wouldn't allow it. He thought
it too dangerous. The less you knew, he said, the better. He
knew we were being watched. We thought no-one would
suspect you.*

*I hope you will not think less of me for holding back. I
know that you, too, are a great believer in George and will
understand the importance of this work. Please deliver it
when you get to London. You will be doing a great service.*

I love you my darling.

Yours always,

Maite

'I love you too,' I whispered as the letter fell from my hands,
knowing that part of me had been left behind.

EPILOGUE

A letter from Ines arrived several months later. Maite was in prison and couldn't communicate directly. Not yet. It was still too risky. She was physically healthy but her spirits were low. Visits were extremely limited.

They'd all been arrested — Patxi, Dr Arriaza and Maite. Patxi had died in prison soon after arrest. There were rumours of torture, but Dr Arriaza, present at his death, insisted it was a heart attack.

Dr Arriaza had been interrogated and finally released. He had somehow managed to explain the charred remains of a discredited book, *The Tree of Gernika*. He was ordered back to the nursing home under strict conditions.

Maite, for reasons unclear, had been detained indefinitely. The case against her was weak, there being scant material evidence — a miniature camera, a series of sketches. A sheaf of documents — a purported manifesto for Basque independence containing plans for coordinated bombings — couldn't be found. But links with her brother and sister couldn't be overlooked.

§

A second letter arrived six months later, this time from Maite herself. She'd been released under a general amnesty for political prisoners. She was coping, readjusting to normal life. Her brother and sister, released soon after, were struggling, particularly her brother. Family and friends had gathered around, and there was endless support from the townsfolk.

Dr Arriaza was soldiering on, but deeply saddened by the loss of his close friend. The project, she said, was bearing fruit.

She thanked me again for what I'd done and looked forward to better days, happier times.

'*Ondo ibili!*' she said, on closing. '*Te quiero.*'

§

In the years that followed Maite's release, life in Mundaca continued — as sure as one season followed another. The tide of fascism turned, a wave of democracy swept through the village and the shadow of Franco gradually receded.

With the monarchy restored, despair turned to hope when a new Spanish government began granting limited autonomy to the regions. A Basque government would be established, eventually calming the turbulent waters that had pervaded their homeland.

And in the river mouth, the tide rose and fell. And the sea was mostly quiet with barely a breeze to ripple the surface. There were storms and the depths would turn dark and uninviting, and on rare, perfect days, there were endless, long, beautiful waves. And, if you were lucky — in the right place at the right time — you might have the ride of your life.

PLEASE REVIEW

Thank you for reading *Mundaca*. If you have a moment, please consider writing a short review of this novel on Amazon, Goodreads, Apple or wherever you engage with other readers online. Your feedback would be greatly appreciated because reviews assist authors more than you might think, as well as helping your friends, family and others to choose their next book.

ABOUT THE AUTHOR

Mundaca is Owen Hargreaves' debut novel. The story is based on his experiences travelling and living in the Basque Country of Generalisimo Franco's Spain in 1975. Owen later returned to Australia to study medicine. He has worked in public health, principally with refugees, in Sudan, Thailand, Pakistan and Zanzibar. In Pakistan he worked for three years as the UNHCR Health Coordinator for the Afghan Refugee Program in Baluchistan. After ten years abroad he returned to Melbourne in 1994 to become a GP. Father of four, and still a keen surfer, these days Owen enjoys riding the waves of creative expression as much as the swells of the world's beautiful oceans and seas.

ACKNOWLEDGMENTS

Eternal thanks go to my writing mentor, the highly talented author and editor Clare Strahan. I met Clare through a formal manuscript assessment of an early draft of *Mundaca* via Writers Victoria. Clare went on to mentor me through a series of drafts to a completed work, while simultaneously working on her own literary creations. Clare's professional and patient guidance led me steadily in a writerly direction. She taught me about the three-act model, story structure and balance, show and tell, pacing, and offered many ideas for improving and tightening the story. As her student I probably taught her only one thing – how to make a leg rope.

My heartfelt thanks to all my family and the various friends who have supported me through the long and sometimes arduous process of writing a novel as a part-time author.

To those who've read one or more drafts of the story and given invaluable feedback, tips and ideas, I thank you wholeheartedly.

My eternal gratitude to Euan Mitchell, who rescued me at the end, when mainstream publishing was unachievable. I tracked him down some two-and-a-half years after completing the novel. He gave my dusty manuscript a polish, coordinated the publication project, and provided great support and timely expert advice. It's all in his book *Your Book Publishing Options*, but there's nothing like the human touch to bring that knowledge and wisdom alive.

My thanks to Robyn Wallace-Mitchell for her proofreading, and to Luke Harris from Working Type for the cover design and layout.

My warm thanks also to Tim Baker, Wayne Lynch and Kevin Naughton (in alphabetical order) for reading the novel and providing encouraging reviews.

To Lady Luck, for leading me to a book in the local library entitled *Telegram from Guernica: The Extraordinary Life of George Steer* by Nicholas Rankin. Serendipity is a wonderful thing! And George Steer was, indeed, extraordinary.

To all those people wandering the streets, mumbling to themselves, who I thought were lost souls, my apologies. I came to realise that some of you, at least, were writers working on dialogue, and happily joined your club.

To the various characters in the book (many based on real people) – we've spent a lot of time together, got to know each other well ... it's been an enormous pleasure.

And, finally, to the central character of the story, the picturesque village of Mundaka in Spain, with its rivermouth and waves, and hearty inhabitants, my endless gratitude and affection. You have a lifelong admirer.